Someone is Trying To Kill Me

A NOVEL

James L. Dickerson

SARTORIS
LITERARY
GROUP

A traditional publisher with a non-traditional approach to publishing

Sartoris Literary Group, Inc.
Jackson, Mississippi
www.sartorisliterary.com

1

"Someone is trying to kill me."

Dr. Rivers Mann gazed across his desk, stone faced.

A very attractive Asian American, about twenty-six — tall, willowy, delicately boned, with enormous eyes, spoke with controlled urgency. She'd appeared at his office without an appointment. A walk-in.

As he looked at her, her words rolled around inside his head like tumbling bowling pins. *Someone is trying to kill me.* Yeah, right. It's a phrase often heard in mental institutions, but seldom encountered in private practice.

"Why have you come to me?" he asked, his brow gently wrinkled.

There was a look of surprise on her face.

"Because it's driving me crazy. That's what psychologists do, isn't it? Stop people from going crazy! You're licensed to do that, right?"

He ignored the question.

"I'm afraid I have a full schedule today," he explained. "But I'll be happy to fit you in later in the week."

She ignored his suggestion.

"Could I please have a glass of water?"

Classic avoidance, he thought. There was an unopened bottle of water on his desk. He unscrewed the plastic top with a click and slowly emptied the contents into a large tumbler, the cascading water the only sound in the office. Then he handed it to her, noticing that she received it with both hands, neither of which was trembling. He was getting more interested by the minute.

"As I said, I'll be happy to see you later in the week. Just work it out with my secretary."

No response. Instead, she sipped the water and lowered the glass to her lap, where she pinged her nail against the glass. She looked down at the glass, her emotions deflating like a balloon with a slow leak. She wasn't one to take rejection well. She'd expected him to drop everything and rush to her rescue, in view of the seriousness of her problem.

When she didn't respond to his suggestion that she schedule an appointment, he followed up with, "What makes you think you're crazy?"

She looked up at him with intense, black-as-coal eyes.

"I didn't say I was crazy," she said, *thinking isn't that just like a man? Why do they take everything we say literally?* "I said people are trying to kill me and it's driving me crazy! There's a big difference, you know. I'm not crazy yet. I've never been crazy!"

"Let's just suppose that someone is trying to kill you . . . "

"You say that like you don't believe me!"

"OK, let me rephrase that. Who do you think is trying to kill you?"

"I have no idea."

"Why do they want to kill you?"

"I wish I knew."

"Have you talked to the police?"

"Of course."

"And what happened?"

"They told me to take a number and have a seat."

"Then what happened?"

"I left without taking a number."

"I see."

Rivers leaned back in his chair, pondering her comments. The woman had a firm enough grasp on reality to debate word usage with him. Her eye contact was strong, yet not fixated. She was much too focused on their conversation to be psychotic. He had a feeling that whatever the source of her distress, it was not an emergency situation.

After a moment, he said, softening, "I have a full schedule today, but I'll ask my secretary to work you in tomorrow."

"If I'm still alive," said the woman sarcastically.

"Let's hope you are still alive—let's hope both of us are still alive."

The woman stood and brushed the hair away from her face. For most of the conversation, her hair had fallen across her right eye.

"Well, if that's the best you can do," she said, smiling weakly. "See you tomorrow."

"Wait a minute," he said. "What's your name?"

"Doe Peterson."

As she was going out the door, Rivers called his secretary and instructed her to set up an appointment for the woman. Moments later the secretary entered his office, flashing a smirk.

"Want the scoop on your new patient?"

"Sure—why not?"

"When I arrived this morning she was sitting in a convertible parked off to the side."

"There's nothing wrong with sitting in a convertible."

The secretary rolled her eyes.

"If you'd let me finish—after you came in I ducked into the hutch to make a pot of coffee. As I started for my desk, I saw her walk into your office and close the door behind her."

"I wondered why you allowed her in."

"I didn't. She must have followed you in while I was away from my desk. I figured you'd send her packing when you got ready."

Rivers grinned.

"I was a little surprised to turn around and see her sitting there in my office."

"Want my advice?"

"Not particularly."

"Well, you got it anyway—I'd watch out for that lady. She's a lot slicker than you are. Most women are."

"We'll see."

As she left the room, she glanced over her shoulder and said, "Can't wait to read your notes on the interview."

"That's confidential, you know."

His next patient was a middle-aged woman who was having a difficult time getting over her divorce. The one after that was an adolescent boy with chartreuse hair who'd been suspended by his high school for trashing the computer room. Then there was the fifty-year-old man who'd suddenly, to his astonishment, become a prolific bed-wetter. Sometimes therapy sucks.

2

At lunch Rivers went to the Mud Pie Café, a hole-in-the-wall eatery on the bluff overlooking the Mississippi River., where he met an old friend for lunch. Every Wednesday, at noon, they met at the café and ordered chocolate pie and African roast coffee and talked about the good old days when they were college roommates and life seemed full of promise.

Jack McCain was already at their favorite table when Rivers entered the café. He wore a suit and tie, though he looked ill at ease in it and the jacket was perpetually wrinkled; it was the standard uniform for newsmen at the *Memphis Press*, where he was an editorial writer.

Rivers pulled out a chair and sighed as he sat at the table.

"Tough morning?" asked Jack.

Rivers shook his head. "No worse than any of the others."

"I've come to understand that changing human behavior comes with the same frustrations as writing about human behavior."

"I've never thought about it that way."

"Either way, you're dealing with Man's failures as a human being."

"Emotional problems shouldn't be equated with failure."

"It's a system failure, if nothing else."

"Whatever."

"Is it true that psychologists have a high suicide rate?"

"For men, it's the same as the general population. It's higher for women. Much higher. Six times higher."

"How do you figure that?"

"No one knows."

"What one group has the highest risk for suicide?"

Rivers smiled. "White males your age."

Brushing off the comment, he asked, "What about women?"

"Asian-American women in their twenties."

It was at that point that the waiter slipped pie and coffee in front of them. "Anything else?" the waiter asked.

"No thanks," said Rivers.

The two men stopped talking and concentrated on their meringue-heaped pie. To hell with blood sugar and cholesterol, the pie had a rich chocolate taste and a silky texture that melted on contact with the tongue. They ate in silence, each gently slicing their fork into the mysterious creamy concoction with a level of deliberation usually associated with intricate brain surgery.

Rivers and Jack were unlikely friends. Since neither had specified a roommate when they entered college, they were randomly assigned to each other. Rivers was blond, blue-eyed, athletic, from a wealthy family that instilled conservative values in him, while Jack was dark, intense, a musician who came from a family with a long liberal tradition. They shared a ten by fourteen room in a high-rise dormitory that students called the "rock." It was unbearably cold in the summer and unbearably hot in the winter.

Rivers was a proud member of ROTC; Jack protested the army's involvement in campus affairs. Rivers joined several academic fraternities; Jack tossed cherry bombs into the room where they met. The two men could not have been more unalike. Upon graduation, Rivers enrolled in graduate school, ultimately receiving a doctorate in psychology before enlisting in the army to serve four years in PSYOP, the psychological operations division.

After leaving college, Jack went on the road with a rock band, playing keyboards, but after a few years he grew tired of that lifestyle and got a job as a reporter at the *Memphis News*. When Rivers relocated in Memphis after leaving the army, he and Jack began their "pie Wednesdays," a tradition that'd cemented their friendship for the past fifteen years.

Once they finished their pie, they both pushed away from the table.

"We may be the only grown men in the city who have pie parties," laughed Jack.

"Not just the only men. The only people, period — look around. You don't see many women stuffing their faces with pie, do you?"

"No, but I've seen a couple of women ask for pie to go."

"So that's what's in those ominous brown paper bags."

"Like alcoholics pirating a bottle of vodka past their neighbors, they take their pie home, where they light a few candles and eat alone."

After lunch, they walked out into the warm sunshine and stood around and talked about sports and politics for a few minutes, watching the river traffic as it proceeded in an orderly fashion up and down the river.

One of the good things about their friendship was that they almost always agreed on all issues, each impervious to imperfection. That made for economical and satisfying conversation. After bandying about a few observations, they went their separate ways, each man vaguely satisfied that their social obligations for the entire week had been met.

When he returned to his office, Rivers found his waiting room filled with patients. A woman who was afraid of lettuce. A little girl who had been sexually abused by her teacher. An Iraq War veteran who couldn't hold down a job because of night terrors that left him exhausted each morning. A married couple who wanted him to give them a reason to stay together (his least favorite type of therapy because it has such a low success rate).

He would give each of them a ray of hope, something they could believe in. Or at least he would try.

3

On his way home that evening, Rivers thought about Doe Peterson. She wasn't like most of his delusional patients. Paranoid schizophrenics who think someone's trying to kill them often deny it for fear of being thought crazy. They tend to be secretive, convinced that they can trust no one.

By contrast, Doe's fear that someone was trying to kill her was the first thing out of her mouth. Whatever else she was, she wasn't paranoid.

Rivers lived about thirty minutes from his office. It only took minutes to get out of the city, so most of the drive was on a two-lane, blacktop country road that hugged the gently rolling hills of pine forests and farmland that stretched all the way to the high bluff that overlooked the river.

He liked the quiet drive back and forth each day because it gave him time to think. He was pondering the challenge presented by Doe Peterson when he became aware of a black SUV with tinted windows closing in on him from the rear. He watched in the rearview mirror as the SUV drew closer and closer.

Each time he looked away from the mirror to see the road — and then looked back into the mirror — the SUV was another ten yards closer. He knew most of the vehicles that traveled the road, but he'd never seen this particular SUV. Within minutes, the vehicle was dangerously close, tailgating him, its front bumper only a few feet away from his back bumper.

Rivers looked into the rearview mirror, straining to look past the tinted windshield, but the glass was too dark and he couldn't tell whether the driver was male or female. Abruptly, the SUV pulled back a couple of yards and then darted to the left, pulling over into the left lane.

Rivers maintained his speed and the vehicle pulled up alongside him. Again, he tried to get a good look at the driver, but all he could see was a silhouette of someone wearing a cap.

Suddenly, the SUV slammed into the side of his car, bumping him off the road so that his right front and rear wheels spun onto the gravel, slinging rocks, struggling for traction, while the left wheels remained firmly on the pavement. He fought to keep his car from leaving the road entirely, but each time he attempted to get back on the road, the SUV bumped him again, the deafening sound of gravel peppering against the underside of his car.

Rivers' heart pounded as he fought to keep control of his car. Once he realized that the SUV would not allow him back onto the road, he braked, not hard enough to send him skidding into the canal, just enough to start slowing the car, at which point the SUV slammed hard into him once again, forcing him entirely off the road and down an embankment into a canal filled with stagnant, snake-infested water that gave off an ammonia-like odor.

He braced himself as the impact set off his airbag, momentarily stunning him as water seeped into the car. He opened his eyes and saw water quickly covering his feet. He gulped air and gasped.

Once he pushed the airbag away from his face, he saw that the water level was up to the base of his windshield. He unfastened his seatbelt and attempted to lower the window, but the electrical circuit was shorted out by the water.

He took a deep breath. Then he removed his cell phone from the inside pocket of his coat and punched the automatic dial button that he hoped would connect him to his wife, Shelly.

The phone rang four times before the voicemail answered and asked him to leave a message. Rivers spoke into the phone: "Honey, it's me . . . I guess you must be in the backyard, or maybe out shopping . . . I'm in a ditch about five miles from the house. The car is filling with water and the window opener has shorted out. I've got to find something to break the glass . . . I'm going to call the sheriff's office. Gotta go. Love you."

Rivers punched in 911 and told the operator what'd happened. She said help was on the way. Advised him to take the leather cover off his phone and use the metal corner of the phone to break the window glass. He'd never thought of that. He did as she suggested and struck the glass with his phone.

The impact jarred his wrist, but it wasn't enough to break the glass. He twisted away from the door to make room for a longer swing. This time, to his surprise, the glass broke, shattering into millions of little pieces that disappeared into the foul water that poured into the car.

The car wasn't completely submerged. The water level was only about chest high, so he pushed and turned to pull himself out of his car seat, lifting his head through the opening into the fresh air, pushing hard as he could with his hands to propel himself from the car.

Once he freed himself, he swam to the bank and crawled out of the water, arms trembling from the strain. He'd only been out of the water for a minute or two when he heard the siren. Exhausted, he walked up the bank and flagged down the patrol car.

The sheriff's deputy pulled off the road and reported her location to her dispatcher before getting out of the car. As she approached Rivers, she asked, "Are you all right?"

"Oh, I'm fine," said Rivers. "Can't say the same for my car."

"Anyone else in the car?"

"No, it was just me."

Together they walked over to the bank to peer into the canal. Rivers' car was about three-quarters submerged.

"You're lucky," said the deputy.

"How's that?"

"If the water had been deeper, you might not have gotten out of the car."

She was right. It was a close call.

As he stared at his car, reliving the event, he couldn't help but marvel at the suddenness of it all. From the time the SUV first slammed into him, until the moment he went into the canal, no more than fifteen or twenty seconds had elapsed. As he gazed down into the canal, the deputy followed his tire tracks back up the road to the point where they first left the pavement. She was young, probably in her late twenties, and she was overweight, not to the point of being obese, but stout with thick shoulders.

The deputy made notes onto a pad and then asked Rivers about the accident. He told her the whole story, from start to finish. She took notes as he spoke and when he finished, she asked, "What make of SUV was it?"

"I don't know. It was black with tinted windows. That's all I know."

"Man or woman behind the wheel?"

"I couldn't see inside the vehicle. They were wearing a cap. I could tell by the silhouette."

"Did you get the tag number?"

"No, it was covered with mud."

"Did the SUV stop when you went off the road?"

"No, it kept going."

"Not even briefly?"

"It was speeding."

"How fast were you going?"

"I don't know . . . probably around fifty."

The deputy quietly took down his comments.

After a prolonged silence, Rivers asked, "Aren't you going to put out whatever you call it—an APB, or something like that—for the SUV?"

The deputy seemed annoyed by the question.

"Yes sir," she answered. "Just as soon as I complete my interview."

"Another five minutes and he will be out of the county," Rivers said, the annoyance clearly showing in his voice."

"Yes sir—I understand."

"Whoever it was tried to kill me."

The deputy looked up from her notes.

"Why do you say that?"

"Because this was no accident. I was driven off the road deliberately."

"Who would do that to you?"

"I have no idea."

"Then why do you think someone was trying to kill you?"

Rivers felt his blood pressure rising.

"Why else would they push me off the road?"

"Sir, please understand that this happens all the time. Maybe the driver's judgment was impaired by substance abuse. Maybe the driver was a senior citizen who suffers from Alzheimer's or something like that. We'll look for the SUV—it should have white paint on the right side—and take it from there."

She looked at the address on the report. "You don't live far from here. Do you want me to give you a lift home—or would you like to wait for the tow truck?"

"Thank you. I'd appreciate a ride home."

When they got into the patrol car, he watched her put on her sunglasses and absently rest her hand on her firearm, a 9mm automatic. She checked in with her dispatcher and they were soon on their way.

"Are you sure you're all right?" she asked. "I can take you to a hospital, if you like."

"No, I'm fine."

When they arrived at his house, a two-story white building at the top of the bluff, the deputy pulled into the driveway and followed the circular drive to the veranda.

"Thank you for all your help," said Rivers as he got out of the car.

"You're welcome," said the deputy.

"We'll want to look your car over before releasing it to you."

"I understand."

The deputy tipped her cap at him and drove away.

Rivers walked over to the side of the house and saw that Shelly's car was gone. One mystery solved. He walked up the front steps, still soaking wet. He thought about going inside to change clothes, but when he saw a patch of sunlight on the veranda, he sat dead center in the light, the sound of Johnny Cash's "Ring of Fire" inexplicably ringing in his ears.

This was a test of some kind — right? he thought. *A rest of grace? A test of commitment? A test of something I don't understand?*

By the time he saw Shelly's Mercedes coming up the driveway, the sun had pretty much dried his clothing, though his hair was still damp and stringy. He waved. She honked the horn. He sat there, looking like a southern-fried Buddha, as she got of her car and then retrieved a small plastic bag from the backseat and started up the sidewalk to the house, swinging the bag at arm's length.

Shelly was what the kids call *really hot*. Blonde hair that fell past her shoulders. Long legs. Movie star face. A dentist who'd earned her medical degree by agreeing to serve in the navy and then in the naval reserves, she'd met Rivers at a mental health workshop for dental professionals. They'd been married ten years, but they had no children. Neither wanted children.

The closer she got to the veranda, the harder she stared at her husband. He'd never greeted her in such a manner. He appeared

15

disheveled. The only time she'd seen his hair like that was when he got out of the shower, or swam in the river or a lake. Starting up the steps, she called out, her voice tightening with concern, "Honey, are you all right?"

He looked at her a moment. If he said no, that'd be an exaggeration. If he said yes, that'd be an understatement. He said nothing, allowing his perplexed face to do the talking for him.

Shelly sat down beside him.

"What in the world happened to you?" she asked. "You look like hell."

Rivers looked up at her, not sure where to begin.

Finally, he said, "I was in an accident."

"What!" she said, her eyes growing large. "Were you hurt?"

Rivers shook his head. "I went into the canal. Got soaked. But I'm fine."

She reached over and hugged him tightly, her voice breaking. "Are you sure? Have you been to a doctor?"

Rivers shook his head.

"Do you hurt anywhere? Did you bump your head?"

"No, no," he said. "The airbag stung a little bit when it hit my face, but that was it."

She pushed away so that she could see him better.

"So how did it happen?"

"I'm not sure."

"You mean you don't remember?"

"I know how it happened. I don't know *why* it happened?"

"I don't understand."

"I think someone is trying to kill me."

4

It was dark by the time Doe arrived at her parents' home in the Ozarks. Before she could even get out of her car, they rushed out to the driveway to greet her, arms outstretched. Benjamin and Anna Peterson had received a telephone call from Doe while she was on the road, informing them that she was on her way. They were overjoyed. They didn't see her nearly enough, at least not since she'd moved to Memphis.

Unable to have children, they adopted Doe while she was an infant. All they knew about her background was that her mother was Chinese and her father was a Caucasian American. Girls weren't greatly valued in China at that time, especially girls of mixed racial heritage, so it wasn't difficult to persuade authorities there to release her for adoption in America. Both in their forties at the time, they'd been passed over by domestic adoption agencies because of their ages. They considered Doe to be a gift from God.

"We're so glad you could come," said Anna, wrapping her loving arms around Doe.

"Home is where my heart is," answered Doe.

"Awe," purred Anna. "You'll always be my baby."

Benjamin patiently waited his turn to hug his daughter. Then the three of them went inside the cabin. After years of running a business in Little Rock, Benjamin and Anna had recently retired and bought a cabin in a secluded mountain area not far from a trout-rich river. Inside the cabin, they sat on the back porch and sipped iced tea as they gazed out at the river that cut through the trees with picture-book clarity.

"We were surprised you didn't call before you left Memphis," said Benjamin. "You usually give us more of a head start."

"I did it on impulse, really. Just got in the car and headed west."

"That's not like you," said Anna, concern in her voice. "Is everything all right?"

Doe was taken aback by her comment.

"Of course, everything's all right," she lied. "You're reading too much into it. I had a couple of days off and decided to pay you a visit. No special reason other than that I love you."

It was all a lie, but she hoped they wouldn't see through it. She wanted to be pampered by her parents, but she didn't what them to know why she wanted to be pampered. Sometimes, the less parents know, the better.

"We're so glad you did," said Anna. "Benjamin and I were talking about you just this morning, wondering how you were doing."

"Oh, I'm just fine."

"How's the modeling going?" asked Benjamin.

"Great. I've been doing a lot of national print work lately, and I've been booked for a magazine feature that'll be shot in three weeks."

"That's wonderful, honey. Where will you have to go?"

"Miami."

"I wish you didn't have to travel so much," said Benjamin. "Airline travel is not as safe as it used to be, not with all the terrorists . . . and the diseases that seem to be popping up everywhere. I wish you had a regular nine-to -five job."

"Well, Dad, you know that's not the life I've chosen."

Anna came to her daughter's defense.

"Benjamin, you know good and well that most girls Doe's age would love to be able to travel the way she does."

"I know that," he growled. "Doesn't mean I have to like, does it?"

Doe rose and hugged her father around the neck.

"You old bear—you just love me too much, that's your problem."

Benjamin blushed and coughed, embarrassed at the attention.

* * *

That night Doe sat knotted in a ball on her bed, her knees pulled up to her chest. Outside, rain fell in torrents as waves of thunder swept through the forest, rattling the windowpanes with the storm's fury.

After a particularly loud crash of thunder, she went to the window and pulled back the curtain to peer outside. She saw nothing but pounding sheets of black rain. Her bedroom had a door to a private, ground-level balcony that overlooked the river. She checked the lock on the door, just to be safe. Then she turned on the radio, turned down low so it wouldn't bother her parents. The only clear station she could find was a country music format. As George Jones whined about a broken heart, she curled up again on the bed and opened a book.

Outside the cabin, footsteps made their way across soaked leaves. The steps were hesitant, stopping often. Each time they stopped, the rain cascaded over them, pooling around them in deep puddles.

Doe put down the book and brushed her hair. Then she started undressing. By the time she went into the bathroom she was wearing only her bra and panties. She peered out the bathroom window into the night. The window did not have curtains and she always looked outside before fully undressing. Seeing nothing, she turned on the water and finished undressing before stepping into the shower.

Outside the cabin, footsteps walked up to a lighted window and stopped. From inside, shadows could be seen moving across the window. Unfortunately, Doe was not looking in the direction of the window.

Doe stood in the shower, the refreshing water pouring over her hair and face. She closed her eyes and enjoyed the soothing warmth of the soapy water. There was something about the roar of the water rushing from the shower nozzle that gave her a sense of well being, even during a rainstorm.

Outside the cabin, the footsteps approached the balcony and stopped. A hand reached into a pocket and pulled out a plastic credit card. The hand expertly worked the card between the lock and the door frame.

After a moment, the door clicked open, allowing light from inside the bedroom to fall across the balcony. The footsteps moved into the bedroom and the door closed shut behind them.

Doe turned off the water and stepped out of the shower. For a moment, she thought she'd heard something. She paused, listening hard. Hearing nothing but the dripping of rain, she shook her head and dried off with a towel. Then she wrapped the towel around her waist and used a second towel to dry her hair. As she walked into the bedroom, she stopped abruptly.

There was a knock at her door.

"Doe, you still awake?" asked her father. "I brought you some warm cocoa."

Before she could answer, she saw something out of the corner of her eye. Someone was standing inside the curtain at the balcony door. In the dim light, only legs and feet could be seen. Doe gasped and backed against the wall.

Then she screamed.

Whoever was behind the curtain bolted onto the balcony and jumped over the rail into the night.

Benjamin burst into the room, the warm cocoa spilling from the glass onto the floor. "What's going on?" he demanded, his eyes wide with alarm.

Doe ran toward him and embraced him.

"There was someone in my room!" she said excitedly. "They ran out the balcony door."

Benjamin gently pushed her aside and hurried over to the balcony door. He looked outside and saw nothing. He closed the door and locked it.

"What did they look like?" he asked.

By that time, Anna was in the room. Before she could ask the obvious question, Benjamin said, "We've had a prowler. Inside the room. Doe said he ran out onto the balcony and jumped down. Stay here with Doe. I'm going to get my gun and look around outside."

"Benjamin, don't do that—it's not safe."

But he was already gone. First into his bedroom, where he retrieved a 12-guage shotgun from his closet. Then out the back door into night. He shined a flashlight over at the balcony. Then he swept the light beam through the trees. Nothing. Whoever it was had fled. Doe and Anna turned on the balcony light and walked outside and waved to him.

"See anything?" asked Anna.

"Not a thing," he said, and then turned and walked back inside.

Doe and Anna greeted him in the kitchen. By then Doe had slipped into a terry cloth bathrobe.

"Shouldn't we call the police?" asked Anna.

Benjamin shook his head. "Wouldn't do any good. They're long gone. I'll stop by the sheriff's office tomorrow and tell them what happened."

Too keyed up to sleep, they made more hot cocoa and sat around the kitchen table and talked for a while. Benjamin asked Doe several times if she had any idea who the intruder was and she said she didn't have a clue.

"Well, did you see his face?"

"He had on a black, knit cap and I only saw his back for a second. It all happened so fast."

After they finished their cocoa, they returned to her bedroom to see if anything had been taken. Everything was in place. Doe looked though her overnight bag and found nothing missing. Her cash and credit cards were still in her purse. Doe knew why the intruder had entered her room, but she was afraid to tell her father and mother. Afraid that the knowledge of it would put them in danger. *Someone wanted to kill her!*

* * *

Sometime after midnight Doe sat up in bed. She couldn't breath. Her life was collapsing inward. Her heart raced. Her face was covered with sweat. She wondered if she was dying. The dream had seemed so realistic. She was adrift on a raft and land was nowhere in sight. The waves rose high all about her and the wind howled, peppering her face with tiny grains of sand.

Moonlight danced all through her bedroom, an alternating breeze though an open window creating a kaleidoscope of fluttering images as the curtains gently whipped from side to side. She was drawn into luminous patterns that were creepy and beautiful at the same time.

Suddenly, she saw something unexpected. She gasped and stared into the darkness, holding her breath as she waited for the light to again illuminate the corner by her dresser. What had she seen? Her heart raced as the curtain fluttered, bouncing light rays about the room as if they were gently lobbed tennis balls. There, she saw it again. Something on her dresser she'd never noticed.

She slipped off the bed and slowly made her way over to the dresser. She picked the object up in her hands and carried it over to the window so that she could examine it in the light. Once she saw what it was, she gasped. It was a picture frame that contained a photograph of her in a compromising situation.

She screamed. For the second time that night.

The picture fell to the floor, the glass breaking into a hundred tiny pieces.

Quickly she reached down and scooped the photograph from behind the broken glass, nicking her index finger in the process, and stuffed it into a dresser drawer. Within seconds, her bedroom door was open and her father and mother were rushing into the room, her father brandishing his shotgun.

"What is it, honey?" he asked breathlessly.

Anna said nothing, but reached out and put her arms around her daughter and pulled her into her, squeezing her tightly.

When Doe didn't answer, her father fired off another question: "Is everything all right?"

"Yes—yes!" Doe said, gently pushing away from her mother. She knelt and picked up the two largest pieces of the broken glass.

"What is that?" asked her mother.

Finally getting her wits about her, Doe said, "It's a picture frame I found at a yard sale in Memphis." *Lies, lies. More lies.* "I unpacked it last night and put it on the edge of the dresser. In the dark I knocked it to the floor.

"What's this all about?" asked her father.

"I just told you, Dad. I'm so sorry I screamed."

Anna noticed blood dripping from Doe's finger. She reached out and gently grasped her hand, lifting it for a better look.

"Why you've cut yourself on the broken glass."

Doe instinctively yanked her hand away and reached for a tissue, which she wrapped around her finger. "It's nothing, Mother. Just a little cut."

"Well," she said, her voice trailing off. "You need some ointment on that finger so it doesn't get infected."

"I know, Mom. I've got some in my overnight bag."

"It's probably expired. You know how you are about keeping track of those things."

Anna padded out of the room in her bedroom slippers and returned seconds later with a tube of antibiotic ointment. "I just bought his yesterday."

Anna took Doe's uninjured hand and led her over to the bed, gently nudging her down onto the sheets.

"Now let me see your finger."

Doe dutifully held up her hand and watched as her mother cleaned her wound with a tissue, squeezed ointment on the cut, and attached a band-aid.

"Thank you, Mommie."

"Now, now," said her mother. "I want you to go to sleep. I'm going to sit in the rocker and stay with you all night." She nodded to Benjamin so that he would leave the room. As he left, he said, "Good night, honey."

"Thank you, Daddy."

Anna pulled the sheet up to Doe's shoulders and tucked her in.

"You go to sleep now. I won't let anything happen to you."

Doe watched her mother settle into the rocker across the room, quickly drifting off to sleep.

"We're here for you," Anna said, barely speaking above a whisper.

5

Shelly drove Rivers in to his office the next day. She dreaded going to work, so she was delighted to have Rivers for company on the way into town. From the time she was a very small child, becoming a dentist was all she could think about. She hated her time in the Navy because of all the sexual harassment that she endured. It was constant. Day after day.

Once she was at a morning briefing when a cocky visiting officer crossed the room, grinning arrogantly, wrapped his arms around her, and kissed her full on the lips, to the applause of the men in the room. She felt humiliated.

After she made it through all of that, she thought it'd be easy sailing. Not so. Male patients in the dentist's chair sometimes moved their arms so that they would touch her breasts as she leaned over them. They told her dirty jokes. They didn't floss before coming in, so she had to spend time picking bits and pieces of decayed broccoli, bacon, and spinach from between their teeth.

It amazed her that patients, male and female, used such bad judgment when making cosmetic choices. It was at the point now that she wanted to scream when patients told her they wanted gold teeth or diamond inlays.

Worst of all was the way her work made her back ache by the end of each day. Leaning over to peer into open mouths put stress on her back, whether she was standing or seated on a stool. She was at a point in her career where she was seriously considering pursuing a new career in computer science, or perhaps joining a university faculty, where she could talk about dentistry instead of actually doing it. Then there was the other option. Adopting a child and taking a couple of years off to enjoy life more fully.

"Have a good day," Rivers said, as he got out of the car. She'd complained about her work from time to time, but he had no idea how much she really hated going into her office. "I'll let you know if I get my car back today."

"Love you," she said, and drove away.

Rivers was early, something he daily aspired to because he didn't have a back entrance and he had to enter through his waiting room. Seeing anxious patients before it was time to see them was not among his most favorite things to do. He picked up his messages from his secretary and went into his inner office and poured himself a cup of freshly brewed coffee.

After sipping his coffee, Rivers called the sheriff's office.

"What's the verdict?" he asked.

"We've gone over it for evidence," said the deputy in charge. "You're free to tow it to a repair shop."

Rivers asked, "What do you mean by evidence?"

"We found black paint on the side of your car and broken plastic at the site of the accident, probably from a turn-signal light."

"Oh," said Rivers. "Have you made any progress locating the other vehicle?"

"Not yet."

"You'll let me know when you do, right?"

"First, we'll check out all the leads."

"So you'll let me know if you come across anything suspicious."

"Not necessarily. People have a right to privacy, even criminal suspects. Plus, I'm sure you understand that there are two sides to every story. We'll let you know if we make an arrest."

"Are you telling me that if you suspect a particular person, you won't tell me their identity until you make an arrest?"

"Yes. That's the way the system works. Being a professional person, I'm sure you can understand that we have rules we have to follow."

"Yeah. Sure."

Rivers turned off his phone and thought for a moment. Perhaps he was overreacting. The police have more experience with such things, he reasoned. Perhaps they are right to wait for absolute proof before jumping to conclusions. Even so, the fact that the other vehicle didn't stop to help shows a lack of character, if nothing else. Too bad lack of character isn't a crime.

Rivers picked up the stack of files on his desk and glanced through them. First up today was Doe Peterson, the woman who thought someone was trying to kill her. Second was a middle-aged woman who'd been suffering from depression for twenty years. Then there was the alcoholic funeral director who had problems sticking with AA. Each of them wanted to talk about their problems. Most wanted him to massage their egos.

The secretary opened the door and stuck her head inside.

"Doe Peterson is here."

"Show her in," said Rivers.

Doe made eye contact with him the minute she entered the room. That was unusual. Most of his patients talked for twenty minutes before they dared make eye contact, so fearful were they of his disapproval.

Some patients thought he had the ability to read their minds. Others thought he had mystical analytical powers. Rivers fed those thoughts by doing what all good therapists do: He said as little as possible to contradict his patients' perception of him as a shaman.

Doe sat in the chair across from his desk. She wore jeans and a white, pullover sleeveless top. He couldn't help but notice how tanned her squared shoulders were and how beautiful her arms were—muscular, yet pretty much straight lines from shoulder to elbow. He had a ballet dancer's body.

"How are you today Ms. Peterson?" he asked.

"I've been better," she said, a look of distress in her eyes.

"Tell me about it," he said.

Doe told him about visiting her parents. About the broken picture frame. About all the lies she told her parents. About the intruder.

"I don't know if I'm going crazy or not," she said.

"Are all the things that you told me true? Is there any doubt in your mind that they actually happened?"

"Of course, they happened," she said, somewhat offended.

"Do you see a link between the incident in Arkansas and what you told me when you first came into the office?"

"That someone was trying to kill me?"

Rivers nodded.

"I don't know—maybe."

"Let's talk about Arkansas. I'll assume that everything you told me is true. Is it possible that the intruder was a random act? A drifter maybe?"

26

"I don't think so."

"Why?"

Doe paused, losing eye contact.

"Because the picture frame had a photograph of me in it. Something that I should not have posed for. If my parents had seen it, they'd been terribly hurt."

"Was it a published picture that anyone could have come across?"

"No."

Rivers paused, doodling on his notepad.

"Who had possession of the picture?"

"I did. It was in a box in my closet."

"Here in Memphis?"

"Yes."

"That is interesting."

"You're not making me feel any better."

"I'm trying to separate the two issues."

"OK. I see your point. It's possible that the incident in Arkansas is unrelated to what has been happening here."

Rivers nodded approvingly. Listening to himself talk, he couldn't help but compare himself to the deputy who interviewed him after the accident. Perhaps the deputy was brighter than he realized. It's amazing how many people make a living talking.

As a therapist, he didn't really believe in coincidence. Things happen in our lives for a reason. Conspiracy is the foundation of life, whether biological or emotional. But that doesn't mean that *everything* that happens to us is the result of a conspiracy. Much of life is random. Shit happens.

Perhaps the deputy was right. Perhaps his accident was caused by a senile driver, or by someone who'd had too much to drink and was afraid to stop to help for fear of going to jail.

Oh, God, I've done it again, he thought. *Me, me, me.*

Trying to stay focused, Rivers continued, "Did you report the incident to authorities to Arkansas?"

"Daddy reported it. He'll follow up on it. It shook him up pretty bad."

"OK, so let's put that aside for a moment. What makes you think someone is trying to kill you?"

"It all started a couple of months ago. First, let me say, I don't know of any enemies that I have."

"What about men? I assume you have broken up with men before?"

"Of course," she said. "But I would never date a killer."

"Every serial killer has a mother, and most have sisters and former girlfriends. I know you wouldn't intentionally date a killer, but killers aren't always who we expect them to be. Have you ever broken up with a man who took it badly?"

"A time or two."

"Did they ever send you threatening messages or stalk you?"

"A time or two."

"And you don't associate any of your problems with them?"

"No."

"Why not?"

"I told you. I would never have a relationship with a killer."

Rivers could see that she wasn't ready to accept that she would ever date someone who was capable of doing bad things.

"Looks like we're going round and round on that issue. Tell me about the things that have happened to you that make you to think someone wants to kill you."

"Well, the first thing that happened was that someone left a dead bird on my doormat."

"Is it possible that the bird flew into the door and killed itself?"

"Possibly."

"Are their any children in your neighborhood?"

"Yes."

"Do you think they may have done it?"

"Possibly."

"So what else happened?"

"My car caught on fire."

"Tell me about it."

"One night I went to a restaurant to meet a friend for dinner. Later, when I returned to my car, it was on fire."

"Really? I assume you called the fire department."

"The fire department and the police."

"What did they say?"

"They said the fuel line had pulled loose. I told them that it must have been working fine when I arrived at the restaurant because I didn't smell any gas."

"What did they say?"

"They said they get called out to car fires everyday."

"Did you tell them that someone was trying to kill you?"

"Yes."

"What did they say?"

"They laughed. They said I'd been watching too much television."

"Well, Ms. Peterson, I must admit that I've found dead birds at my house—and I've known people who had cars that caught on fire while they were parked. Anything else happened?"

"Last week I was out driving in the country, on my way to the lake, when this car pulled up next to me and ran me off the road."

"Oh," said Rivers, his curiosity aroused. "What color was the car?"

"Well, actually, it wasn't a car. It was one of those SUVs—and it was white."

Rivers smiled. "Yesterday I was run off the road by a black SUV. Knocked me over into a canal filled with water. I could have drowned."

"Oh, my god! Are you serious?"

Rivers nodded.

"I'm so sorry! They must have followed me here. Now they're after you."

Rivers sighed. Talking to patients is a selfless endeavor. It's difficult to sustain a mutually satisfying conversation. He turned and looked out the window a moment, allowing the silence to dampen Doe's expectations. Finally, he said, "That's not really the point I was trying to make."

"Oh," she said.

"Let's put murder aside for a while and talk about you."

"If you think it will help. All this does have me very upset. I'm sure you can see how it would drive even the most ordinary person crazy."

"You have no idea how much I empathize with you."

Rivers s started at the beginning, by asking about her childhood. At this point in her evaluation, he felt that she probably had BPD, borderline personality disorder. It's a diagnosis for people who fall short of meeting the criteria for psychosis, but still display symptoms that exceed the clinical definition of neurosis. It's called borderline because it falls between the two.

In many respects, Doe appeared to be a classic borderline. She had a difficult time accurately interpreting the actions of others. She was bright, witty, extraverted, when it came to interacting with others, yet, always fearing the worst, she possessed a strong urge to isolate herself from the very people who wanted to get close to her.

Before Doe told him about her childhood, she explained that she was adopted and had no brothers or sisters. He thought it interesting that she defined herself as adopted, even before she defined her childhood. Obviously, adoption was a big issue with her, as it is with most adopted children.

"I was born in China," she explained. "My father was an American who didn't want me or my mother. He put me up for adoption and returned to America. My adoptive mother and father couldn't have children, so they went to China and toured the orphanages and found me and brought me back to this country. I'm a chosen child. They love me very much."

"Have you had any contact with your birth mother and father?"

"No. My birth mother died under mysterious circumstances and I have no idea who or where my birth father is. I don't think I want to know. He abandoned me and my mother. He can go to hell."

"Are your adoptive parents Asian?"

"No, they're white."

"How did you feel growing up with white parents?"

"I'm half white myself."

"Of course."

"I didn't notice a difference until I started school and other children asked me where I was from. They asked me why I looked different."

"Children can be cruel."

"It wasn't too bad. I like being different. It works to my advantage in my profession."

30

"I can see that," Rivers said. He made a note on a legal pad and then he continued: "Tell me about your adoptive parents."

"They are wonderful people," she said. "They tried having children of their own, until they were in their forties, and then they decided to adopt, only they were told they were too old to adopt an infant in this country. They found me in a Chinese orphanage."

"Do you know your Chinese name?"

"Yes. It's Yao Ta. My birth mother's name was Yao Bai. "

"Who named you Doe?"

"My father. On the day they heard from the orphanage that the adoption would be approved, my dad was out deer hunting. He saw a buck and a doe and he passed up the buck because of the doe. When he returned home that day and mom gave him the good news, he told her about the deer and they decided that the doe was a sign from God—and so they named me Doe for good luck."

"How was your childhood?"

"Wonderful—I was the center of their universe. They gave me everything I wanted."

"Everything?"

"Well, within reason."

"How do you think you were different from the other children your age?"

"I was bored more often than they were. I understood the other children, but I don't think they understood me. When I talked to them about my feelings, they acted like they didn't know what I was talking about."

"What kinds of feelings did you try to talk to them about?"

"Growing up, I felt like a part of me was missing. That made me feel empty sometimes. When I told my friends, they said they'd never heard of anyone feeling empty. They'd poke fun at me and it'd make me cry and they'd apologize and we'd go on playing and they'd forget about it. But I didn't forget about it. It stuck with me."

"How would you describe your personality?"

"Outgoing. The life of the party. Sometimes shy. Withdrawn. It all depends."

"Depends on what?"

31

"On who I'm with. Don't laugh, but since I was a very young child I've had this ability to take on the personality of whomever I'm with. Maybe I don't have a personality of my own. Maybe I'm a lost soul."

"Interesting," said Rivers. He paused to write a couple of lines on his legal pad. "How does that apply to the men in your life?"

"What do you mean?"

"Do you take on their personality?"

"You know, I've never thought that, but I guess I react differently to my boyfriends than I do to my friends. When I'm with a man, I tend to become the opposite of them. If they are outgoing, I become shy. If they are shy, I become outgoing."

"What is the longest relationship you've ever had with a man?"

"I don't know—four or five months, I guess."

"Why do the relationships end?"

"All different reasons."

"For example?"

"I once dated this man who lived his life by a schedule. He ate at a certain time. He went to sleep at a certain time. He wanted to make love at the same time every week. The more schedules he put me on, the more tense it made me. We had lots of fights. He said that I made him feel that he always had to walk on egg shells when he was around me. I was an hour late for dinner once, because I was on a modeling assignment that ran late, and when I arrived he became so angry that I broke up with him."

"Did he try to resume the relationship?"

"No—I guess he knew better than to try."

"This other man I dated was very abusive to me. Emotionally and physically. I knew I should stop seeing him, but I couldn't—I loved him too much. He loved me too, I think, but it seemed like everything I tried to do to please him backfired. I tried to be the person he wanted me to be. I really did. But it got to the point where we couldn't have a conversation without me crying and him pounding the wall with his fist. Finally, he said he couldn't take it anymore."

"So he broke up with you?"

"Yes."

"How old were you when you had your first sexual experience?"

"Fourteen."

"That's young, isn't it?"

"I was in love and he was much older. Sex seemed like the thing to do."

"How much older was he?"

"He was twenty three."

"Did your parents know about that relationship?"

"Oh no, they would have killed me if they had known."

"Let's talk about your father. What does he do for a living?"

"He's pretty much retired now, but he used to be a contractor."

"What kind of contractor?"

"He traveled around the world building installations for the government."

"Earlier you said you assumed the opposite personalities of your boyfriends. How did that work with your father?"

"Oh, we're like two peas in a pod."

Rivers leaned back in his chair. "I think we've covered enough ground today."

Doe smiled. She looked more relaxed now than she did when she first entered the office. "OK, so I've got a question?"

Rivers nodded approvingly.

"Are you saying you *don't* think someone is trying to kill me?"

"No, I'm not saying that at all. Attempted murder investigations are beyond my area of expertise. What I am saying is that there could be many reasons for the bad things that have happened to you. I'm not the right person to help you sort through that. If you are still concerned about someone trying to kill you, I recommend that you talk to a private investigator."

"Thank you Dr. Mann," she said, rising to her feet. "Before I leave I have one last question." She paused. Then she lobbed the question at him as if she were serving a tennis ball. "Do you think I'm crazy?"

Rivers rose to his feet before he answered.

"No, I don't think you're crazy," he said emphatically.

"But you do think I could benefit from talking to you more?"

"Yes, I do. On your way out, why don't you make an appointment to come back next week."

Doe extended her hand and shook hands with him, using a grip he found to be unusually strong for a woman. "I will. Thank you."

Once she was gone, Rivers scribbled a note on the legal pad.

"Possible borderline personality . . ."

6

Preston LaGrange was one of the least known famous men in America. To be totally honest, the only people who understood his contribution to society were those who possessed top-secret clearances in the United States government. They knew him as the inventor of the Mack 222, a computer software program that allowed the government to simultaneously screen tens of thousands of emails and telephone conversations of private citizens. Computer geeks worshiped him.

Mack 222's search engine was similar to the ones that Internet users make use of everyday. With his program, the government designated several combinations of words—for example, "explosive," "radiation," and "fuse"—and allowed government computers to listen in on conversations or filter emails for combinations of those words. Once they were located, emails were copied and telephone conversations were recorded and sent to computers that held them in abeyance until human screeners could examine the messages for context.

Preston made a fortune from his invention. He invested in various public Internet ventures, all of which were successful, and he expanded his financial empire by purchasing a hotel casino in Las Vegas. The Nirvana Hotel was one of the tallest buildings in the city. It offered computers in every room that allowed guests to play the slots from the comfort of their bedrooms, sitting rooms, and, yes, even their bathrooms, where it was possible to sit on the toilet and gamble, even while taking care of business.

Guests could reserve rooms on any floor of the hotel, except the top floor where Preston lived in an opulent penthouse. The most notable room in the penthouse was not the living room and any of the five bedrooms, but the computer room, a mini-bunker built of steel-reinforced concrete. Bombproof, fireproof, and microbe-proof, the room had the most sophisticated air-filtration system available. Inside the computer room was the Mack 222, with a continuous feed into the government's top-secret system.

As Preston quickly discovered when he sold Mack 222 to the government, all sales are not final—it required a lifelong commitment to the project. The government set up a compatible system in his penthouse so that he could troubleshoot on a twenty-four-hour basis, and it assigned to him a special handler, Secret Service Agent Cefalu, whose job it was to keep an eye on Preston and run interference for him in situations in which the project's integrity might be compromised. He was granted that most coveted of designations, a license to kill. His was made simpler by the fact that Preston lived alone in the penthouse. His wife of more than two decades, Edith, had died recently of cancer. They had a daughter, but she no longer lived at home.

Agent Cefalu had an apartment on the floor immediately below the penthouse. From his apartment he was able to keep the penthouse under surveillance with the use of cameras on the elevator, at the entrance to the penthouse, and inside the front door, the only entry to the penthouse. In addition, there were cameras mounted on the roof that covered all the windows of the penthouse, making it impossible for anyone to scale up the building or repel down the outside wall without being observed.

Preston complained about his lack of privacy all the time.

"What if I wanted to sneak a hooker into my penthouse?" he once jokingly asked Agent Cefalu, to which the agent replied, "Hookers aren't good for your health." But he understood that it was needed and he didn't give Agent Cefalu a hard time about it, except when he wanted to good-naturedly razz him.

By temperament, Preston was quiet and studious, the archetypical computer nerd. Most women considered him handsome, but he wasn't adept enough at small talk to do well with women in social situations. If put into a roomful of women, he invariably avoided eye contact and clamed up, causing some women to wonder if he was mentally challenged, prompting him to once tell Agent Cefalu, "I love women—but only in small doses."

Agent Cefalu responded that he understood perfectly.

One day they were sitting on the observation deck, smoking illegal Cuban cigars and sipping imported scotch, when Preston confessed that he was saddened by the fact that he had so little contact with his daughter.

"Most of the time daughters worship their fathers," he sighed. "But sometimes father and daughter don't bond."

"I've heard about cases like that," said Agent Cefalu.

"I have no idea why she'd be like that. I tried my best to be a good father. Gave her everything she asked for. Never once spanked her, not even when she was defiant. Her attitude toward me is one of the great mysteries of my life. She hates my guts—and she's not shy about saying so. "

"My wife and I never had children," said Agent Cefalu. "It's one of the great disappointments in my life. If we'd had children, our marriage might have lasted longer."

"Don't you think your work might have had something to do with your divorce?"

Agent Cefalu nodded and took a swig of scotch.

"You know, they'd can my ass if they knew I was drinking on the job."

Preston grinned at him. "What are you talking about? You're always on the job."

"They don't see it that way."

"To hell with *they!*"

"I'll drink to that."

The men clinked their glasses together. They sat in silence for a long while, savoring their cigars. Finally, Agent Cefalu pulled away from his cigar and turned to Preston, looking him squarely in the face.

"There's something I don't understand."

"What's that?"

"The doctors told you that if you keep drinking it will kill you. Why won't you listen to them?"

Preston didn't answer right away. It was an intelligent question. It deserved an intelligent answer. Six months ago Preston was diagnosed with cirrhosis of the liver. Doctors told him that if he stopped drinking the disease would stop progressing. If he continued to drink, they told him he could expect complete liver failure within twelve months. He gave it a lot of thought.

He wasn't an alcoholic, but he genuinely enjoyed the taste of scotch. For as long as he could remember he had ended the day with a couple of drinks. He didn't doubt that the doctors knew what they were talking about, but he rationalized that if the trade-off was one year with scotch, versus two years without scotch, he'd take the scotch.

Preston puffed on his cigar and said, "I'm older than you are, but mark my words, you will come to a point in your life when you become so damn tired of comprising that you'll decide, 'Hell, I'm going to do this no matter what!' I guess that's the only way I can explain it. I know that scotch is bad for me. I'm not addicted to it, I swear. But here's the thing—this damn disease is going to take away everything I love in life. Holding onto my scotch is the only way I have to fight back. I've lost a lot over the years. The scotch lets me know that I'm still in the game. Does that make any sense to you?"

Agent Cefalu nodded. "When you put it that way it does make sense. I just hate to see you do something that hurts you."

Preston laughed. "Life itself hurts! From the day we are born, it's a fool's game to see who can make the slowest trip to the finish line. You're not among those who think there's a way to get out of life alive, are you?"

"No, I'm with you. It's a death sentence from day one."

"I'm curious. Are you reporting my drinking to your superiors?"

Agent Cefalu looked at him, a mischievous grin creeping across his face. "Are you reporting my drinking? Or the fact that I'm smoking Commie cigars?"

"No."

"Then how can I report your guilty pleasure?"

"You know, this is one hell of a fine system we've built in America."

"Damn right!"

7

Faith Holiday was not the most famous lounge singer in America, but she'd done well for herself in Las Vegas, where she performed on a regular basis. Growing up she had all the advantages you'd expect of a child born to wealthy parents. But she rejected all that after graduating from high school.

She fell in with the wrong crowd, experimenting with drugs and indulging in petty crimes such as shoplifting and vandalism, finally doing stints as a topless dancer and making an x-rated video or two before discovering that she could carry a tune well enough to front a lounge band.

At twenty-four, she'd already lived a full life, though it didn't show in her face. Still pretty, she had long blonde hair and a decent figure, though she was probably a few pounds overweight. She had a sultry voice that worked to her advantage when she sang ballads, but it wasn't the kind of voice that sent record executives into a tizzy. She'd never have a hit record, and she knew that and it didn't matter because she knew that she someday would inherit a fortune.

Faith was backstage in her dressing room, applying her makeup, when there came a knock at the door. She froze. Drunks sometimes made their way backstage and harassed the female performers. Once the police showed up to serve her with papers. No, a knock at the door did not belong on her Top 10 list of favorite things to hear.

After a moment the knock repeated.

Finally, she said, "Who is it?"

"Tony," said a voice on the other side of the door.

"Oh, come on in," she said, relieved.

Tony Apple was a low-life hood who liked to tell people that he was Faith's manager. In truth, the only booking he ever got for her was the gig with the porno video producers. He took ten percent of her paychecks for the videos and then pocketed the other ninety percent by selling her cocaine.

She tolerated him because he knew people in low places and enjoyed doing favors for her. He was in his mid twenties, had a smoothly shaven head, and wore several gold rings clustered on each ear. On his forearm was a tattoo of a naked woman in a pornographic embrace with a hooded cobra.

"What took you so long to answer?" he asked, pulling up a stool next to her at the makeup mirror.

"I didn't know who it was."

Tony laughed. He had a peculiar way of laughing. It started deep in his gut and rolled up to his throat, sort of like an avalanche in reverse. Once you heard it you never forgot it.

"You're not sleeping with some other guy, are you?"

"No, and I'm not sleeping with you either."

"Don't hurt to try."

"The closest you'll ever come to sleeping with me is when you watched me having sex with that prick the video producers chose for me."

"He done you real good, didn't he?" he said cheerfully.

"Oh, yeah, he done me real good," she said sarcastically. "You ass!"

"That's something you got to get right in your head. Any man you're around is gonna want to do you. It's the law of the jungle."

"I thought the law of the jungle was about killing your dinner."

"Sex . . . killing . . . it's all the same thing."

Faith sighed. "That reminds me of the shit I heard when I was a dancer. You've got to listen to it because they're paying you to listen. Believe me, there are some screwed up men out there."

"And you think women aren't screwed up?"

"Oh, I know damned well that women are screwed up. The difference is that women take their craziness out on themselves, while men take it out on each other — or on women."

Tony shook his head. "You think too much for your own good."

"It wouldn't kill you to do a little thinking yourself."

"It might."

Tony watched her apply makeup to her eyes, fascinated by her concentration and her ability to transform her appearance. Stuff for her lips. Stuff for her eyes. Stuff for her skin. He jumped in the shower, jumped out, and looked the same every day. He wondered what it would feel like to change his appearance on a daily basis. To become someone else.

40

Faith interrupted his line of thought with a question: "So what brings you around today? Any news?"

"I'm just doing my job. Speaking of which I need some more money. Travel expenses."

"I just gave you some money last week."

"All gone. I got expenses."

She stopped doing her eyes long enough to look him in the eye. "OK, fine, I'll have money for you tomorrow. First, I want to know how things are going."

"Don't worry. You're getting your money's worth. When I do a job, I do it right. You know that."

"I'm going to need details at some point."

"I understand. Now's not the time. Some things you don't need to know for your own good. Follow me?"

Faith nodded. Then, satisfied with his answer, she went back to doing her eyes. "Check with me tomorrow. I've got to finish this and then get dressed."

"Yeah," said Tony, coming to his feet. "Enough of this chit chat. I ain't no chick. Do I look like a chick? I don't do chit-chat." He leaned over and kissed her on the cheek and walked out of the room, swinging his arms like a drum major.

Faith smeared makeup over where he kissed her. Then she finished up and changed into a tight-fitting red dress that showed off her cleavage and her legs. She brushed her hair and fluffed it down around her shoulders, brushing it away from her cleavage. One last look into the mirror. Perfect.

She left the dressing room and walked down a long, dimly lighted corridor that took her to stage left. The band was already set up on stage behind a closed curtain. She waved at them, but the drummer was the only person who saw her. He smiled and returned her wave. She walked over to the announcer, who leaned into a podium with a microphone attached to it, and she whispered, "I'm ready when you are."

Without checking with the band, the announcer leaned into the microphone and said, "Ladies and Gentlemen . . ."

Frankly, he didn't give a damn.

The guitarist and bass player hurried to get in place as the curtain pulled apart. They immediately started into a pre-selected fast-tempo song, playing several bars before Faith strode across

41

the stage and stood in front of the microphone. There was mild applause, but she couldn't tell how many people were in the room because of the lighting.

As she began singing, she looked to her left and saw Tony sitting alone, guzzling a beer. She hated it when he came to her performances. Once, using an annoying voice that was loud enough for her to hear on stage, he told everyone seated around him that she was his girlfriend.

When she looked to her right, she saw the last person she wanted to see in the audience — Preston LaGrange!

8

Doe Peterson had this way about her. She brightened a room simply by walking into it. Oscar Ross noticed that right away when she strolled into his office. It was a second floor office, located above a strip mall bakery, and he didn't get many walk-in visitors. As a private investigator, most of his customers contacted him by telephone and asked to meet him in a crowded public place. Didn't hurt his feelings in the least.

Doe caught him with his feet up on his desk, watching a soap opera on television. When he saw her walk in the door, he slammed his feet to the floor, scrambling for the remote so that he could turn off the television. He hurriedly slipped on a plaid sports jacket that he'd hung on the back of his chair.

"Yes ma'am," he sputtered.

Doe extended her hand.

"My name is Doe Peterson and you've come highly recommended."

He took her hand and held it briefly, noting how beautiful her fingers were. "Sit down, please."

Doe sat on the other side of his desk, with her purse planted securely on her lap. She crossed her legs and looked him full in the face.

"What can I do for you Ms. Peterson?"

"I won't mince words. Someone is trying to kill me—and I want to find out who."

"What makes you think someone is trying to kill you?"

Doe told him the same story she told Dr. Mann.

When she finished, she sat quietly and awaited his response.

He was an older man, probably in his early fifties, and he had a stocky build. His hair was thinning on top, but he wore it long, pulled back into a foot-long ponytail. A former city cop who'd been busted for wrecking too many patrol cars during pursuits, he had a seedy, weather-worn look about him.

That was the first thing Doe thought when she saw him. *He'll be perfect!*

43

"That does sound suspicious. I'm not one to believe in coincidences. Who on earth would want to kill a pretty thing like you?"

"If I knew that, I'd go to the police."

"I see."

"Have you gone to the police?"

"Yes — they told me I was being silly."

"I've heard all I need to hear. I'll be glad to take your case. I'll need a retainer, though."

Doe reached into her purse and withdrew an envelope. She tossed it over onto his desk. He picked up the envelope and looked inside, counting the bills.

"Thousand dollars. That'll do."

He opened a desk drawer and dropped the envelope into the drawer and slammed it shut. Then he sat up straight in his chair, pulling himself up close to the desk so that he could take notes on a legal pad.

"Since we don't have any suspects, I'll need to tail you for a week. Once we have a suspect, I'll tail him. I want you to give me your schedule every day for the next week."

Doe told him everything she could think off — all her modeling assignments, her planned lunches with friends, her next visit to Dr. Mann.

"Wait a minute," he said, looking up from the note pad. "You're seeing a shrink?"

Doe nodded.

"Did you tell him that you thought someone wanted to kill you?"

Again she nodded.

"What did he say?"

"Not much. He said he needed more information before he reached a judgment."

"You're not loony, are you?"

Doe was so certain that she wasn't loony that his remark didn't offend her. "No," she said softly. "I'm not even close to being loony."

Oscar grinned. "Glad to hear it. I can't help you if you're loony."

When he got all the information he needed from her, he stood and offered his hand. She rose and shook hands with him, suspecting that he enjoyed the touch of her hand more than she wanted him to. She turned to leave, but then stopped and turned.

"You said you'll be following me?"

"That's right."

"Following me where?"

"Everywhere."

"What kind of car will you be in?"

"You'll see it in the parking space downstairs that has my name on it."

"Thanks," she said, and left. She walked down the stairway and looked for his car. It was a silver, nondescript Altima. Old enough to have several dents on the driver's door. She smiled as she got into her car and drove to her first modeling assignment of the day.

*   *   *

One of the things that Doe liked about being a model was that it required almost no preparation on her part. She simply showed up for work and submitted to whatever the photographer had in mind. She didn't mind being a human canvas.

The hair stylist did her hair the way the photographer wanted it done. The makeup artist applied her makeup to the photographer's specification. And she wore what the photographer selected for her.

No decisions were required on her part, other than the obvious ones such as getting a good night's sleep the night before, not eating a large meal, checking her teeth, and foregoing breath saboteurs like coffee and cheese.

Doe was sitting in the makeup chair when the photographer, Wesley Jones, came into the room and greeted her. He was a pleasant man in his early forties, the only African American photographer in the city who got assignments for high-end projects. Women liked working with him, not just because of his photographs, but because he never hit on them. Some wondered if he was gay.

"So what do you want me to wear today?" asked Doe.

45

"Nothing but a pretty smile."

Doe looked him squarely in the face. Was he joking?

"Don't give me that look," he grinned. "I don't make the rules. I just follow them."

"Maybe you'd better explain what we'll be doing."

"The Dover Bath Company—you know, they're the ones who make all those fancy bathtubs and showers—wants a sensual image for a magazine campaign. You won't be nude in the photograph, but you'll have to be nude for me to get the right shot."

"Will I be in the tub or standing in the shower?"

"Both. It's just a matter of where you hold your hands and arms. OK?"

Doe shrugged. "Sure. I'm fine with it as long as it's done in good taste."

"You're a peach, Doe. Just come out when you're ready."

When he left the room, the makeup artist said, "He's a nice man, isn't he? Wouldn't hurt a fly."

Doe nodded. "I've worked with him several times. So far so good."

With her makeup done to perfection, Doe undressed and put on an oversized terrycloth robe that'd been left out for her. She walked out into the studio, the upper floor of a downtown office building that had been gutted except for the essential structure. The walls were old brick. The floors were hardwood. The ceiling had been stripped so that skylights could be installed the full length of the room.

In the far corner, Wesley had constructed two separate bathrooms, one with a tub and the second with a shower. He elevated a thirty gallon plastic container on a reinforced wooden platform onto which he ran a garden hose from a nearby sink. The principle was simple: the water tank was high enough to give adequate water pressure to the shower and the bathtub.

Wesley was busy adjusting his camera when Doe approached.

"Just have a seat. I'll be ready in a minute."

"It's your nickel," she quipped.

A few minutes later, Wesley said he was ready.

46

"Let's do the shower first. The water won't be hot, but it won't be cold either. When I give you the signal, turn the water on the way you would in your shower at home."

Doe slipped off her robe and her shoes. She had one of the most perfect bodies Wesley had ever seen, which is why he chose her for the project. Her legs were long and lean, and her buttocks were rounded and firm. Her c-cup breasts moved with each step she took, but in a good way.

Once she stepped into the shower, she folded her arms across her breasts, covering herself, and said, "Just tell me what you want me to do."

"You'll need to turn at a slight angle away from the camera. I want a full view of your body from head to foot, but since it's for a magazine ad it can't show pubic hair or too much breast. Certainly not nipples."

Doe turned to her left, twisting slightly to the back wall of the shower.

"How's that?"

"Perfect."

He turned on a smoke machine that created an illusion of steam and he returned to his camera and said, "OK, now turn on the water."

Doe did as he asked, shocked at the initial coolness of the water.

"It's cold, Wesley!"

"You'll get used to it," he grinned, snapping the shutter.

Doe knew the routine and seldom needed direction. She closed her eyes and pretended she was in her own shower. He was right. She got used to the water temperature after only a couple of minutes.

"Beautiful," Wesley said as he snapped frame after frame.

Fifteen minutes later he told her she could turn off the water. She did as he asked and reached for a towel that he'd placed on a nearby stool.

"So what's next?" she asked as she dried herself off.

"We'll do the tub next."

As she finished drying off, he turned on the faucets in the tub.

"We aren't going to use anything hokey like bubbles. Instead, we'll protect your modesty by taking advantage of the way water

47

reflects light. So I'll want you to lean back in the tub and slip down into the water, just enough so that your nipples are covered by the water. I want some cleavage, but not a lot."

Doe wrapped the towel around her and walked over to the tub and watched it fill with water.

"Did you clean this tub out?"

"Of course," he said. It was a lie. "But before you get in there's something I want you to do."

"What's that?" she said, eyeing him suspiciously.

"I want you to you rub baby oil onto your shoulders, upper arms and chest. He held the bottle of oil out to her.

Doe looked at the bottle, but she didn't reach for it.

"Do you have any rubber gloves?"

"Rubber gloves? No, why?"

"If I rub baby oil onto my skin, it will get under my nails. Why don't you do it?"

Wesley looked at her a moment, wondering if he should. He lowered the bottle to his side. "I really need the oil so that your skin doesn't appear dry."

"I understand. But if you want me to use oil, you'll have to apply it yourself."

Wesley worked almost exclusively with women, but he would be the first to admit that he didn't understand them. He'd worked with models that made it clear that if he touched them, even accidentally, they would sue his ass. He'd had affairs with other models, but never touched them at work. He looked at Doe, his eyes pulled down into a squint.

"This is not some kind of trick is it?"

Doe laughed. "Wesley, it's no big deal. Just do it so I can get out of here. I'm meeting my boyfriend for lunch."

Still wrapped in the towel, she sat on the stool near the shower.

"Let's do it!"

Wesley reluctantly walked over to the stool and took the cap off the baby oil bottle. He squirted a small amount of oil on her shoulders and smoothed the oil out with his hands, spreading it down each arm. Then he squirted oil onto her chest and smoothed it out, working his hands down to her breasts as she lowered the towel. He was surprised at the firmness of her breasts because he knew that they had not been augmented.

48

Once he finished, he stepped back and admired his work.

"Not bad," he said.

Doe looked down at her breasts and said, "Cool!"

"Why don't we do the tub now?"

Doe dropped the towel and walked over to the tub and stuck her finger into the water to test the temperature. She frowned. "It's cold."

"You'll get used to it."

She slipped into the water, letting out a subdued squeal.

"Just hurry up. I don't know how long I can stand this."

Wesley looked through the viewfinder and gave her instructions about how to position her neck and head when she leaned back. He never had to ask her anything twice. Once he set the scene, all he had to do was work the shutter. She was the best he'd ever worked with.

She'd get into a zone and the rest of the world ceased to exist.

* * *

After she left the studio she looked for Oscar, but she couldn't find him. *That's odd,* she thought. *Maybe I misunderstood him.*

Disappointed, she pulled out into the street and drove south to an old part of town where Trent had a second-floor condo. The buildings on the street once had been thriving retail shops, but as urban blight had spread through the city the businesses had disappeared, one at a time, replaced thirty years later by boutique shops that catered to young couples without children that thought it was hip to live downtown.

Trent didn't own a boutique, but he had offices wedged in between stores that sold scented candles, artwork, designer clothing, and pottery. He owned an insurance agency that sold a variety of policies that targeted young couples. His condo was across the street from his office. Next door to his condo was a parking garage that had an entrance into his building.

As Doe pulled into the garage, she glanced into her rearview mirror and saw the silver Altima she'd seen outside Oscar's office. She smiled. He'd been there the whole time. *Silly me,* she thought.

Doe parked her car and looked around for the Altima. She didn't see it. She figured he must have parked out on the street. She walked through the dimly lighted garage to the exit door, which was not so much an exit as it was an entrance to the condo building.

The walk to the door always gave her the creeps because of the way her footsteps slapped against the concrete and echoed throughout the garage, reminding her of the grade-B horror movies she saw as a child.

Looking over her shoulder, she punched in the security code and entered and took the elevator to the second floor.

Trent was waiting at the door when she arrived.

They kissed and stepped inside, after which he locked the deadbolt.

"Hungry?" he asked.

"Sure," she said, following him into the kitchen.

"How was the session?"

"Soggy."

"What do you mean?"

"It was for a bath company and I had to pose in a shower and a bathtub."

"You mean, like in a swimsuit?"

"No—I mean, like buck naked."

"Really," he said, a sudden look of concern on his face. "Who was the photographer."

"Wesley Jones."

"I don't trust him. He didn't try anything, did him?"

"Never has."

"He must be queer."

Doe thought about the enormous bulge she saw in his pants while he was putting on the baby oil and she smiled. "Whatever."

They sat at the kitchen counter and ate the sandwiches that Trent had ordered from the deli down the street. He was a considerate man, or so Doe thought. There were rumors that he had ties to some of the city's major drug dealers, but he'd never been arrested or even charged with a crime.

Doe rationalized that people who said that about him were jealous. A former star college quarterback, he was tall and muscular, with long blonde hair that fell down to his shoulders and icy blue eyes that women often found irresistible. Doe was no exception. She often told him that it was he who should be the model. Her eyes got all dreamy when she looked at him.

50

They were still eating when Trent's cell rang.

"Hello," he said. "Sure — forty five minutes? Me, too."

He turned off the phone and looked at Doe.

"Guess you heard that. I've got a meeting in forty-five minutes. Mind if we skip lunch and go straight to dessert?"

"No problem."

Trent put his arm around her and led her into the bedroom. The covers were pulled back on a bed that had sheets that matched his eyes. Doe thought it was a nice touch, but she didn't say anything. Instead, she unzipped the back of her dress and slipped out of it and tossed it onto a nearby chair.

Then she unfastened her bra and looped her thumbs into either side of her panties and slowly twisted them down her legs and over her feet. She twirled the panties on her index finger and tossed them onto the bed.

"Don't move a muscle," said Trent.

He'd already taken off his shirt. Now he was removing his slacks. He walked across the room to where Doe was standing. After a long, passionate kiss, he gently nudged her toward the window, where the blinds were open but just barely, allowing only a sliver of outside light into the room. He placed his hands on her waist and gently turned her to the window.

"Lean over and put your hands on the window sill," he whispered.

"Why?"

"Just do it."

He slapped her buttocks.

"Awe! That stings."

"A little pain enhances the experience."

"If you say so."

She braced herself against the window sill as his movements went from slow and deliberate, to hard and fast, causing her to stiffen to keep from being pushed into the window. As he made love to her, roughly and without whispered words of encouragement, she gazed out the window

Oscar sat in his Altima, eating what appeared to be a hot dog.

She closed her eyes, thankful that he wasn't looking up at the window. Ordinarily, she loved having sex with Trent, but this time she just wasn't that much into it, especially after she looked

51

back over her shoulder and saw him glance at his watch. He could be a son of a bitch, even without trying.

When he finished, he whirled her around and kissed her breasts. Then he lifted her into his arms and carried her to the bed, where he stretched her out and smothered her with kisses. After a few minutes of that, he sighed and leaned back and lay beside her on the bed, exhausted.

"I love having lunch with you," he said.

"But we didn't finish lunch."

"Yes we did."

"That's what you think."

They lay in silence for a while longer and then he looked at his watch and said, "I hate to tell you this, but I'm going to have to run in a few minutes."

"I understand," she said.

He jumped out of bed, a move that looked more like an Olympic maneuver than a lover's farewell, his feet landing flat on the carpet. He hurried to the bathroom, talking without looking at her. "Got to get a quick shower. Just let yourself out. Thanks for coming by. Talk to you later."

Then he was gone.

She heard water running in the bathroom. She slowly got out of bed and searched for her panties. Getting dressed only took a minute. She was thinking . . . *it's me that needs the shower.*

She left the condo and took the elevator down to the first floor.

The garage had a dark, musky smell to it. She looked around. The first floor of the garage was almost empty. Chills raced up her arms. She started for her car, convinced that someone was watching her. She turned several times to look behind her, but she saw nothing unusual. As soon as she got into her car, she locked the doors and started the ignition.

As she drove out onto the street, she saw Oscar in the Altima, but she quickly looked away so that he wouldn't see her looking at him. For some reason, she thought she wasn't supposed to acknowledge his presence.

All this was so new to her that she didn't fully understand all the rules, not that she would follow the rules if she did understand.

She didn't appreciate Trent having rough sex with her. It would have been nicer if he'd discussed it with her first. In case she had some good ideas of her own. Even so, she had to admit that it was exciting. Actually, she felt more aroused thinking about it than she'd been while they were doing it. It was one of those delayed reaction orgasms. She gripped the steering wheel tightly as she touched her thighs together. Her breathing quickened and her eyes widened.

For the first time in her life, she realized that the memory of sex is sometimes more powerful than the act itself. For a minute she thought about turning around and going back for more. The only thing that stopped her was the image of Oscar's Altima in the rearview mirror. If she turned around, she'd have to explain it all to Oscar later and she very much didn't want to do that.

Doe drove on, no longer thinking about death.

Oscar saw a white Mercedes convertible approach the garage entrance and turn inside. The blonde behind the wheel wore a scarf. He only saw her for an instant, but his first impression was that she was quite attractive. He considered staying to check her out, but then he saw Doe going through a traffic light up ahead and he sped after her.

Blondes. Convertibles. An identity-covering scarf.

Maybe it was the PI in him, but that combination usually meant trouble.

9

One of the things that troubled Rivers was the increasing number of women who came into his office to talk about abusive boyfriends or husbands. Five years ago, he'd see maybe two cases like that a month. Today he saw two or three cases a week. He was at a loss to explain the increase.

The woman who just left his office, his last patient of the day, could intellectualize the things she needed to do to have a better life, but when it came down to day-to-day choices she seemed powerless to choose men who would be good for her. As he got ready to leave the office, her explanation continued to ring in his ears: "I can't explain it. I just prefer bad boys—they make me hot!"

When he stepped out of his office into the outer office, he was dismayed to see that his receptionist had gone home and left the door unlocked.

Someone could have come into the office he thought.

He'd asked the receptionist a hundred times to lock the door if she left before he did. Not once had she ever complied. Rivers shook his head as he walked out and locked the door behind him.

Perhaps I'm the wrong person to counsel women he thought. *They never seem to listen to me.*

His restored car had been dropped off at his office earlier that day. He walked around the car, checking out the repairs. To his surprise, it looked as good as new. He unlocked the door with the remote and tossed his briefcase inside. Then he sat in the driver's seat, closed the door, and put his key into the ignition. He turned the key, but nothing happened. The starter turned over, but the car didn't crank. He was about to try again when he smelled smoke. He looked over the steering wheel and saw smoke pouring from beneath the hood.

As he hurried out of the car, there was a loud pop and flames leapt high into the air from beneath the hood. He whirled to run away and tripped, falling hard to the pavement.

Everything went dark.

When he woke, his head was cradled in the arms of the hairdresser who had the beauty shop next door to his office. He tried to get up but the hairdresser pulled him back into her arms. He rubbed the corner of one eye.

"Honey, take it easy," she said. "You knocked yourself clean out."

Rivers raised his head and looked for his car.

Firefighters had sprayed it with foam, creating a billowing black cloud of smoke that rose fifty feet into the air. From out of the chaos a couple of paramedics ran toward him and dropped their gear to the pavement as they asked him how he felt.

"I feel fine," he said.

"No pain?"

"Just my head."

One of the paramedics shined a flashlight into his eyes.

"Follow my finger," he said, moving his index finger from left to right.

Rivers complied and the paramedic nodded.

Rivers asked, "Can I sit up?"

"Sure, if you feel like it."

Rivers sat up and stared at his car.

"Was it a bomb?" he asked.

"You'll have to ask the Fire Officer."

"Who's that?"

The paramedic pointed to a man standing off to the side.

As Rivers watched from a distance, the Fire Officer approached the car once the flames and smoke had been knocked down. One of the firefighters opened the hood so that the Fire Officer could peer at the engine. He pointed at a couple of places and then stepped back. He looked around the parking lot, spotted the paramedics with Rivers, and walked over to them.

"You own this car?" asked the Fire Officer.

"Yes," answered Rivers, rising to his feet. "What the hell happened?"

"That's a good question," said the Fire Officer. "Have you had any problems with the car?"

"None. It was in an accident a few days ago, but there was no problem with fire."

"Did you send it to the shop?"

"Yes."

The Fire Officer nodded knowingly.

"That might be the problem. Something could have happened in the shop during repairs. It looks to me like the gas line was pulled apart from the carburetor. When you tried to start the car you pumped gas out onto the engine and it must have caught a spark."

"So you think it was an accident?"

"What else could it be?"

"Maybe someone sabotaged my car."

"Do you know anyone who'd do that to you?"

Rivers shook his head. No point in telling a firefighter that someone was out to get him. The firefighter had no power to protect him.

"You need to call and have your car towed to a repair shop," said the Fire Officer. "You might want to check with your doctor, too. Good luck."

As the Fire Officer turned away, Rivers said, "Thanks for your help."

Rivers also thanked the paramedics and the hairdresser. Then he retreated to his office. The first person he called was Shelly, but she didn't answer her phone. Then he called to make arrangements to have his car towed to a repair shop. All that remained was getting home. He called a car rental agency and had them deliver a car to his office.

On his way home in the nondescript rental, Rivers replayed the day's events over and over again. What was he missing? He didn't believe in coincidence. Things happened for a reason. Usually, it was just a matter of putting the pieces together. Human behavior follows a pattern. The bad things that had happened to him not only didn't follow a pattern—they made no sense.

When he got home, he pulled a beer from the fridge and went out on the back porch and put his feet up and gazed out at the barges on the river. They plowed through the water with quiet deliberation, bearing mysterious, tarp-covered cargoes that seemed insignificant when compared to the majestic surge of the river. He couldn't hear the sounds of the water from his perch on the bluff, but the moist breezes that flowed off the river found their way to his porch.

Rivers hadn't been on the porch long before he heard Shelly come in the front door.

"Honey, I'm on the porch," he called out. He heard her open the fridge and then walk out onto the porch.

She leaned over and kissed him on the cheek.

"Whose car is that out front?" she asked.

"It's a rental."

"Your car not ready yet?"

"They delivered it this morning."

Shelly looked at him, perplexed.

"They did a great job with the repairs. There was only one problem."

"What's that?"

"When I turned the key, the car blew up."

"What?" said Shelly.

"Yeah, it blew up and burned to a crisp."

As he spoke, she noticed the scrape on his forehead. She leaned over and examined it. "What's this?"

"As I was getting away from the car, I tripped and knocked myself out."

"Oh, my God! Are you all right?"

"The paramedics checked me out."

She sat on his lap and put her arm around his shoulder.

"Why did your car blow up? Was it a bomb?"

"I asked the firefighters and they said it looked like the gas line pulled free and poured gas onto the engine."

"Do you think that's what happened?"

"I don't know what to think, honey."

She pulled herself into his chest, hugging him tightly. He kissed her and said, "Let's go inside."

She smiled. "Now you're talking."

By the time they got to the bed, they both were naked, leaving a line of clothing from the porch to the bedroom. After a few minutes of kissing and touching, he said, "You must have been thinking about me on the drive home."

"Why do you say that?"

"Because you're already so excited."

She nuzzled into his neck, kissing him, moving down across the chest, and then back up to the other side of his neck.

57

"What can I say," she purred. "You have a thermal affect on me."

Later, as they lay in bed, gazing out at the sunset over the foot of the bed, Rivers said, "I tried to call you after my car blew up, but your phone was turned off."

"Oh," she said, looking puzzled. "I don't know why. I must have been with a patient or something."

"I was beginning to feel loveless and homeless—certainly carless."

"Oh, you poor baby!" she said, descending into baby talk. "I feel *soooo* sorry for you."

"Sometimes it's hard being me."

"Whatever."

10

Jack McCain was surprised to see Rivers walk unannounced into his newspaper office. He glanced at his watch.

"Pie time already?" he asked.

Without being invited, Rivers sat in the only empty chair in the room. "It's amazing how quickly the weeks are passing."

Jack looked at his friend, not liking what he saw.

"You're early — what's on your mind?"

"There's something I want to talk to you about. I didn't want to talk in the restaurant."

"Are you all right? I mean, from a health standpoint."

"Oh, sure," he said, forcing a brief smile. They'd lost a mutual friend to cancer the previous year and it still bothered both of them, not so much losing him as watching him fade away a little bit at a time, day by day.

"It's nothing like that."

"That's good."

"My problem is that someone is trying to kill me — or at least I think they are."

Jack stared at him, waiting for him to continue.

Rivers paused, thinking that a well-paced question from Jack would be in order, but when it didn't come, he told him the rest.

"The sheriff's office and the fire department say both incidents are accidental. What do you think?"

Neither men would admit it, but Jack was Rivers' shrink. His experience as a journalist, dealing with a wide variety of people, gave him the kind of insight you couldn't learn in school. Jack pondered the question.

"If I was a police officer or a firefighter, I'd probably tell you not to worry about it, playing the odds, you know. Besides, what police officer or firefighter do you know that wants more work? Of course, if I were you, I'd be concerned."

"Really?"

"Well . . . yes! How many years have you been driving?"

Rivers paused, doing the math. "Twenty-six years."

"Ouch! During that twenty-six years, how many times have you been run off the road into a ditch by a hit-and-run driver, and how many times have you had your car blow up?"

Rivers looked surprised. "That's not what I wanted to hear."

"What did you want to hear?"

"That I had nothing to worry about."

"All I can tell you is that if it were me, I'd be concerned."

"You'd have reason to be concerned. Through your writing, you've ruined careers and sent people to prison. I'm the one they came to for counseling before going to prison. You've got powerful enemies. I don't have an enemy in the world that I know about. Do you think I've got enemies?"

"I wouldn't know who they'd be."

"Neither do I. I'm not like you. I've played it safe my entire life. What should I do?"

"Do you own a gun?"

"I've got a shotgun that belonged to my father."

"What about a pistol?"

"No."

Jack yanked open his desk drawer and pulled out a chrome-plated .44 magnum that he slammed down on his desk top. Rivers' eyes widened.

"Take this one, then."

Rivers shook his head. "No, no . . . "

"Then get one of your own—and learn how to use it."

"Do you think it's that serious?"

"Do you?"

Rivers nodded. "Life sure has a lot of crap in it."

"You only get to play it once. That's why you've got to do it right."

"OK, I've got that off my chest. Let's go get some pie."

"Now you're talking," Jack said.

They walked past the other editorial offices to the elevator and rode down in silence. Since the restaurant was only a few blocks away, they decided to walk. It was a beautiful day. Blue sky. White clouds. Hot, but not too hot. They passed a homeless man playing a harp and they tossed some change into his tin cup.

"That fellow had a hit record thirty years ago," said Jack.

"No kidding."

"After I started work here, I saw him about town quite a bit. He had the town's only Rolls. Always had a blonde on each arm. Apparently he's not too good with a budget."

"I get musicians coming in for therapy from time to time. Usually it's drug related. Most of them, if they have any degree of success, have a difficult time coping with the loss of that success. They go through a grieving process similar to what people go through when they lose a loved one. Many people who lose loved ones expect them to miraculously come back. Same way with musicians who lose fame and fortune. Sometimes they do rebound, but not often. Music is not a business I'd want a kid of mine going into."

When they arrived at the restaurant, they sat at their usual table and ordered their usual pie. The waitresses and waiters all dubbed them the cocoa twins. They didn't care. They figured they could be called worse.

After the pie arrived, Jack said, "I know you don't want to discuss your problem here, but if there's anything I can do, just let me know."

"What could you do?"

"I don't know. But if something comes up that you think I might be helpful dealing with . . . you know, with the police, or with some of my sources. Just let me know. Meanwhile, watch your back."

Rivers didn't respond. His eyes were riveted on something in the distance. Jack followed his line of sight and saw Shelly being seated at a table with a man he'd never seen before. His long blonde hair was pulled back into a ponytail.

Rivers asked, "Who's that?"

Jack didn't answer.

Rivers looked at him, perplexed.

Jack said, "Are you going to sit here and stare? Or are you going to go over and say something?"

This time Rivers didn't answer.

Jack continued, "Tell you what—let me finish off my pie and we'll leave together."

Rivers nodded. He couldn't take his eyes off Shelly. Not once had she looked around the room. Her eyes never left the eyes of her lunch companion. He wondered if she did this sort of thing every day.

Finally, Jack said, "Let's go. This one is on me."

They stood and Jack tossed a couple of bills onto the table. Then they started across the room to where Shelly was seated. As they approached, she turned and looked Rivers squarely in the face. She froze for a moment. Then she gave him her most radiant smile. She rose from her chair and embraced Rivers and spoke to Jack. Then she said, "Honey, this is Trent Boggs. He's an insurance agent and he'd like for us to switch our home insurance over to his company."

Trent stood and extended his hand, first to Rivers and then to Jack. "Pleased to meet you, Dr. Mann. Do you have time to join us?"

Rivers glanced at his watch.

"No, I don't think I can. I've got an appointment in ten minutes." He smiled and then continued, "If I'm late, my patients tend to worry."

"I understand," said Trent. "I'll just make my spiel to your lovely wife."

Jack remained silent for as long as he could.

"How long have you two been doing business?"

Shelly glanced at him, a fleeting look that told him she didn't appreciate the question.

Before Trent could answer, Shelly said, "One of the girls in my office has insurance with him. She told me we could save a lot of money if we switched."

Rivers thought about that a moment. No one likes to have an awkward conversation with a loved one in front of others. He wondered why she didn't tell him about the insurance. Perhaps she was discussing his two accidents with her staff and someone asked her if they had enough insurance to cover my losses. It could be as simple as that. Finally, he said, "I really have to run. Why don't you give Shelly all the information and we'll discuss it tonight."

"That sounds good," said Trent.

Rivers leaned over and kissed Shelly and said, "See you tonight, honey."

"Love you," she said.

As they were going out the door, Jack whispered, "Do you know who that was?"

"What do you mean?"

"He's got an insurance agency all right, but he's a pretty shadowy figure."

"Really? So you don't think I should let him have my insurance?"

Jack looked at him and shook his head. Rivers was a brilliant psychologist, but sometimes he couldn't see the big picture.

"If it was me, I wouldn't want him involved in my life. Trust me. You should keep your distance."

"If you feel that strongly . . ."

"I do."

"Should I go back now and tell him I'm not interested?"

"No — let it go for now."

11

Preston had become reclusive since the diagnosis of his illness.

When you know you're going to die, you don't so much seek out new experiences as you try to understand old ones. He'd done well for himself but he had regrets. He no longer awoke each morning excited about the possibilities of a new day. His first thought each morning was always, "Oh, I see I'm still here."

Wouldn't it be nice if we lived forever?

Well, maybe not. All life comes with baggage. Who wants to carry baggage for all eternity? Not Preston LaGrange, that's for sure. It was three years ago that doctors handed him his first real baggage. He'd had indigestion for years. Not until his urine turned brown did he go see a doctor. They ran a urinalysis and found that his bilirubin levels were elevated. Then they ran a blood test and his liver enzyme numbers were sky high. They prodded him from head to foot, and then asked him to undergo a liver biopsy. When the results came back, his doctor sat him down and gave him the bad news—cirrhosis of the liver.

At first it was no big deal. He felt fine. You couldn't tell that he was sick. His doctor told him that if he quit drinking he'd be a candidate for a liver transplant. Preston promised he'd quit drinking, but he never did.

As the months went by, his body underwent changes. He started itching a lot. He began to lose his hair. Spiderlike blood vessels appeared on his chest. Disturbing symptoms, but not terrifying. It wasn't until his ankles started swelling that he went back to see his doctor.

"Fluid is starting to build up in your body," the doctor explained. "I can give you some pills to take care of that. If you don't take the pills, your gut will be the next thing to swell. We call it ascites."

"So you can take care of all these things?"

"Yes, for a while. Did you stop drinking like I asked you to?"

Preston shook his head.

"If you stop today, there's a chance you'd be approved for a liver transplant."

"If I don't?"

"Then you don't get a new liver."

"If I keep going like I'm going, how long do I have?"

"If you keep drinking? I'd say six to nine months."

"What happens next?"

"It's not a pretty picture."

"I can handle it."

"One of your liver's important jobs is to filter toxins out of your blood. Especially ammonia. When a liver is sick, like yours, the amount of toxins that get past the liver and go to your brain gradually increases. If that happens, your behavior starts changing. Whereas once you showered each morning, you rationalize doing it every few days. You lose interest in keeping up your appearance. You start forgetting things. In the later stages, you may experience hallucinations and not recognize old friends."

"Anything else?"

"Yes," said the doctor, and he walked over to a chart that had an image of the human liver. "All your blood passes through your liver," he explained, pointing to the image on the chart.

"When you have cirrhosis, it creates a roadblock for some of that blood. When that happens, the blood pressure inside your liver increases to a point where it causes the veins in your throat and stomach to balloon out like varicose veins. If the blood pressure inside those veins gets too high, they explode, filling your throat or stomach with blood. If that happens, it's a life threatening emergency that has to be addressed with surgery."

Preston shook his head, rattled, but not willing to admit it, not even to himself. "When it comes to dying, what's the best case scenario?"

"You have a heart attack or stroke. There's no good way to die from the complications of cirrhosis."

"What are the chances it will clear up on its own?"

"About the same as you waking up as a woman."

"Oh."

You'd think Preston's conversation with his doctor would've forced him to give up his scotch. Sadly, it had the opposite effect. Scotch became even more of a crutch to get through day to day living. His talk with his doctor did have one major effect. It made him determined not to drown in his own blood, or to die locked up in some funny farm because his brain was pickled in ammonia.

12

Faith rode through a one hundred degree wall of heat. Her tomato-red Honda C90 purred along at 50 miles-per-hour, its top speed. She seldom left town on her motorbike. Mostly she drove it around town. She loved the freedom it afforded her, especially when it came to parking and gas mileage. It wasn't unusual for the bike to get 100 miles-per-gallon.

What she didn't like about taking it out on the highway were the 80-mile-per-hour jerks in the limos who zipped past her and shouted profanities at her for cruising below the speed limit. She didn't care. The purr of the motor. The feel of the air, however hot and stinging against her face. The smell of the roadway. It all came together in a good way for her.

Tony Apple was on the seat behind her, his arms wrapped about her bare midriff. They were on their way from Vegas to Lake Meade to do some scuba diving. She couldn't stand the guy, but he did favors for her and trips like this were the price she paid for those favors.

She didn't mind having his arms around her midriff, but every now and then his hands wandered up inside her tube top. She'd learned while working as a dancer that when men grabbed her boobs the best way to handle it was to ignore it. Men feel foolish if they're squeezing boobs and the woman acts as if she's totally unaffected. That happened to her once in the club and she leaned to one side so that she could watch television. When the man saw her do that, totally oblivious to his efforts to molest her, it deflated him totally and his hands dropped to his side.

Same song, different verse when Tony started messing with her boobs on the motorbike. She said nothing, just kept watching the road, grooving on the rough grind of the tires against the pavement, wondering what kind of man would get off on a woman wearing a helmet.

After a few seconds, Tony felt wimpy and slid his hands back down to her waist, acting like it was no big deal, though she herself knew it was burning at him inside that she didn't respond, as if his hands were nothing more than bugs on a windshield.

Time passed quickly on the road. By the time they arrived at Lake Mead, she'd barely had time to ponder the things in her life that'd turned sour on her. She liked to think about them because thinking about them made her feel that she had some control over them. She didn't, of course. She was like a leaf caught up in a tornado. Her destiny was no longer in her hands, if it ever had been. She was oppositional to that thought, convinced that if she kept trying, she would eventually win life's game. But since when has life ever given points for effort?

Faith chained her motorbike to a gate. They were greeted by a one-eyed man who took their rental fee and then fished the change from his front pockets. Once he walked away, they loaded their scuba gear aboard a pontoon boat that was badly in need of paint. From a distance, the one-eyed man watched their every move, trying not to be obvious.

"They're biting pretty good over at the west end!" he shouted.

"We'll give it a try," said Tony.

"Need bait? I got plenty."

Tony shook his head and waved him off.

With Faith at the throttle, they slowly pulled away from the dock and headed for open water. A short distance from the dock, Faith opened up the throttle and locked it into place. As the boat chugged along, she slipped off her jeans, revealing a black bikini bottom. Then she turned her back to Tony and slipped off her tube top and quickly put on a black bikini top.

"Let me know when you see a good place," she shouted to Tony, who was at the other end of the boat.

"It all looks the same to me," he shouted back.

Faith throttled back and then killed the engine. Without saying a word to Tony, she tossed an anchor overboard and leapt into the lake. She'd brought gear for him, but he wasn't sure if he wanted to use it. He wasn't about to put on the gear and jump into the water without her supervision. He waited, walking around the boat, looking at the water for some sign of her.

Twenty minutes later, Faith bobbed into view, her golden hair glittering in the bright sunlight. She looked around to get her bearings. The pontoon boat was less than fifty feet away. When she spotted it, she swam leisurely over to the boat and latched onto the boarding ladder.

Tony peered over the rail at her. With one, quick gesture, she slipped off her diving mask and tossed it into the boat. She said, "It's dark down there, but I can make my way around."

Tony reached out to help her aboard. She stepped onto the deck and slipped off her scuba gear and shook the water from her hair, looking like she belonged in a television travel ad for the Caribbean. She had just the right look: large, pale-blue eyes, high cheekbones and a square, masculine jaw, features that blended into a package that was practically impossible for anyone to ever forget.

"Don't you want to dive?" she asked. "I thought you'd follow me in."

Tony shook his head.

"I'm not sure if I want to."

He was embarrassed to tell her that he couldn't swim. He'd tried to learn when he was young, but it didn't work out. Each year after that, it seemed, there was always something that kept him from resuming his lessons.

Faith didn't care one way or the other if he went into the lake. She didn't ask him to explain further. His answer would have bored her and distracted her from her main pursuit in life—pampering the person she loved the most, herself. She stretched out on the deck, face down, and unfastened her bikini top. She lay in the sun for a long while before speaking again.

Finally, she said, "You going back tomorrow?"

"Yeah," he said. "Tomorrow night."

"Don't mess this up."

"I'm not."

"It's got to go down exactly like I told you."

"There's no need for you to talk down to me like I'm a kindergartner."

"I'm not, Tony. It's just that when I pay for something, I want it done the way I want it done. Understand?"

Tony didn't respond. He hated it when women bossed him.

Soon she dozed off, her back soothed by the warm rays of the sun. Thirty minutes later, when she awoke, she felt refreshed. She raised up and saw Tony sitting on the edge of the boat, his legs dangling in the water. She fastened her top and got to her feet.

"I'm going back in," she said. "Why don't you come with me?"

"Naw, I'm enjoying what I'm doing."

"But you aren't doing anything."

"Exactly."

"Suit yourself."

Faith slipped on her scuba gear, adjusted her mask, and jumped into the lake. As she descended into the murky waters of the lake, she held a battery-powered spotlight in front of her. She swam along the floor of the lake. It was remarkably smooth, covered with a thick carpet of dark, tangled vegetation.

Beyond the beam of the spotlight, the lake was a pitch-black wall of darkness. It reminded her of driving on a rural road on a moonless night. Occasionally, fish swam in and out of the light beam, red eyes sparkling.

Suddenly, the spotlight went dark as it was knocked from her hand and a shadowy figure swam past, nearly brushing against her. Frantically, she kicked her way to the surface, her head bobbing straight up out of the water near the boat. She saw Tony, but his back was turned. She yanked the mask from her face.

"There's something down there!" she screamed.

Tony rushed to the side of the boat. "What are you talking about?"

Faith swam to the side of the boat.

"Something went past me in the dark. It knocked the light out of my hand." Before Tony could answer, she turned and nervously glanced about the lake. "Were any boats in the area?"

"There's no one else around." Faith's story gave credence to his worst fears about underwater experiences. It made him sick to his stomach.

"Strange," said Faith, a puzzled look on her face.

"Probably nothing to it."

Faith managed a smile. "Yeah. Probably nothing to it."

Tony helped her into the boat. "What do you want to do now? Do you want to go back to the dock and get another light?"

Faith thought a moment, her chest still heaving. Finally, she shook her head. "I don't think so. I've had enough for one day. I want to go back to the dock."

13

Preston wasn't interested in leaving the penthouse. He had a DVD collection of more than three hundred classic movies and a music collection that contained every song ever recorded by the Beatles, the Rolling Stones and the Animals. If he wasn't in the mood for music or movies, he surfed the Internet or played around with Mack 222 to see what the government was up to.

They didn't like it when he did that. He was only supposed to enter Mack 222 at their request to solve a specific problem. Each time he violated that rule, some anonymous government official always contacted Agent Cefalu and blessed him out, as if it was somehow his fault, and demanded that Agent Cefalu question Preston about the incident and fill out a report and send it to Washington in triplicate (no emails accepted).

Preston had a number of icons on his computer screen. One was for his Internet service. One was for his word processor program. Another was for music downloads, but he never used that program. The icon for Mack 222 was a skull and bones depiction. He found it amusing. It was his way of slapping the government's wrists. He didn't particularly like the government, mainly because it was so totally without a sense of humor. Agent Cefalu was the only government man he'd ever met that could take a joke. He liked that about him.

Preston clicked on the Mack 222 icon and waited for it to download from his hard drive. Then he entered his username, followed by his password. He knew that Agent Cefalu would be knocking on his door within the hour, but he didn't care. The Mack 222 was his baby. He'd rock it anytime he damned pleased. Once he entered the top secret system, he monitored the traffic for a few minutes, curious about what the government was doing.

One scan was not surprising. Using the words "surprise, mosque, Iraq, Iran, flight and explosive," and then opening the gate to any pairings that used three of the six words, the scan picked up thousands of emails and telephone calls. He read some of the emails and listened in on some of the telephone calls.

One telephone call was from a daughter to her mother.

Said the daughter, "My **flight** to Pittsburgh was two hours late, but when I arrived at the **mosque** it was a pleasant **surprise**."

Preston moved on to another scan that had the words "money, secret, campaign, New York, and voters." Like the other scan, it produced thousands of catches. Again, he listened in on a conversation: "**New York voters** are essential to her **campaign**, but the **money** simply isn't there. Senator Jackson is her secret **weapon**. I'm sure there will be a public statement later this month."

Disgusted by what he overheard, or more to the point, disgusted that he was able to overhear such a confidential conversation, Preston left the scan toolbar and started working the search engine to initiate a scan of his own. He entered the words he wanted located and waited.

Within seconds he had a response: no hits.

Preston sighed. If there was no current activity, he'd have to search various government archives, some of them public, others top secret. The Mack 222 was super software that knew no boundaries. But to find what he wanted, he had to know where to search. This time he went to the State Department archives of confidential documents. He entered the same words and phrases. Within seconds, he had more than two dozen hits.

About that time his door bell rang.

He knew damned well who it was.

He looked at his watch. Only thirty minutes this time. He quickly logged off, shut down his computer and left the room, locking the door behind him. He looked through the peephole and saw Agent Cefalu. He opened the door and greeted his friend with a broad smile.

"What can I do you for?" he asked.

"You know."

"Come on in. What'll it be, beer or scotch?"

"It's kind of early in the day for drinking, isn't it?"

"Late — early — they're just words."

"I expect you know why I'm here you old son of a bitch."

Preston laughed. "Damn it Cefalu! You take all this too seriously."

"You would to if that was where your paycheck came from."

"Oh, I got my money from them in a lump sum. Well, most of it—they still pay me monthly to keep myself available."

"You're a little too available if you ask me," grumbled Agent Cefalu.

"Oh, hell. What is it this time?"

"You know damned well."

Preston put his arm around Agent Cefalu's shoulder.

"I was just doing a routine check," he lied, knowing full well that Agent Cefalu knew it was a lie. That was a big part of their friendship: a mutual agreement that it was Ok to lie as long as it was to keep the other person out of trouble.

"So when I fill out the report I should say that you were given the system a routine checkup?"

"Absolutely."

Agent Cefalu continued, ". . . as a means of detecting problem areas at an early stage of their development?"

"I couldn't have explained it better myself. Do you want that drink now, or do you want to come back after you write out the report?"

Agent Cefalu thought a minute. "Maybe I'll come back for the drink."

Preston walked him to the door and watched him make his way to the elevator, thinking, with a tinge of remorse in his heart, *my last friend.*

14

When Tony Apple arrived in Memphis, the first thing he did was to rent a white-panel truck at the airport. It had tinted windows and an automatic transmission. He preferred trucks to cars. Something about the way they fit the road. Personal preference aside, panel trucks better suited his professional interests. Independent contractors, like him, needed extra space.

Driving to the Commodore Hotel, he played around with the radio. He was impressed. It even had a CD player. The truck had only 1,263 miles on it. He took a deep breath and sighed. Still had that new truck smell. Nothing better.

He realized he was driving too fast, and he eased up on the accelerator and slowed down. Didn't want a speeding ticket, that's for sure. He turned on the radio. It was pre-set to FM-100, a pop station that didn't have much use for guitars. No problem. He liked the deejay, a fast-talking man with a Southern accent who seemed to be upset about something. He decided to stick with him. When a man hears another man who's upset, he naturally wants to know what he's upset about in case it's something he needs to be upset about.

He exited the Interstate and turned onto Union Avenue, going east instead of west. Wrong way. He turned around in a liquor store parking lot, but not before purchasing a fifth of vodka that was dutifully fitted into a brown paper bag upon which someone had lost a game of tic-tac-doe.

As he drove west toward the river, he went past Sam Philip's Recording Service, where Elvis got his start. Even with the air conditioner on, the heat was unbearable. Vegas was hot, but not this sticky kind of hot. The back of his shirt stuck to the seat.

Since he didn't want to be associated with the truck anymore than necessary, he parked on the street at the front of the hotel, where he'd have to turn his keys over to a valet. Once parked, he slid his suitcase off the passenger seat and strolled along the sidewalk. He walked past a man with a guitar who was seated on a crate pulled over into the shade of a skyscraper.

Next to him was a sign that read **I used to be SOMEBODY! Now when I look in the mirror, I see somebody else!**

Tony flipped a coin into the metal cup at his feet and kept walking, the music of the man's guitar in rhythm to his footsteps.

Tony nearly fainted when he walked into the hotel lobby; the wall of cold air that greeted him was intense, like walking into a meat locker. The lobby had an ornate, marble fountain at one end, around which were gathered a group of tourists. The furnishings looked expensive. Exactly what you'd expect in a five hundred dollar a night hotel. He could've stayed in a cheaper place, but he knew that the cops would be less likely to hassle him at the Commodore.

After he checked in, he went straight to his room and stretched out on the king-sized bed. He didn't especially care for traveling. It made him sleepy. He pulled the pillows from beneath the covers and arranged them in a special way.

Then he dropped off to sleep.

The phone was ringing when he awoke.

"Hello," he said, groggy.

"You all right?" asked the voice at the other end.

"Oh, yeah . . . I was taking a nap."

"Nap!"

"What's wrong with that?"

"For starters, it's eight in the morning."

"I was up all night, and the flight in tired my ass out."

"Oh."

"Shouldn't you be calling on my cell?"

"I tried, but it's turned off."

"That's because I was taking a nap."

"I guess there's nothing else to talk about. Just wanted to make sure that you arrived OK."

"You aren't having second thoughts, are you?"

"No, it's not that at all. I've got to go now. Let me know if you run into any problems."

"I will."

He hung up the phone, shaking his head.

Maybe this whole thing was a mistake.

15

Doe awoke and saw the gentle, morning light creep fog-like around the mini blinds into her bedroom. Her eyes welled with tears. She didn't have to raise the blinds to know that it was going to be a beautiful day. She lay on the bed with her feet lazily spread apart, surrendering to the moment.

Doe had been dating Trent for only three months, but she clearly saw the potential for a long-term relationship. At twenty-six, she'd had her share of relationship misfires, but each failure only gave her more hope for the future. At least that's what she told herself. She believed that where there is smoke there is hardly ever fire. Lord knows, she'd ploughed through enough smoke in her life to provide special effects for the average Arnold Schwarzenegger movie. What she wanted most in life was a raging fire. Passion. She craved it.

She thought about the day that awaited her. She had a photo session for an ad campaign for a local department store. She had an appointment with Dr. Mann. For her, that was a full day.

She heard her roommate, Flutie, stirring in the next room.

"Did you remember the coffee?" Flutie called out, her voice whinny with sleep.

"It's in the refrigerator," answered Doe.

"Thank God," said Flutie, her voice trailing off as she padded from her bedroom to the kitchen.

Doe and Flutie had been friends since their early twenties, when they dated men who were best friends. The relationships fell to the wayside after the boyfriends completed medical school and announced that they were gay and in love with each other and planned to move to New Orleans to find their happiness; but the women's friendship blossomed, even though they chose different career paths.

Doe became a model. Flutie opened the Mud Pie Café, one of the most popular pastry and coffee shops in Memphis. Sardonically bubbly, she soon found that she was a natural-born hostess.

Hearing Flutie clank around in the kitchen made it difficult for Doe to lie in bed and daydream, so she reluctantly got up and began the rituals that defined her mornings. She looked in the mirror and fluffed her hair. She felt older than she looked. She had a flawless complexion that was the envy of every woman she met, including her best friend, Flutie. When she entered a room, men *and* women noticed. Beauty was her curse.

"I wonder what Trent sees in me," she thought, running her fingers through her hair. She gathered her curls up into a ball and held it on top of her head. In an instant, she knew that would not do. It made her look older.

Flutie's voice wafted out of the kitchen.

"I'm making pancakes. Want some?"

"Not today. Thank you." She ran her fingers over her stomach. "I want to look my best today."

Doe ran her bath water into an old tub with ornate legs and tossed in a sprinkling of bath oil beads. Their upscale condo was in a renovated midtown building that dated back to the 1920s. She took her clothes off, removing the paper-thin cotton gown that was her trademark. She swore that it guaranteed her sweet dreams, even under the worst of circumstances, but Flutie said that the gown made her look like a little girl and she didn't mean that in a nice way.

She tossed the gown onto the door hook and gently lowered herself into a tub filled with steaming hot water. The sound of the faucet screeching as she turned it off was her cue to lean back and savor the upcoming day.

Doe had soaked in the tub for only a minute or two when Flutie appeared, wearing the Springsteen T-shirt that she always slept in.

"Coffee is on the way," announced Flutie. She hiked up the T-shirt and sat on the toilet.

Doe hated it when she did that. She complained about her lack of modesty often, but Flutie was not a woman who easily changed her behavior. Criticisms were jokes meant to be tossed aside and pondered from a safe distance.

Doe closed her eyes and sank deep into the water as Flutie tinkled in the toilet. She heard Flutie wipe and waited for the sound of her footsteps leaving the room. Instead, Flutie stood over

77

the tub, waiting for Doe to open her eyes. After a moment passed, Doe said, "Is there no soap in the lavatory?"

Flutie turned and looked. "Yeah, you got soap."

"Why don't you wash your hands?" Doe asked.

"I'll wash them later. I always wash before I handle food."

"I hate to tell you Flutie, but you don't fit the profile for a cultured woman."

"How's that?"

"Women, statistically speaking, wash their hands immediately after using the bathroom, not *later*."

"You may be right. Maybe I'm more like a man. I know that when it comes to sex, I'm more like a man."

Doe opened her eyes and saw Flutie's smiling face gazing down at her. Flutie and Doe were about the same height, but Flutie had more curves and wore her naturally blonde hair in a loose style that brushed against her shoulders. Most men found her beautiful, especially when she slipped her dazzling smile into overdrive.

"What on earth do you mean?"

"I mean I don't have to be in love with a man to sleep with him."

"Is that the way men think?"

"Oh, you know it."

"Well," Doe said, her thoughts wandering. "I guess I'm the same way, but I have to be in love with a man to keep on sleeping with him."

"That's a different story entirely."

There was a long pause, the two women smiling at each other. Finally, Flutie asked, "Is that all?"

"What do you mean, is that all?"

"Can I go now? I've got pancakes on the griddle."

Doe sighed. "I never invited you to share this private moment in the first place."

"Are you sure?"

"Damned sure."

"Well, in that case, you'll have to finish that bath in silence." As she went out the door, Doe screamed, "Flush the damn toilet before you leave!"

78

Flutie grinned at her. "Sorry, but I haven't washed my hands yet and I know how picky you are about your toilet."

Then she was gone. Flutie was like that. It was as if she had radar that picked up silence and drew her to it like a hammer to fine china. Doe and Flutie bickered a lot, but it was done in a playful way because they loved each other dearly and would never intentionally say anything to hurt the other person.

Doe had just slipped into her bra and panties when the doorbell rang. She hurriedly walked into Flutie's bedroom and found her sitting on her bed drinking a cup of coffee, a pillow between her legs.

"Would you get the door, please, so I can finish dressing?"

"Sure," said Flutie gleefully, whipping the pillow aside to reveal that she had on no panties. "Anything else you want me to do."

"No, no, no," said Doe, breaking out into laughter. "You just finish your coffee. I'll get the door."

"Whatever," said Flutie, returning the pillow to its place of honor.

Doe slipped on a housecoat and went to the door and peered through the peephole. She saw a man with a bouquet of flowers. Her heart raced and she threw open the door.

"Flowers for Doe Peterson," said the man, holding a dozen long-stemmed, red roses.'

"That would be me."

The man handed her the roses and told her to have a nice day.

Doe closed the door and looked for a card. There was none. She was looking for some indication of the florist's name when Flutie walked into the room.

"Nice," said Flutie. "From Trent?"

"There's no card," she said, a puzzled look on her face.

"Maybe it fell off."

Doe looked at the floor around the door. "No . . . nothing."

"Don't they usually send those over in a box?"

"I don't think they were from Trent," said Doe. "He'd want to make sure that I knew they were from him."

Flutie laughed. "Maybe you've got a secret admirer."

Doe grimaced. "I've got all the secret admirers I need, thank you."

Flutie walked away, talking over her shoulder, "Your friend Trent seems to have an admirer of his own. Saw him in the café with a good looking blonde."

Doe shouted after her, "He told me about that—it was a business lunch."

"Whatever," Flutie said, disappearing into her bedroom.

16

Oscar Ross drank coffee from a thermos as he sat outside Doe's townhouse, scrunched down in his seat so that the outline of his head couldn't be seen against the background of the headrest. Actually, he was about half a block away, far enough that he could see someone coming and going from the townhouse, but not so close as to be obvious.

The stakeout was his specialty. He especially like it when he was a cop and on the city's payroll. Some days he spent weeks at a time, just sitting outside houses, drinking coffee, reading magazines, listening to the radio, watching people enter and leave. Sometimes he took photographs.

He was there when Doe received the roses, but he didn't think anything about it. Just a guy in a truck with flowers. He rang the doorbell, handed over the flowers, and left. Nothing out of the ordinary.

When Doe left the house, he followed her to Dr. Mann's office.

17

Doe was beaming when she walked into Rivers' office.

"You look unusually chipper today," he said. There's nothing a psychologist likes better a smiling patient.

"That's because I'm dating the most wonderful man in the world."

She sat in the chair opposite his desk. In her hand was a folder.

"This morning he sent me a dozen of the most beautiful roses you've ever seen."

"What was the occasion?"

"That's the best part. There was no occasion. He did it because he's got a big heart. He didn't even enclose a card."

"Really," said Rivers. "Why didn't he enclose a card?"

"Because, to him, that'd be bragging."

"Oh. That's unusual. Most men like to brag when they send flowers."

"Really?"

"Sure."

Rivers wasn't sure what to make of that. He doodled on his note pad. One of the emotionally painful things about being a psychologist was the frequency with which patients subjected their therapists to an unending array of highs and lows. The smile that first appears to be an indication of improved emotional well-being can sometimes be nothing more than an inappropriate reaction to a stressful situation. He'd had patients lose loved ones and come into the office smiling, only to quickly break down into hysterical crying.

Doe had wrapped her entire face about a smile, but he wondered if the reason for the smile was appropriate. If he'd received an anonymous gift, he'd be curious about the intent of the sender.

Once she appeared comfortable, he asked if she'd had any more problems.

"No, I feel safe now."

"Why's that?"

"I hired a private investigator to keep an eye on me."

"Who'd you hire?"

"Oscar Ross."

"Used to be a cop, didn't he?"

"Yeah, that's him."

"What did he say about the flowers?"

"I haven't talked to him about it."

Rivers offered her a glass of water, but she declined. He poured a glass for himself. He hoped he wasn't too transparent. Water was a useful tool to pace an interview. He suspected some patients probably knew what he was doing. He didn't care. Sometimes he was thirsty.

"Let's talk about your boyfriend."

"Good choice of topics."

"You've been together how long?"

"About three months."

"At any point during your relationship, have you ever broken it off?"

"Sure. Several times."

"Why did you break up?"

"Because he gets so jealous. Sometimes I get tired of him following me to photo sessions. I get tired of him criticizing me for posing in little or nothing for male photographers. I get tired of him telling me who I can be friends with."

"So he's done things like that more than once?"

"Yes, but he's got my best interests at heart."

"Why would he follow you to a photo session?"

"So that I get there safely."

"And why does he tell you what friends to have?"

"So that I won't be hurt."

"And that doesn't bother you?"

"Of course, it does. A few times I broke up with him."

"Why do you go back to him?"

"Because I love him. I can't help it. He's a wonderful man."

"Has he ever hit you, pushed you, or yelled at you?"

"Yes."

"Which?"

"All of the above. It sounds bad, I know. But he'd never do those things if I didn't give him cause to. When you get down to it, most of the things that happen are my fault. He loves me so

83

much it drives him crazy and he does things he wouldn't ordinarily do."

Rivers sighed.

"I want you to understand that there is nothing you can do that justifies him hitting you or pushing you or emotionally abusing you by telling you that you are worthless. Has he ever told you that?"

"Yes. But you're making him sound bad and he's not that way. He's a wonderful man."

"What does he do for a living?"

"He owns an insurance company."

"What's his name?"

"Trent Boggs."

Rivers doodled on his notepad. He wondered if Trent Boggs was behind the unfortunate incidents Doe had experienced. Perhaps he wants to frighten her so that she will be more dependent on him. Then, again, perhaps someone really is trying to kill her.

Being a therapist is a little bit like being a cop. Anytime a woman is murdered, the husband or boyfriend is always the prime suspect in the eyes of the cops. Whenever a woman comes into a therapist's office with emotional complaints, the husband or boyfriend is always at the top of the list of possible causative factors, along with the woman's parents. For Rivers, this Trent fellow was a definite "person of interest," as the police are so fond of saying.

Rivers put down his pen and continued, "What is there about Trent that attracts you?"

"Everything . . . The way he looks. They way we share the same view of life. The sense of loyalty he feels toward loved ones." She paused, twirling her finger in her hair. "I don't know if I should say this or not, but we're like two peas in a pod when it comes to sex."

"How so?"

"Well, we just like the same things. He likes to surprise me, and I like being surprised."

"Are you faithful to one another?"

"Absolutely."

"Do you see him as a potential life-long mate?"

84

"I do. I really do. We've had our ups and downs. But everyone goes through that. I bet even your marriage is not perfect."

"My marriage?" the reference stilled him as his thoughts went in a hundred different directions at once. A moment later, he said, "It's true that all relationships go through cycles. Good days. Bad days. Ordinary days. But the difference in a good relationship and a bad relationship is that the partners in a good relationship never resort to abusive behavior during the down times. Can you say that about your relationship?"

Doe thought a moment. "Look—here's the thing! When Trent is abusive it's because I drive him to it. It's all my fault. I want you to teach me how not to do the things that make him abusive."

Rivers had a sinking feeling in his gut. Doe was a lovely woman. It saddened him to see her engage in self-destructive thinking. If he could write her out a prescription for happiness, he gladly would do so. Unfortunately, his healing powers were limited to what he could persuade her to do for herself.

"I want to help you. But I'm afraid I can't teach you that. Instead, I'll help you to better understand your own needs."

Doe nodded, accepting his words for what they were worth, which was not very much in her mind if they didn't help her solve a practical problem. She looked at him with an inquiring expression.

"You aren't going to forget why I came to see you, are you?"

"Not a chance."

Doe got up to leave, but instead of going to the door she approached his desk and dropped a folder in front of him.

"What's this?" he asked.

"It's the media package that my modeling agency sends out to clients. It's got my bio. List of clients I've worked for. A sampling of my photos."

"Why are you giving me this?"

"So that you'll know more about me," she answered.

Once she left the office, he thumbed through the portfolio. Her photos were stunning. She was different in each image. A chameleon.

18

It was so hot the air conditioner ran nonstop.

Trent greeted her at the door and kissed her as he pulled her inside his condo. With their lips still locked, he gently backed her against the wall and lifted her skirt so that he could run his hands over her hips. He loved the heat of her skin on a hot day. His lips moved from her mouth to her neck, where he kissed her lightly, his lips skimming across her skin.

Moments later he pulled back and started unbuttoning her blouse. With her arms dangling submissively at her side, she surrendered to the moment, her eyes following the movement of his fingers with eager anticipation. Without saying a word, Trent patiently unfastened each of five pearl buttons, slowly opened her blouse and slipped it over her shoulders and down her arms, allowing it to drop to the floor. Then he reached around her and unfastened her bra and pulled it over her arms. It, too, fell to the floor.

As cold air from the air-conditioner blew against her bare skin, he gently kissed her breasts, twirling his tongue against her flesh. She sighed and ran her fingers through his hair. She loved the way he took nothing for granted and seemed to genuinely cherish each moment they spent together.

He pulled away, causing her skin to erupt with chill bumps as the cold air flowed over the wetness left by his kisses.

Then she watched as he unfastened her skirt and unzipped it ever so slowly, allowing it to fall past her legs to the floor. Before removing her panties, he dropped to his knees and planted a warm kiss where she least expected it.

As he slipped her panties down her legs and over her toes, she ran her fingers through his hair, her head tossed back, her chest heaving with each breath.

Just when she thought she knew what would happen next, he surprised her and turned around so that his back was facing her. He leaned over and put his hands on his knees.

"Hop on," he said gleefully.

She burst into laughter and leapt onto his back, wrapping her arms around his neck as he grabbed hold of her legs and held them in place. He made a circle in the living room, riding her on his back as if he were a pony, around and around. Then he galloped into the bedroom and gently dumped her onto the bed. She lay on her back, legs parted, one thigh raised higher than the other, prompting him to tell her that she took his breath away.

Trent did a strip tease for her, mimicking the moves he'd seen female strippers perform. He didn't know if she'd ever watched a stripper, but he was pretty sure she'd appreciate the moves. She did, shouting her encouragement each time he removed an article of clothing. Once he finished, he slid onto the bed, serpent-like, making love to her, the first time face to face, and the second time with her face pushed down onto the sheets.

Afterward they lay side by side, exhausted, neither speaking for several minutes.

Finally, she asked, "Do you ever think about it afterwards?"

"All the time. Do you?"

"All the time."

Trent turned and looked at her. "I'm going to ask you a question and I don't want you to take it the wrong way."

She gazed into his eyes, waiting.

"I don't understand why you're sleeping with me."

"What do you mean?"

"Do you love your husband?"

With that, Shelly propped up on her elbow.

"Of course, I love my husband. Why would you ask a question like that?"

"Because you're sleeping with me. Does he know that you're sleeping with me?"

"God no," said Shelly.

"Are you going to ever tell him?"

"Never."

"Do *you* understand this?"

"No. I don't need to understand it. I love my husband. I like having sex with you. It's exciting."

"It's two different things?" he asked.

"Now you've got it."

She got up out of the bed and went into the living room. Seconds later she returned with her clothing gathered up in the arms. She dumped her things on the bed next to him and picked through the pile until she found her panties.

"Get over it—I don't need two therapists in my life."

She slipped on her panties and bra, dressing quickly.

Trent found her ability to dress while carrying on a conversation highly erotic. He reached up and pulled her down to the bed.

"You're hurting me," she protested.

"I want one more."

"You've had enough for one day," she said, smiling.

"There's no such thing."

He pulled her down to his face and kissed her.

She responded by straddling him, his skirt hiked up to the waist. Her eyes said no—and yes.

Without removing her panties, he made love to her while she was fully dressed. She leaned over, pressing both hands to the sheets, struggling to keep her balance as he bounced her over and over again, her hair cascading as her head rocked front to back. Being a medical person, she sometimes worried about brain damage during sex. She'd read case studies about people who'd injured themselves during sex.

"Oh, well," she muttered to herself.

19

After her visit with Dr. Mann, Doe had lunch with Flutie and spent the afternoon shopping, spending the money she'd earned at her last modeling session. She loved to model. She loved to shop. One passion fed the other.

The sales clerks in all the boutiques and high-end department stores considered her a celebrity and it was rare to see her looking over merchandise without at least three sales clerks hovering over her, catering to her every whim. Young girls looked up to her as a role model. As she left the mall, she called Trent several times, but he didn't answer and his voice mail was turned off. That didn't concern her. He had a very successful business and it was often difficult to get in touch with him.

Every time she glanced into the rearview mirror she saw Oscar looming in the background, pacing himself, keeping about a half block away from her car. She sped up, he sped up. She slowed down, he slowed down. He made her feel safe. Worth every penny she paid him.

When she arrived at her townhouse she waited to get out of her car until she saw Oscar pull into place. Despite his gruffness, she figured he was the fatherly type. Good with kids. But then what did she know? She'd be the first to admit that she wasn't a great judge of character when it came to men.

The routine was that she was supposed to enter the house and walk through each room and then flash the light at the front door to let Oscar know that everything was all right. The first thing that hit her when she stepped inside was the scent of the red roses. It was a scent that made her feel warm inside.

Flutie wasn't home, of course. Her schedule was dictated by the needs of the café, which required her presence from seven in the morning until ten in the evening. For Doe, that was a good thing and a bad thing. A good thing because she had the house to herself all day and most of the evening. A bad thing since Flutie always came home wired, eager to talk and drink wine, if she wasn't in the company of a man, in which case there would be music into the wee hours and perhaps a guest for breakfast, something Doe always hated.

Doe put away the clothes she purchased, tossing the lingerie into the laundry hamper and the blouse and skirt into the dry cleaners basket. She refused to wear anything before it was washed or laundered, the main reason being that she had no way of knowing who tried on the clothing first, but also because she'd read a magazine article that said clothing always fit better after it'd been washed or dry cleaned. Seemed reasonable to her.

She had a dinner date with Trent at seven, but she had plenty of time to get ready before then. She hadn't told him about Oscar, mainly because Oscar asked her not to, but also because she liked having a little mystery in her life. She'd about made up her mind that perhaps Dr. Mann was right. He'd never said that no one was trying to kill her, not straight out; but she felt that probably was what he was thinking. Maybe she'd keep Oscar another week or two, and then let him go.

Doe slipped out of her clothes, dropping them into the laundry hamper; then she went into the kitchen and poured herself a big glass of orange juice. She'd once dated a man who scolded her for drinking big glasses of orange juice. He insisted that orange juice had to be enjoyed in small glasses. He berated her for drinking it in a large glass. She told him he was crazy.

Ever since they broke up, she'd made it a point to drink at least one big glass of orange juice each day. Once she'd gulped down her juice, she smacked the glass onto the counter and looked out the window into the back yard. It wasn't much of a yard. Just enough space for a couple of small trees and two flower beds.

As she walked back to her bedroom, she paused in the hallway to look at herself in a full length mirror. Turned left, right. All the way around. Any objective person would say she had a perfect body, but she wasn't objective and all she could see were flaws. Her back was too fat. Her hips weren't firm enough. Her breasts weren't large enough. They weren't small enough. Her thighs were too large for her body. She wasn't above playing head games with herself.

Doe went into the bathroom and turned on her shower. While the water heated up, she sat on the toilet seat and thumbed through a fashion magazine. She loved fashion pictures, even when she wasn't in them. She liked pictures of clothes. Pictures of people. Pictures of cars and homes. Pictures of animals. She was considering taking photography lessons so that she would have a profession to fall back on when she was too old to model.

Once at a photo session she commandeered the camera and ordered the photographer to pose for her, wearing the same clothing she'd worn moments before. "Now smile!" she said, working the setup. "Make love to the camera."

The photographer must have had some gender issues because he loved the attention. Before it was over, she had him buck naked on a bearskin rug as she walked circles around him, urging him to be super pouty or down-and-dirty seductive or lovingly sexy. Once she commanded him to suck in his gut, an order that made him blush.

When she saw steam wedging around the curtain, she tossed the magazine aside and stepped into the shower, turning the nozzle so that the water stream narrowed and came out hard against her skin. To her, a shower was almost as good as sex. She twisted and turned in the water, relishing the feel of it against her skin. The way it warmed her, caressed her. It aroused her, made her think about her evening with Trent.

What on earth did women do before God created men? she wondered, not bothering to ponder the scriptural contradictions of her question. Contradictory analysis was not really her thing. *Men are a hell of a lot of trouble, but when you think about the alternative . . . well, what's a girl to do?*

She stayed in the shower until the water temperature started dropping. Then she turned off the water and stepped onto a bathmat. She rubbed her hair with the towel and then used it to dry off her body. She looked at her hair. It was damp only along the edges. She plugged in her hair dryer and turned it on.

Almost immediately, there was a flash of light, followed by a loud pop. She dropped the hair dryer to the counter, horrified to see foot-long flames leaping into the air. She backed away just as the flames engulfed a hand towel next to the sink. She ran out of the bathroom and down the hallway.

Then, realizing that she was naked, she hurried back into the bathroom and grabbed her towel and wrapped it around her. She ran down the hallway, all the way to the front door.

Oscar was drinking a cup of coffee when he saw her run from the front door, waving her arms and screaming at the top of her voice. Shaken, he spilled the hot coffee onto his lap, giving added energy to his awkward exit from the car.

Doe ran toward him, screaming, "Fire! Fire! Fire!"

As he approached, she yelled out, "Just follow me," and she turned and ran back into the house, with Oscar huffing and puffing to keep up with her. He followed her into the bathroom and saw the flames.

"Where's your fire extinguisher?" he exclaimed.

"In the kitchen!" she responded, literally jumping up and down.

Oscar dashed into the kitchen and returned with the fire extinguisher, which he proceeded to empty onto the fire, foam spewing all over the bathroom, covering the mirror with a thick coat that looked like shaving cream.

Once the fire was out, he dropped the fire extinguisher to the floor and leaned against the wall, catching his breath. Finally, his face flushed, he asked, "What the hell happened?"

"I turned on the hair dryer and it just exploded!"

Oscar stared at the hair dryer a minute or two before approaching it.

"Was there any kind of warning? Did it click on and off? Make an unusual sound?"

"No. There was no warning. It just blew up in my face."

Oscar shook his head. He didn't like the way that sounded. He unplugged the hair dryer and rolled the appliance from side to side, examining it. "Got a screwdriver?" he asked.

Doe went into the kitchen and got a screwdriver from the utility drawer and gave it to Oscar. As she watched, he disassembled the hair dryer.

"Just what I thought," he said. He turned around and showed the hair dryer to Doe. "Look at this—someone has tampered with this hair dryer so that it would catch on fire. Look at the way those wires are crossed. I assure you it didn't come that way from the manufacturer. How long as you have this hair dryer?"

"I don't know. Maybe six months."

"Yeah—it's been tampered with all right."

Doe's eyes widened. "You mean someone really is trying to kill me?"

Oscar nodded. "It sure looks like it."

20

Preston knew that he'd have to work fast. Thirty minutes tops. He logged onto the Mack 222 program and typed in the names he gathered during his previous search.

The names he entered, Yao Bai and Yao Ta, led him into the archival vaults of the U.S. State Department, U.S. Citizenship and Immigration Services, and the Federal Bureau of Investigation — and, much to his surprise, the China Public Security Bureau. That shocked him because he had not programmed Mack 222 to penetrate the records kept by foreign governments. Someone had added that feature to the software after he turned it over to them.

He whistled aloud.

No wonder the bastards don't want me poking around in their business.

Feeling a little bit guilty, Preston searched through the archives of the China Public Security Bureau until he found a folder on Yao Bai. She was born in 1960 in Shanghai. Served on numerous youth committees in the Communist Party. Worked as typist at U.S. Consulate. Married in 1980. Had a daughter, Yao Ta, in 1981. Died 1981. Preston sighed and leaned back in his chair.

Just then the telephone rang. He hurriedly logged off before he answered the telephone. He immediately recognized the voice of the female caller.

"No," he lied. "I'm not busy. Come on up."

He put down the telephone and pressed a button that unlocked the express elevator to his penthouse. No sooner did he do that than he heard his door buzzer. He knew who that was — Agent Cefalu. He turned off the lights in his computer room and walked out, locking the door behind him.

Agent Cefalu was shaking his head when Preston opened the door.

"Man, you're killing me," said Agent Cefalu. "Maybe I'm getting too old for this job. Or maybe they need someone older, I don't know."

He looked at Preston, the sort of look a father would give a naughty child. "You know why I'm here, don't you."

"I can guess."

"What were you doing this time?"

"Just doing a little research."

"Research! Why don't you go to the library if research is your thing?"

"It's easier to do it online."

"Then why don't you hook up to a commercial Internet provider? That would be so much easier for all of us."

"I feel more comfortable with my own program."

"But it's not your program anymore. You sold it. Remember?"

"I'm not a robot that they can turn on whenever they get the urge."

"OK, I can see I'm wasting my time. So what do I tell them this time?"

"Tell them I remembered a possible flaw in the system and I entered to check it out."

"Oh, that's a good one," said Agent Cefalu. "Are you keeping track of all your excuses? You need to be careful not to use the same one twice."

Preston tapped his index finger to his temple.

"All right here."

They heard the elevator door open and turned to see a young woman walk down the hallway, swinging a beaded purse at her side. She smiled, but it wasn't a friendly smile. She walked like someone who was dragging a ball and chain behind her. She shouted out, "This my welcome party?"

Neither man answered.

When the woman walked up to them, she thrust her purse into Agent Cefalu's mid-section, and said, "There—knock yourself out."

"How are you today, Faith," said Agent Cefalu, trying his best to be polite.

Faith looked at him as if it were a silly question.

"How am I doing?" she mocked. "Poor—that's how I'm doing."

Agent Cefalu didn't answer. He looked through her purse and handed it back to her. "You're good to go."

"What's the deal with checking my purse every time I come here? You think I've got a rocket launcher in there or something."

"It's just procedure," said Preston. "Nothing personal."

Agent Cefalu gave Preston a sympathetic look.

"I'll be in my apartment if you need me."

Then he gave Faith a half-smile and walked away.

"Come in, Faith," said Preston.

She swaggered into his penthouse, swinging her hips in a defiant manner, and tossed her purse across the room into a chair.

"I see nothing has changed since my last visit."

"Nothing needs changing."

"Most people like change."

"I'm not most people."

"Tell me about it."

He reached out to hug her, but she pushed him away, saying, "Don't touch me."

He recovered quickly and asked, "Would you like to have a seat?"

"Yeah, why not?" She sat in a chair across from a dark-blue leather sofa.

There was obvious tension between them. Neither looked very comfortable in the other's presence. Faith twirled her finger into her hair as she looked around the room, avoiding eye contact.

After an awkward few moments, Preston asked, "Are you doing all right?"

The question seemed to catch her off guard. She paused, feeling the prick of a question laced with emotional pratfalls.

"No," she said. "I'm not all right. I need money."

"Why do you need money?"

"Because I've got expenses."

"What kind of expenses?"

"Just things I need to pay for."

Preston looked out the window, this thoughts lost in the white clouds that raced past, a stark contrast to the intensely blue sky. "How much do you need?"

"Ten thousand dollars."

"That's a lot of money."

"It's what I need."

Preston looked at her a minute, a dozen contradictory thoughts cruising through his mind, all at the same time. Saying no to her was not an option. He slowly got up and went into his bedroom.

Minutes later he returned with a bundle of cash in his hand, which he gave to her with the admonition, "Put it to good use. Just make sure that whatever you use it for is legal."

Faith took the money without comment, without really even looking at it.

Preston sat back down and looked at her, waiting for her say something that would make him feel better about giving her the money.

After a long pause, during which neither could think of anything to say, Faith stood and walked to the door, pausing just long enough to stuff the money into her purse. Then she was gone, without saying goodbye or I love you or thank you, the quiet deliberation of the door closing behind her echoing in Preston's head, a comment that spoke volumes about their relationship.

The visit had exhausted him. He leaned his head onto the back of the sofa and closed his eyes. The pain in his right side was intense. There was a bitter taste in his mouth. The memory of a better life haunted him to the point that he no long could remember the point in his life that he decided to settle for less.

21

When Trent arrived at Doe's townhouse, the first thing she did when she opened the door was to leap into his arms. As she wrapped her arms around him, she surreptitiously glanced down the street and saw Oscar sitting in his car.

Once she pulled away from the embrace and closed the door behind them, he asked, "What's wrong, Doe?"

"My hair dryer caught on fire and it scared me to death."

"You're kidding!"

"No, no—it just burst into flames. It was terrifying."

"That's crazy."

He took her in his arms and held her for a moment. To his surprise, he found the scent of her fear intoxicating. The moment ended abruptly when she announced that she needed a tissue to wipe her nose. Sniffing, she dashed into the bathroom and then returned looking more composed.

"Where is the dryer?" he asked.

"Still in the bathroom."

"Mind if I take a look?"

"No, not at all."

Trent went into the bathroom and examined the hairdryer, with Doe leaning over his shoulder. She pointed to one of the wires.

"Look at that," she said. "See how it pulled away from where it was screwed down. That's what caused the fire."

Trent looked at her in astonishment.

"How did you know that?"

Not wanting to tell him about Oscar, she lied and said that the fire officer explained it to her.

Trent put the hairdryer back down on the counter.

"You need to get rid of that thing," he said. "You can't use it now."

"I haven't had a chance yet."

They went into the living room and sat on the sofa.

"So what do you want to do now?" she asked.

"I though we'd pick up some sandwiches and go out on the river."

"Cool! I'll just change into some shorts."

While Doe was changing, Trent returned to the bathroom and reexamined the hairdryer. No doubt about it. Someone had tampered with it. It made him realize that there are hundreds of ways to kill someone. The trick is to make it look like an accident.

"Smart," he mumbled to himself, lowering the hairdryer back to the counter. "It took a smart son of a bitch to do that."

On their way to the river marina, they stopped at a deli and picked up a bag of sandwiches and chips. Then they pulled into a convenience store and got two six-packs of beer and a bag of ice that Trent put into a cooler.

The marina was located south of the city in a still-water inlet that protected docked boats from the strong currents of the river. Trent had a baby-blue, 25-foot, Marathon Cruiser with a rebuilt Volvo engine. It slept five and had a stove, fridge, shower and head.

Doe loved going out on the boat, but she preferred the lake to the river, mainly because when they went upstream the rough river currents sometimes bounced the boat like a rubber ball.

There was still plenty of sunlight when they arrived at the marina. They put the sandwiches and the cooler on the boat and cast off. As they were leaving, Doe saw Oscar pull up and get out of his Altima. He looked very angry. She knew it was because she hadn't told him about the boat ride. He'd made her promise that she wouldn't throw any surprises at him.

Once they got out on the river, Doe changed into her swimsuit and climbed out on the bow. She was there for only a minute when Trent shouted for her move to the stern, where she'd be safer if the boat started bouncing against the currents. Her eyes flashed with anger.

"I can't do anything right today, can I!" she snapped.

She walked past Trent to the stern and spread out her towel and stretched out to catch the last rays of the day's sun.

Trent was used to her outbursts. Sometimes he felt he had to walk on eggshells when he was with her. The best way to respond, he'd learned by trial and error, was simply not to respond at all. He knew she'd be smiling in a few minutes. He ignored her and piloted the boat out into an easy riding channel.

As he watched for floating debris and submerged tree tops, he reached into the bag of sandwiches and withdrew two, one of which he flipped back to Doe. The sandwich landed on the blanket next to her. Then he pulled a couple of beers from the cooler.

"Want a beer?" he asked.

Doe sat up and reached for the beer, a broad smile on her face.

"It's good and cold," she said, wrapping her fingers around the bottle.

"Packing beer is an art," he responded.

They went several miles up river, staying close to the riverbank. The sun set on the Arkansas side of the river, casting a warm orange-and-red glow across the water. Trent pulled into a small cove and dropped anchor in still water, away from the currents. They kissed and made love, the motion of their bodies rocking the boat. Water splashing in the dark. The scent of honeysuckle from the shoreline. The whir of birds coming in to roost for the night.

Afterward they lay in the dark for a long time, looking up at the stars.

"Trent, what do you want more than anything else in life?"

At first, he was hesitant to answer. He'd never known a woman who didn't have a battery of tests that she administered to her boyfriend or husband, tests that always were disguised as innocent questions.

"To be with you," he lied.

"Correct answer," she said, smiling.

"What do you want more than anything else?"

Her eyes sparkled. "To be with you, of course. I love you very much. But there's something else I also want. I want to be one of those."

She pointed into the heavens.

"A star?"

"Absolutely."

"What about children? Do you see that in your future?"

"Not now."

They lay in silence for a while.

Then they got up and dressed.

Trent loved the way her bare skin looked in the silver moonlight. He loved the way she took her time when she dressed, waiting until the very end to cover her breasts. He loved the way she allowed him to watch, without making eye contact with him, as if she was alone and didn't know he was there.

He hated it that he couldn't love her the way he loved Shelly.

Life would be simpler that way.

22

When Doe entered Rivers' office, she slapped the charred remains of her hair dryer on his desk and said, "Now, tell me I'm crazy!"

Rivers looked at her and blinked, not sure what to say. As it turned out he didn't have to say anything. She did all the talking. Before he could respond, she told him the story about the hair dryer from start to finish.

"Someone really is trying to kill me. Oscar, the private eye I hired, he thinks so, too. What do I do now?"

Rivers' first thought was that someone trying to kill her, and her being borderline, were not competing possibilities, not entirely. Both could be true. He picked up the hair dryer and examined it. Then he withdrew a handful of tissues from the box that he kept on his desk for his patients and he wiped the char from his hands. "Did you show this to the police?"

"Are you kidding? They'd just laugh at me. They are better at investigating murders than preventing them."

"Did you show it to your private eye?"

"He was parked outside when it happened. He put out the fire. He said the hair dryer definitely had been tampered with."

"So what are you going to do next?"

Doe looked puzzled for a moment. The answer to that question had not yet entered her head. She sighed. "I guess I thought everything would be all right when I proved to you that someone is trying to kill me."

She paused long enough to snatch a tissue from his desk and dab it to her eyes. Then she said, "That's silly isn't it? You can't do anything about it, can you?"

Rivers shook his head.

"Not personally. But there is someone I want to talk to so that I can get a better perspective on what's happening. My job is to help you through this emotionally. Speaking of which, how do you feel about what's happening to you?"

"I'm frustrated. If I knew what they wanted from me, I'd be happy to give it to them to make this nightmare end. What do you think they want?"

"I don't know."

"See, here's the thing. I can change. I can become the person they want me to be, if only they let me know. Call me. Send me a letter. Anything."

"I don't think that's what they want from you."

"If not that — what?"

"Think back. Are there men in your life who are bitter about breaking up with you? Someone who might think that if they scared you, you'd go running back to them? Someone who is jealous of your current relationship? What about enemies of your parents? Is there anyone they know who might be behind this?"

"No, no . . ." she said excitedly, "They're wonderful people."

"I'm sure they're wonderful people. But do they have any enemies?"

She barked, "Absolutely not!"

Rivers maintained a stoic expression on his face, but inside he was smiling ear to ear. Flashing anger one minute. Contrition the next. Very typical of borderline personalities. He looked away, saying nothing, giving her a blank canvas to fill with the dysfunctional colors of her choice.

Thirty seconds later, she said, "I'm sorry! I didn't mean to snap at you!"

"No problem," he answered. "You're upset and you have a right to be. I understand."

"Oh, Dr. Mann, you're the best!"

Rivers knew that he had his hands full with Doe. She was undergoing trauma, while still struggling with an underlying condition that'd tormented her for many years, even though she had no idea that was the case.

Borderline personalities may or may not understand that something inside them makes them different from other people, but the one characteristic they all share, the one thing that sets them off, is a short emotional fuse. Depending on their level of self-awareness, they go through life either constantly apologizing or constantly demanding apologies from others. Sometimes both at the same time.

"Doe, let's shift gears here for a minute," said Rivers. "Was there a time in your childhood when your life seemed to change?"

"What kind of change?"

"Was there a time when you began to doubt your ability to make new friends, or to hold on to your old friends?"

Doe thought a moment.

"Seems like it was easier to make friends when I was younger. It got harder when I became a teenager."

"Why do you think?

"My mother was very protective. When my friends came over, she liked to participate in whatever we did. That wasn't so bad when I was eight or ten, but when I was a teenager, it made my friends not want to come to my house because Mother always found an excuse to be in the next room so that she could listen to us. We'd make plans to do something at my house and one of them would ask, 'Is your mother going to be home?' If I answered yes, they always found reasons to go to someone else's house."

"Did that upset you?"

"Sometimes. But that's just the way Mother was. She didn't mean anything by it."

"Do you remember getting angry a lot as a teenager?"

"Yes."

"What kinds of things did you get angry about?"

"It's hard to remember, really. Sometimes I got angry for no reason."

"Do you see any similarities between the reasons you got angry as a teenager and the reasons you get angry when you are in a relationship with a man."

"Not really."

"What are some of the reasons that you get angry at the men in your life?"

"All the usual ones—they lie, they're inconsiderate, they're messy, they don't pick up their things, they criticize you for no reason, they think their time is more valuable than yours. You're a man. You know all that."

Rivers smiled. "Not all men are alike."

"True. But they are all alike in the ways that drive women crazy."

Doe suddenly put her hands to her face, covering her mouth.

"I'm sorry. I didn't mean to use that word. I don't think I'm crazy. Do you?"

Rivers shook his head.

"You're not crazy. You've got some complicated problems to deal with, but you're not crazy."

"Thanks for that."

"Let's talk more about your concept of men. Have you had relationships with many men that you felt were in the middle, when it came to being good or bad?"

"That's a good question, Dr. Mann. No, all the men I've ever known were either good or bad. Never in between. Sometimes the same men are good one day and bad the next. I've never known a man that was partly good and partly bad."

"So when you're in a relationship, you sometimes love the man you're dating and you sometimes hate the man you're dating?"

Doe's eyes brightened. "That's it! That's it! I've never felt middle of the road with any man I'm involved with!"

"Let's take that love-hate approach a step further. How does it feel when you get close to a man that you have a love-hate relationship with?"

"What do you mean?"

"When you're getting close to a man, do you ever feel it's too close for comfort, so that you feel the need to put some distance between you, even though you care about him?"

"That happens to me all the time."

"Have you noticed that when you feel close to a man, you find excuses to be angry with him so that you can push away and get some air? Then you feel guilty because you've pushed him away, so guilty, in fact, that you go out of your way to be nice to him?"

Doe nodded, her head lowered. "Is that a bad thing?"

"It's neither bad nor good. It's just who you are. The question is whether you should change the behavior that is causing you problems. That's what therapy is all about."

"That makes sense."

"I see that we've run out of time."

Doe seemed disappointed. She got up and reached over and picked up the remains of her hair dryer. "You don't want to keep this, do you?"

He wasn't sure if she was joking, so he played it straight.

"No, I think you should take it with you. You might need it for evidence."

"That's what I'm thinking."

Rivers walked her to the door.

"The next time you think someone is trying to hurt you, I want you to call the police, even if your private eye is nearby."

Doe nodded. "I will."

Rivers watched her walk from his office, through the waiting room, impressed by her regal carriage. The woman knew how to make an exit, that's for certain. Before closing his door, he asked his receptionist to give him a couple of minutes before she sent in the next patient.

Back at his desk, he punched a familiar number into his telephone.

When Jack McCain answered, he seemed surprised to hear Rivers's voice on the other end of the line. "What's up?" he asked.

"I need your advice," Rivers said. "Actually, I may need your help."

"Is what you want legal?"

"For the moment, yes."

"What's on your mind?"

Rivers told him about Doe's hair dryer.

"So do *you* think it was an accident?"

"She becomes more credible each time I see her. I looked at the hair dryer myself. She brought it into the office. I could see how the wiring had been tapered with."

"No shit."

"She's got a private eye, but I'm not sure if he's on the up and up. You've got a lot of sources in low and high places. Would you mind checking on the guy?"

"Sure—what's his name?"

"Oscar Ross."

"Did he used to be a cop?"

"Yeah, I think so. He retired and started up a private investigation business."

"You sure he retired?"

"You sure he wasn't pushed out?"

"I'm not sure about anything. That's why I called you."

106

"What about that incident you had going home? Your car catching on fire? You think there's any connection?"

"I don't see how? I don't think someone would try to kill me just because I'm treating Doe. That doesn't make sense."

"Any other reason someone would want you dead?"

"None that I can think of."

"I'll see what I can find out."

Rivers hung up the telephone just as the next patient entered his office and sat in the chair across from his desk, wiping her eyes with a wadded tissue that had seen better days.

23

At the end of the day, Rivers left his office and approached his car with extreme caution. This time, while the car was in the shop, he had one of those remote starters installed so that he could unlock the door and start the engine with the touch of a button. It worked perfectly. The engine started without incident and purred like a kitten.

He exited the parking lot and drove until he hit Poplar Avenue. Then he turned right on Danny Thomas Boulevard and drove north past Chelsea, where the old American Studios was located, the sacred ground where Elvis recorded "Suspicious Mind." The studio was long gone, but the song's theme endured.

These days, everyone Rivers knew was suspicious of someone for something. He included himself in that mix. As he left the city limits, he thought about Doe and her problems, and then he wondered, as strange as it seemed on the surface, if their problems were somehow intertwined.

He realized he was driving too fast and he slowed down. When he glanced into the rearview mirror to see if a cop had spotted him speeding, he noticed a white van that maintained a distance of about ten car lengths. Had he noticed the van on Poplar? He wasn't sure. There could have been a white van behind him on Poplar. He wasn't sure. White vans were a dime a dozen.

He turned on the radio and listened to the news on NPR. He wondered what the announcers were like in person. He liked their voices. Were any of them in therapy? That was always the first question he asked himself when he met someone new, or listened to someone on the radio, or watched a movie. There are some professions that require you to be a little bit crazy. Radio announcer. Movie actor. Television weather person. Loose screws are a prerequisite.

Danny Thomas Boulevard blended into Highway 51, and the roadside businesses thinned out to an occasional fruit stand. Before he took the road that would take him past Shelby Forest and to the river bluffs, he checked his rearview mirror. The white van was still there. He turned on his blinkers to make a left turn off the highway. The white van did not turn on its blinkers.

Once he completed the turn, he looked into the rearview mirror and saw the white van continue on past the turnoff. Thank God. He smiled, something he rarely did when he was alone. He was wrong to be suspicious of the white van. He liked it when his own human foibles proved to be inconsequential. Ninety-nine times out of a hundred, he told himself, a suspicious mind is unworthy of consideration. If everyone who was suspected of wrongdoing actually committed a wrong act, the human race would be an endangered species.

The drive the rest of the way home was totally uneventful. No one tried to kill him. No one even came close to killing him.

When he pulled into the circular driveway at his house, he was disappointed not to see Shelly's car parked out front. He liked it when she arrived home first. It made his arrival seem more like a homecoming. There's not a man living who doesn't fanaticize about having a beautiful woman greet him at the door with a moist kiss and a cold can of beer. Shelly had been working longer hours in recent weeks. He looked forward to her return to her old schedule.

The first thing he did when he walked inside the house was to toss his keys on the table in the front hallway. He stopped to listen. The house seemed unusually quiet. He was glad he wasn't one of those guys who went home to an empty house at the end of each day. A man needs kitchen noises. He needs for someone to ask if he remembered to pick up a jug of milk. He needs to be told that he's only got fifteen minutes to get a shower before they leave to go to a party that he's forgotten all about.

Rivers went upstairs and changed into shorts and a Grateful Dead T-shirt. Then he went back downstairs to the kitchen and poured himself a big glass of ice-cold grape juice. It really hit the spot. He was glad his T-shirt was black because whenever he drank grape juice he always dribbled a few drops onto his chest. He was the kind of guy that felt compelled to change shirts if he spilled something on it. He didn't care for the spotted look.

The den was populated with leather. There was a sofa. A loveseat. A couple of chairs. All arranged around an oversized coffee table with stout oak legs. He turned on television to catch the news and sat in one of the chairs and propped his feet on the coffee table. It was one of his favorite places on a hot day because it was right beneath an overhead air vent. Whenever the air-conditioner kicked on, cold air poured out of the vent onto the chair below. He was only in the chair for a few seconds when he heard the familiar roar of the air-conditioner motor. Cold, soothing air was on the way.

By the time he finished the grape juice, he heard the front door open and close, keys jingling.

"Honey, I'm in the den," he called out.

Shelly didn't respond right away. She waited until she entered the den, at which point she said, "Hi, dear—you beat me home today."

She went to his chair and kissed him lightly on the cheek. Then she plopped down in the chair opposite him, her skirt askew, showing lots of leg.

"Rough day?" he asked.

Shelly nodded.

"I think it's a tossup as to which of us sees the most disturbing sights. You looking into depraved souls. Or me looking into mouths filled with yesterday's dinner."

Rivers smiled. It was an ongoing discussion they had.

"Obviously, you saw more gunk today than I did."

"Oh, yeah," she said, sighing. She shifted her skirt so that he could see more of her legs. She loved to tease him.

He knew that she was doing it intentionally, but he didn't care. He fanaticized that she wasn't aware of what she was doing. That's what made it fun. He drank in her legs like a wanderer just in from the desert thirsting for water. Each year, he feared that her thighs would enlarge, the way it happens with most women her age. But her calves and thighs were as shapely today as they were when they first met. He was thankful for that.

She leaned back, allowing her head to rest on the back of the chair as she gazed up at the ceiling, a movement that brought her skirt even higher. This time her skirt raised high enough so that he could see all the way up her skirt.

That's odd, he thought. *I would have sworn that she was wearing blue panties when she dressed this morning.*

110

He started to say something about it, but then thought better of it. A question like that would totally break the mood. Besides, what difference did it make whether she had on panties? Rather than satisfy his curiosity, he decided to savior the moment.

Finally, Shelly rose to her feet and said, "What's for dinner?"

They spent the next hour in bed, making love, and then lay without talking on top of the covers to watch the last thirty minutes of a classic movie, *My Dog Rusty*. Rivers thought she seemed unusually subdued in bed. He sometimes worried that she wasn't as happy with their sex life as she once was. After ten years of marriage, he reasoned that all relationships lose a little bit of excitement in the bedroom. Statistics backed him up.

Shelly leaned over and planted a long, lingering kiss on his lips.

"I love you," she purred. "But that wasn't exactly what I meant by dinner."

She got up, walking around the room naked, picking up the clothing she'd dropped to the floor in the heat of passion and rummaging through her dresser for a clean pair of panties.

"I'm going to take a shower," she said, smiling. "When I get out I hope you'll have the dinner problem solved."

The late afternoon light was very flattering as it painted her naked body with pastels of abstract designs.

"I'm the hunter in this family," he said. "I'll go hunt."

She laughed and disappeared into the bathroom.

He hurriedly got up and dressed. Then he went downstairs and got into his car. They lived so far out of town that none of the pizza places would deliver. If he wanted a cheese pie, he'd have to go get it himself. He didn't mind the drive, especially after sex. It reminded him of his teen years. Sex and cars were inseparable. For most men, it is a lifelong association.

The girl at the pizza counter flirted with him when she handed him the pie. On the ride back he questioned the flirtation, wondering if adult men always considered a smile from a young girl to be a flirtation.

When he got back home, he found Shelly working on a soft drink in an oversized plastic tumbler filled with ice. She wore one of Rivers' shirts and nothing else.

"Ah, my weekly passion," she said softly.

They had pizza once a week, but they also had sex only once a week. Was she referring to the pizza or their sex life? One thing Rivers learned as a therapist was this: never ask all the questions that come to mind.

They sat at the kitchen table and began dishing pizza onto their plates.

"Should we eat here or outside?" asked Shelly.

"Let's go outside."

"Yes, let's have our pizza in the wild where it was meant to be enjoyed," cracked Shelly.

Rivers smiled. One of the things he loved about her was her ability to make life fun.

Outside on the porch, they sat in wooden lawn chairs with pizza in their laps. One of the things that endeared her to him was the way she ate. Invariably, she zeroed in on her food while it was still on her plate and followed it with her eyes all the way into her mouth, at which point she closed her eyelids as if she were in the midst of an orgasm.

By contrast, Rivers, like most men, removed the food from his plate without once ever looking at it, guiding it to his mouth as if by radar, making certain that his eyes were wide open to see television, the river, or, in this case, the person he was dining with.

Shelly interrupted his train of thought, which already had jumped from food to the curvature of her thighs, with a statement that sucked all the air from around his pizza.

"Let's talk to someone about adoption. It's been on my mind a lot lately."

"You don't like things the way they are?"

It was a silly question, one that he instantly regretted.

"Don't you think our lives would be enhanced by having a child in our home? Don't you think it would bring us even closer together?"

"I'm sure you are right," he said, taken aback by her suggestion that they could be brought closer together. He didn't realize they needed to be brought closer together. "You just caught me off guard."

"I think we have a lot of love we could give to a child."

They talked about adoption a little more, reaching agreement that they would pursue it with one of the local adoption agencies. As the sun set across the river, their conversation tapered off into a comfortable silence.

Crickets chirped in the distance. The wind off the river smelled of rain. As the night closed in around them, they acquiesced to the loss of another day. Tree frogs punctuated long periods of silence. Tug boats sounded their horns. Lights moved up and down the river.

A light at the bottom of the bluff caught Rivers' attention.

"What's that?" he asked, looking down at the meandering light.

Shelly looked at the light and said, "Probably a fisherman who's got his boat pulled up just off the riverbank."

"Maybe. But look at the way the light keeps moving in one direction. Actually, it looks like it might be moving to the left, but slanted in our direction."

"Then it might be someone walking along the riverbank."

"At night?"

"Happens all the time. I've seen it before."

Shelly got up and took his plate and started for the kitchen.

"I've going up to bed," she said, casting a flirtatious glance over her shoulder.

"It's early," protested Rivers, and then added, "Oh . . .oh."

She laughed. He laughed.

He took one last look at the moving light and went inside.

Upstairs, Shelly was already in bed, naked on top of the covers, studiously reading a magazine. He hurried across the bedroom into the bathroom. "Don't go to sleep—I'll be right back!" There was a tinge of desperation in his voice.

Shelly smiled and turned the page.

Rivers looked in the mirror and ran his fingers through his hair. He was a long way from going bald, but his hair seemed to thin a little more with each passing year. He took the top off the toothpaste and squeezed a dab onto his electric toothbrush. When he turned it on, there was a loud pop.

He was knocked to the floor.

"Rivers!" Shelly shouted. "What's that noise?"

No answer. She rushed into the bathroom and saw Rivers on the floor. Eyes closed. Drool dripping from his half-open mouth. The toothbrush burned on the counter top, flames rising a foot or more. She turned off the light switch and quickly unplugged the toothbrush. Smoke filled the air. The flames died, even as she knelt to the floor and took his pulse. Nothing.

A part of her wanted to panic, but she couldn't. Should she call 911? Should she start resuscitating him? She paused. Seconds mattered. She turned him flat on his back and pressed both hands against his chest, pushing in and out. Then she cupped her mouth over his mouth and breathed air into his lungs.

Pushed again. Breathed again.

After the third time, he lurched and coughed. His eyes opened.

"Honey, don't move," she said. "I'm going to call 911."

She rushed into the bedroom and made the call. She was back at his side within seconds.

"How are you feeling?" she asked, and then quickly added, "No, don't say a word. Just lie still."

Rivers rolled his eyes, looking up at the counter.

"What the hell happened?"

"You were shocked by your toothbrush."

"Is that what I smell burning?"

"Yes. I unplugged it."

"Why don't you run some water over a towel and pick it up and put it in the bath tub where it can't do any more damage."

Shelly did as he asked and then knelt at his side again. He seemed fully alert now. He moved his arms to get up, but she pushed him back down.

"No, don't move," she said.

She convinced herself that everything would be all right. Then she attempted to convince him. He was a tougher sell.

It seemed to take forever, but soon they heard the siren in the distance, Growing closer. Finally pulling into their driveway and abruptly stopping.

Shelly got to her feet.

"Don't you move. I'm going downstairs to let them in."

Rivers laughed. "Like that?"

Shelly had forgotten that she was naked. She ran into the bedroom, quickly slipped into a pair of jeans and a shirt, and then

114

ran out into the hallway, nearly tumbling down the staircase as she rushed to get to the door.

Rivers sat up anyway, ignoring her instructions. He looked around the room. Smoke still hovered near the ceiling. What a freakish thing to happen, he thought. Embarrassing as hell.

When the paramedic arrived they took his vitals and placed him on a stretcher and rushed him out of the house into the ambulance. Shelly went with them, locking the door behind her.

"Where you taking him?" she shouted as she hurried to get in her car.

"City Hospital," one of the men answered.

24

The light from the river slowly made its way up the bluff, twisting and turning as it maneuvered among the trees. It was a steep climb. The only way to ascend the bluff was to take a zigzag route, moving right and then left, moving up by small degrees. Occasionally, the light stopped and shone through the trees, making its way to the house, moving from the porch to either side of the house and then back again.

Lights glowed in two upstairs windows.

The light swept the steps leading up to the porch, moving side to side. The wind snaked though the treetops and twisted down into the flowers on either side of the steps, causing them to sway and then abruptly stop once the wind dissipated.

Steps moaned under the weight of the intruder, who wore crisp, clean sneakers. The screen door creaked open. The light moved from side to side and then went dark. Yellow light from the kitchen fell through the door window and onto the planking of the porch.

The back door was not locked. The intruder eased into the kitchen and looked around. He thought he heard voices upstairs, but he wasn't sure. Walked lightly through the kitchen and into the hallway. The upstairs voices came into focus. Nothing to worry about. Someone had left the television on. The staircase was carpeted, making the ascent soundless.

Bedroom door was wide open. Clothes draped over a chair and on the floor. Vapid game show contestants barked like small dogs on television. The intruder looked at the photographs on the dresser.

The intruder opened each drawer, slowly inspecting the contents. Fingers danced across silken fabric. He looked through the closet, finding a box filled with photographs. He found a picture of Shelly in a swimsuit and admired it for a minute. Then he put it in his back pocket, carefully so that it would not bend.

The bathroom still smelled of smoke. The intruder picked up each bottle on the counter top and read the labels and sniffed the contents. When the saw the toothbrush in the bathtub, wrapped in a wet towel, he lifted it to the counter and unwrapped it. He examined it closely and returned it to the counter. He used a screwdriver to open the casing of the toothbrush, careful not to smudge the char marks on the plastic cover.

Working ever so slowly, he moved the wire he'd attached to a metal brace inside the toothbrush and loosely attached it to its former contact point. He carefully smoothed out the smudges inside the casing so that it would not be apparent that it had been opened. Then he reassembled the toothbrush and screwed the cover back into place. He purposefully left the toothbrush on the counter because he knew it would drive them crazy when they tried to remember who moved it and when.

Except for the picture in his back pocket and the relocated toothbrush, he left everything in the house exactly as he'd found it. On his way out, as he passed the fridge, he opened the door and removed a can of beer and took it with him back down the hillside.

Midway down, he sat on a log and drank the beer, tossing the empty can into a nearby briar bush.

25

At the hospital, Shelly paced beside the bed, ignoring his frequent requests that she please sit in the chair in the corner.

"You're driving me crazy with that pacing. Sit, please! "

Pale green walls. Grey floors. Monitoring screens stacked along one wall. Sickly smell of disinfectant.

By the time the doctor arrived, Shelly was so hyper that she looked like a cat clawing its way up a tree.

"How's he doing?" she asked, barking her question before he even had time to cross the room to reach Rivers' bed.

"His tests were all good," said the doctor, a young intern from India. "But I want to keep him overnight for observation."

"I'm fine," protested Rivers. "I want to go home."

"Not a chance," said the doctor. "If I let you go home and you suffered a heart attack, a delayed reaction to the shock, your lovely wife would sue my Hindu ass."

Shelly couldn't help but laugh.

Rivers smiled broadly.

"I didn't know Indians talked that way."

"They don't," responded the doctor, his face devoid of any semblance of humor. "I've lived in Memphis for five years. Sometimes I talk Memphis."

"I'll stay if you really think I should."

"I do."

The doctor left the room without another word. In his wake, Shelly laughed, "Well, I guess he put your Memphis ass in its place."

"I guess he did."

"How do you feel?"

"Fine. Like always."

"He said the burns on your hand are minor. The redness should go away in a day or so. What a freak accident."

"We don't know it was an accident."

"Do you think someone is trying to kill you? Like when that car forced you into the ditch?"

"I'd like for the police to take a look at that toothbrush."

"What do you think they will find."

"That it's been tampered with."

Shelly sighed.

"I don't know about that, honey. That's sort of farfetched. I think if someone was trying to kill you they'd find a better way to do it."

"Maybe you're right, I don't know."

"Do you want me to stay with you in the hospital tonight?"

"Could we pull the curtains and do it on the hospital bed with you on top?"

Shelly shook her head.

"I'm a medical professional. I couldn't do that. What if we got caught?"

"Unless it was that nurse out there who's the size of Godzilla. I don't think she'd be too impressed."

"Well, if you're not in the mood to play, I see no reason why you should stay. Why don't you go home and call the police. Get them to come out and take a look at that toothbrush."

"Oh, do I have to?"

"Yes. I'll feel better if you do."

"OK, I will if it will make you happy, I'll do it."

"Thanks."

Shelly leaned over and kissed him on the mouth. Then she turned, headed out the door. Over her shoulder she whispered, "I'm going to get naked and sit in your chair to watch television. What do you think of that?"

Before he could answer, she was gone. She was such a tease. It was one of the reasons he loved her. A woman without a sense of humor is like a boat without a rudder. Only one way for those rudderless women to go. Straight ahead. Not Shelly. She relied on sharp turns to make life interesting. He couldn't imagine life without her.

On the drive back home, Shelly used her cell to call Trent.

No answer. She left a voicemail.

"You aren't going to believe what happened to us tonight. Rivers' electric toothbrush exploded on him and almost killed him. I had to revive him. He's staying at the hospital tonight. Nearly scared me to death. I don't know what I would do without him. Call me if you get a chance. Have a good evening. Bye."

119

Once she hung up, she grimaced, not believing she'd left a message. What was she thinking? There was not a doubt in her mind that she was still deeply in love with Rivers. Why was she risking that for a fling? She didn't love Trent. She liked him, but she didn't love him. No, she wasn't positive she even liked him.

When she pulled up in front of the house, she called the sheriff's department before getting out of the car. They told her they'd send someone over right away. "Don't touch anything," the dispatcher said sternly.

Shelly was surprised at how many lights they'd left on in the house. She had an eerie feeling about the house as she walked up the sidewalk to the front steps. Once she ascended the steps onto the porch, she paused to look around. Fireflies flickered around the perimeter of the porch. A pair of bullfrogs croaked at each other somewhere in the distance. Wind gusts tickled the treetops.

Inside the house, she heard the upstairs television, the laugh track from a situation comedy, a small comfort under the circumstances since it implied life as usual. She went into the kitchen and got a soft drink, surprised to see that they had left the back door wide open. She closed it and snapped the lock into place.

She was about to go upstairs when she heard the siren. She went out on the porch and watched as the headlights of the patrol car approached and then turned into the driveway. A female deputy, the same deputy who investigated Rivers' accident, got out of the car and walked up the steps, her hardware jingling with each step she took.

Shelly opened the door and introduced herself, expecting someone a little less gruff. The deputy didn't wait to be invited into the house. She bulled her way inside, brushing against Shelly as she entered, her right hand resting on her revolver.

"Let's see what you got," said the deputy.

"Just follow me."

Shelly led the way up the stairway, with the deputy jingling along behind her. She quickly took her through the bedroom and into the bathroom. The deputy whistled. "You called the fire marshal, didn't you?"

Shelly looked surprised. "Why, no — was I supposed to?"

"Yes indeed. It's in the code. You should have called."

"I'm sorry. I was in a hurry to get medical attention for my husband."

"You did what most people would've done. But you should familiarize yourself with all the laws that apply to you and those you love. You've got to become a multi-task civilian."

"What's that?"

"That's someone who can handle three or more mental processes at the same time. If you'd been trained in multi-task delivery, you'd have been able to get medical attention for your husband, call the fire department, turn off your television set . . ."

"Oh, you noticed that the TV was still on?"

"Yes ma'am, I'm trained to notice those things. You know it's a fire hazard to leave your set on when you're not at home. Because of their high wattage they're prone to spontaneously burst into flames on occasion."

"I didn't know that."

"Oh, yeah. Happens all the time."

Shelly abruptly changed the subject. "The toothbrush that exploded is over there in the tub."

The deputy turned and started to the bathtub, but then quickly stopped. "What's this?" she asked, pointing to the toothbrush on the countertop.

Shelly looked surprised.

"That's not supposed to be there. I left it in the bathtub."

She looked it over closely, careful not to touch it. "How did that happen?"

"I wouldn't know," said the deputy. "Maybe your husband moved it while you were calling for help."

Shelly looked at the countertop and then at the bathtub. She was positive she'd left it in the bathtub. Rivers was the only person who could have moved it. "I suppose that's the only explanation."

The deputy picked up the toothbrush and looked at it.

"Shouldn't you be careful not to leave fingerprints?" asked Shelly. She wanted to snatch it away from the deputy, but fortunately she was able to restrain herself.

The deputy shot her a condescending look that was one part surprise and one part disgust.

"So do you think this was an accidental fire—or a crime?" asked the deputy.

"I don't know what it is."

"So you think it might be a crime?"

"Honestly, I don't know what to think. Besides this incident, my husband was forced off the road and a few days later his car caught on fire."

"I was the investigating officer when his car went off the road. We never found the party responsible, but I don't think it was intentional. The fire must have been a city matter."

Shelly nodded.

"What did the fire officer say about it?"

"They said it was caused by a mechanical problem under the hood."

"And you don't believe them?"

"It just seems like too much bad luck for everything to be an accident."

"Your husband is a psychologist, isn't he?"

"That's right."

"Do you think that maybe his work might be affecting him? He probably works with paranoid people all the time. Maybe it's rubbed off on him. I've heard of that happening before."

"Oh, I don't think so."

The deputy shrugged, indicating she'd given it her best shot.

"There's nothing here that looks like a crime to me. But, if you want me to, I can open up the toothbrush and take a look at it."

Shelly was still concerned about the fingerprint issue, not completely convinced that someone wasn't trying to hurt her husband and not completely convinced that the deputy knew what the hell she was doing.

"Do what you need to do," she said reluctantly.

The deputy took out a pocket knife that had a screwdriver attachment and she used it to open the toothbrush handle. She leaned over the appliance, poking at it like a child picking raisins out of cereal. As she looked over the toothbrush, Shelly noticed how neat and clean her uniform was. Starched shirt. Pressed slacks. Not a wrinkle in sight.

Finally, the deputy grinned and stood erect.

"Look at this!" she said excitedly.

Shelly leaned overtgfgr close to the toothbrush.

The deputy turned it so that she could see it better.

"See, you've got two wires there, both of which are held into place by tiny screws. One of those screws got loose and that let the wire wander over to that piece of metal. The vibrations of the toothbrush probably shook the screw loose."

"It looks like an accident to you?" asked Shelly.

"Sure—it's just a case of equipment failure. If I were you, I'd get a new toothbrush and pretend this never happened. If you ever have evidence that someone is really trying to kill your husband, for whatever reason, then I want to know about it. But I've got to be honest with you. Around here if someone kills another person, they don't run them off the road or tamper with their toothbrush or booby trap their car—they just go after them with a gun or knife. Every once in a while maybe a hammer or an axe. Nothing complicated. Regular people don't put a lot of thought into how they're going to kill someone. Usually, they pick up the first weapon that's handy. The only person who'd think a murder through is a professional. But that's a whole other set of rules. "

Shelly smiled. "Well, if you put it that way."

"You haven't done anything that would get you in trouble with the sort of people that employ professional shooters?"

"Of course not."

"Happens more often that you'd think." The deputy looked around the room. "Anything else I can do for you today?"

"No—you've been a big help. Thanks for coming out so quickly."

"It's my job."

Shelly showed her out of the house and then went back upstairs and cleaned the bathroom, dumping the toothbrush into the trash. She turned on the shower and went into the bedroom to retrieve a pair of panties from her dresser.

She froze when she opened the drawer. Her panties were neatly folded and stacked one on top of the other. She never folded her panties. She just tossed them into the drawer. Rivers likes to make fun of her for being so messy. Maybe Rivers did it as a joke. The last thing Shelly wanted was to spend the night in the house alone. She looked at the clock. It was too late to call Rivers at the hospital to ask if he'd folded her panties. Besides, how crazy would that sound? If you think it's not crazy sounding, just try calling up someone and asking them if they have folded your panties.

26

Jack McCain dropped by High Sass Dames during the lunch hour to eat at their barbecue buffet. The clientele at that time of day was different from the clientele that came into the club at night. During the lunch hour, most of the customers were men in suits, business executives, doctors, lawyers, accountants. The night crowd was more of a blue-collar crowd, sunburned men in overalls, baseball caps, heavy metal T-shirts.

The buffet was set up as far away from the main stage as you could get. When management first got the idea to put in a lunch buffet, they installed it around the main stage, thinking that patrons would want to be close to the action when they piled their plates with pulled pork, ribs, baked beans, and coleslaw; but it didn't work out that way.

As much as the patrons admired the ladies disrobing on the stage, they balked at eating from the buffet. Confused, the manager asked a few of his regular customers why no one wanted to eat at the buffet. The answer made sense when he thought about it. To a man, they were afraid pubes would fall into their food. The manager moved the buffet away from the stage and it was an instant hit.

John loaded up his plate with pulled pork and beans and sat at a table near the door. He was only there a few minutes when one of the waitresses pulled up a chair at his table. Darlene was a tall brunette whose boyfriends all tended to drive Harley-Davidsons.

"What's up, Jack?" she said.

"Not much. I'm meeting some people for lunch."

"Don't worry. I'll get out of your way. I ordered a pizza and I'm waiting for the delivery boy. Don't you like the company?"

"You know I do," he grinned. Darlene had helped him with several news stories. She had a major crush on him. She reminded him of that every chance she got. "Before my friends get here, let me ask you a question."

"Sure," she said, beaming. "I swallow, don't spit."

Jack shook his head in dismay. "Darlene, you aren't even close."

"But isn't that good information to have?"

"Has anyone ever told you that you've told them more than they wanted to know?"

"All the time."

"Well, there you have it—now you've done it again."

"Sorry." She grinned like a kid who's thrown a rock through a window and dares you to do something about it.

"This is serious, Darlene. Will you quit horsing around and listen to me?"

"Sure," she said, feigning seriousness.

"I think there might be a hit out on a friend of mine . . ."

Darlene interrupted, "Who?"

"I can't tell you that. I just want to know if you've heard anything."

Darlene leaned in close across the table.

"There's something coming down. I don't know what. But it's something."

"No idea?"

"I know this. When I approach a table of heavy hitters and they're huddled real close, talking all serious like, and then they shut up when I give them their drinks, I know something is coming down. There's been a buzz in here for days. Lots of intense conversations, if you know what I mean?"

"You don't know anything definite?"

"No, I don't."

"Will you tell me if you do?"

"Honey, you know I will."

"Thanks."

She stopped speaking when the pizza delivery boy approached their table and dumped a box in front of her containing what the pizza company called "The Carnivore." She paid him in wrinkled ones and gave him a two-dollar tip.

As she was paying, Jack's lunch guests walked up to the table. When she saw who they were, she apologetically jumped to her feet and backed away from the table. "See ya, Jack,"

The two men, both wearing expensive suits, pulled up chairs and admired Jack's plate of barbecue. After engaging in chit-chat

126

for a few minutes, the men went to the buffet and returned with plates of their own. The men, both of whom had on wire-rimmed glasses, wore identical pin-striped suits, and identical white shirts. Founding partners of a law firm named Blackberry and Associates, Harry Blackberry and Joseph Blackberry were identical twins. In their early forties, they looked younger than their age.

In addition to guiding Memphis's leading law firm to phenomenal success, the two men were the unchallenged kingpins of the city's underworld. They maintained different codes of conduct for each business. For the law firm, any moral transgression was acceptable as long as it was undertaken with a reasonable expectation of a favorable review by an appellate court.

For the illegal operations, the motto was to do unto them as they would do unto you (murder was never dismissed out of hand). For the adult entertainment businesses (topless bars, escort services, adult bookstores), the Blackberry brothers insisted that they must be operated in a drug-and-violence-free environment. They had a soft spot for the women who worked for them.

You could break their hearts. They saw nothing wrong with that. But you'd better not break any bones or scar their faces. If you did that, you'd hear from the brothers, and not in a nice way. Despite their nerdy, prep-school appearance, the Blackberry brothers inspired fear in those who worked for them—or challenged their authority.

Jack interviewed the brothers on a regular basis for the newspaper. They trusted him to do exactly what he said he was going to do and because of that they didn't get upset when he occasionally stepped on their toes. They wrote bruised feelings off as a cost of doing business.

The three of them ate in silence for a few minutes. In the background, a tall, blonde dancer named Ashley nervously danced on the main stage to the music of Bonnie Raitt's "Something to Talk About."

The dancers were all terrified of the brothers, primarily because they never quite understand the rules of the game. Were they showing too much? Were they not showing enough? Who the hell ever knew?

Finally, Harry, his voice low and his words evenly spaced, said, "What's the matter, Jack. You got a problem?"

"I've got a friend who has a problem."

"And you think we can help your friend?"

"I don't know. I hope so."

"What is it you need?" asked Joseph.

"My friend, Dr. Rivers Mann—do you know him?"

"I've heard the name," said Joseph.

Harry nodded.

"He's been experiencing a series of accidents that I don't think are accidents."

"What kind of accidents?"

"Someone forced him off the road into a ditch. His car blew up in the parking lot of his office when he started it."

The Blackberry brothers shook their collective head.

"I see what you mean," said Harry.

"Have you heard anything about this? Has he stepped on anyone's toes?"

"None of our people would have a reason to have a problem with him."

Harry looked at Joseph. "I say it's either a personal thing, or its coming from out of town."

"My thoughts exactly," said Joseph.

"He's a psychologist, isn't he?" asked Harry. "Maybe it's one of his patients. Or maybe it's a domestic problem. Maybe he's involved with a woman who's got a jealous husband or boyfriend. Is that a possibility?"

"Knowing Rivers the way I do, I'd say no. He's happily married."

"I don't know what to tell you, Jack, except that what we hear on the street, we'll pass on to you," said Harry. "In the meantime, if he needs legal counsel just have him get in touch with us." He handed Jack a business card. "We have been known to work miracles within the legal system."

"Good enough," said Jack, pocketing the card.

The three men went back to the buffet for seconds while the dancers sweated their presence in the club, fighting with each other backstage over who would go on stage next. No one wanted to do it. If the Blackberry brothers didn't like the way you danced, you were done in Memphis. None of the dancers was secure enough to take that chance. It was not a pretty sight backstage.

27

Tony Apple liked to travel because he liked sleeping in hotels. He didn't have to worry about making the bed, or cleaning the bathroom, or unclogging a drain, like he had to do at his apartment in Las Vegas.

In a hotel, he didn't have to worry about being a sitting duck for someone who had a ticket to take him out. If he was feeling heat, for whatever reason, he could simply change hotel rooms each night and not have to worry so much about someone kicking the door down in the dead of night. He liked not having a permanent address.

A movie fan, he liked Woody Allen's line that compares love to a shark that has to keep moving to stay alive. When you were in Tony's line of work, the only way to get a good night's work was to be like a shark and keep moving. Sleep in a different place each night. No problem for Tony. The Three Stooges followed him everywhere he went. He'd never stayed in a hotel where he couldn't find the Stooges on TV. That was the one constant in his life.

After waking several times during the night, mostly because of bad dreams, Tony lay on the hotel bed until mid-morning, watching the Stooges. Then he got up and brushed his teeth. He was fanatic about his teeth. His father and mother both lost all their teeth before they reached forty. He was terrified that he would wake one morning and discover that all his teeth were gone.

He walked around in his underwear for a while, obsessively going back and forth to the window to see if anyone suspicious was lingering out on the street. Then he pulled up a chair to the only table in the room.

On the table was a rather large brown paper bag that contained a jar of cold cream, a fifth of vodka, a pair of plastic gloves, a roll of paper towels, and a small glass bottle upon which was written the words "aconite." Better known as wolfsbane, devil's helmet, or blue rocket, aconite is a white powder that is derived from the leaves and roots of a garden plant, *Aconitum anglicum.*

Tony slipped on the rubber gloves. They had a scent that he liked. He removed the plastic wrapping from a hotel water glass, wadding it into a ball that he tossed into a nearby trash can. Then he poured one finger of vodka into the glass. He raised the glass to his lips. Gulped the vodka with one swallow. Grimaced and stamped his foot.

"Damn!" he said, squinting one eye.

Then he poured another finger's worth of vodka into the glass and carefully opened the bottle that contained the aconite.

He tapped about a teaspoon of white crystals into the vodka, the only liquid in which aconite will dissolve, and he twirled the mixture until the crystals disappeared. He leaned over the glass and sniffed. Nothing. No odor. It was like sniffing water.

The jar of cold cream was next. Before opening the jar, he looked at the digital picture he took of an identical jar of cold cream. Approximately one-third of the cream was missing. He reached over onto his room service tray and picked up a spoon and used it to scoop cream out of the jar until it looked similar to the jar in the picture. He dumped the excess cream into the paper bag.

Before the next step he paused and took a long draw on the vodka bottle. He didn't care for the taste of alcohol, but it gave him courage, or so he believed.

He'd done his research. Aconite was regarded by the ancient Greeks as the "Queen of poisons." In ancient times it was used to poison the tips of arrows and spears. It's a fast-acting poison that kills within eight minutes when ingested or applied to the skin. Death comes quickly because it attacks the cardiovascular and central nervous system and paralyzes the muscles used in breathing.

Tony lifted the water glass and gently poured the contents into the jar of cold cream. By the time he returned the glass to the table, his hand was shaking. He watched as the vodka pooled on top of the cold cream. He watched for ten minutes, but very little of the liquid seeped into the cold cream. Not knowing what else to do, he took the end of the spoon and stirred the mixture, blending the liquid into each fold.

Soon the liquid was no longer visible. The jar looked like an ordinary container of cold cream. Tony screwed the top onto the jar and lowered it into a plastic bag and sealed it with a plastic zipper. Then he slipped the rubber gloves from his hands, pulling inside out so that he would not touch the exposed surface. He put the gloves and the contaminated glass into the paper bag and folded it and tossed it into the trash can. He started to take another swig of vodka, but then he remembered that he had contaminated the bottle with his gloved hand. He went into the bathroom and scrubbed his hands with soap and water. Then he unwrapped a clean glass and, using a washcloth to grip the bottle, he poured a full glass of vodka. After one sip, the phone rang.

"Hello."

He smiled when he recognized the caller's voice.

"Everything is fine. I don't think I'll be here too much longer."

Long pause.

"I understand. It's not as simple as you think. There's a lot involved. No . . . don't get angry. I'm doing the best I can. Soon . . . It will be soon . . . . I know that you are under pressure. I promise this will be done."

After the conversation ended, Tony lay on the bed and watched television for most of the day. The problem was that people didn't understand his line of work. They had unrealistic expectations. When people didn't understand him, it gave him a migraine and that usually put him in a bad mood.

28

Shelly was the first thing that Rivers saw when he opened his eyes. She sat in a chair to his right. Elegantly dressed in black. Perfumed. Lots of leg showing. The instant his eyes opened, she said, "Good morning."

Rivers raised himself up and blinked. "How long you been here?"

"Just a few minutes."

"Damn, you look good."

"Thanks honey. How do you feel?"

"Totally normal."

"I checked with the nurses and your doctor released you. I thought I'd drive you home and then go in to work."

"That's a nice surprise."

Rivers bounded out of bed, feeling a little silly in his hospital gown. He dressed quickly, foregoing his socks, which he stuffed into his back pocket, slipping his expensive loafers onto his bare feet.

"I'll be glad to get out of this place," he said, hopping on one foot as he struggled to force a resistant loafer onto the other foot.

"I'm glad the doctors were here for you," she said. "It could have gone the other way, you know."

"I know."

"It's made me thankful for what I've got."

"Me, too."

Driving home in Shelly's car, they rode in silence for a long time. He thought about the accident, if indeed it was an accident. How would he have reacted if he'd found Shelly stretched out on the floor? Was he prepared for any emergency that could happen around the house? He doubted it. He vowed to do his homework so that he would be prepared.

Shelly thought about how much she cared for Rivers. She'd be lost without him. She thought about her affair with Trent and she almost had a panic attack. How could she have been so stupid?

Shelly reached over and placed her palm on Rivers' thigh and drove with one hand. He smiled and put his hand on top of hers.

Small gesture. Spoke to the heart. Sometimes, during the down time between patients, Rivers reflected on his marriage. None of his friends were still married. Most of his patients were divorced, separated, or about to be. He didn't know the secret to his marriage to Shelly. Luck, probably.

Shelly dropped him off in front of the house. He closed the car door and looked like he wanted to say something. She rolled the window down and he stuck his head in the window.

"I almost forgot," he said, grinning. "I love you."

"I love you, too," she said, her heart racing.

"Bye." He turned and went into the house as she drove away.

When he closed the door behind him, he stood for a moment. The house was quiet, eerily so. No television or radio. No air conditioner struggling to keep the air cold. No creaks. No running water. It occurred to him that Shelly was right. What was missing in their life was a child, someone to explore the house with wild abandon and make it come alive.

He walked through the hallway and into the kitchen. He got a soft drink from the fridge and opened the back door to go out onto the porch. The heat was stifling. He sat on a porch swing and looked out at the river. No barges or boats in sight. The currents were stronger than usual. Whitecaps. Giant whirlpools that moved down the river like underwater tornadoes.

Wouldn't it be nice if the rough water in our life could be viewed from a distance? he thought.

The cell rang. He could see from the caller ID that it was Jack.

"What's up, Jack?"

"Where the hell are you?"

"What do you mean?"

"I called your office and your receptionist told me that you were in the hospital."

"That's right—well, I *was* in the hospital. I'm home now."

"Are you all right?"

"I'm fine."

Rivers told him about the toothbrush. Shelly bringing him back to life. The trip to the hospital. His release. For some reason, the events sounded so much worse, more ominous, when he explained them to Jack.

Jack was silent for a moment, processing the information. Rivers had told him about the incident without assigning blame or voicing an opinion about why the toothbrush malfunctioned. Finally, he said, "You sound very matter of fact about the toothbrush. Do you think it was an accident?"

"No."

"So you think someone is trying to kill you?"

"I've thought so from the day I was run off the road."

"What did the police say about the toothbrush?"

"I was in the hospital, but the sheriff sent someone out to investigate. They interviewed Shelly and then they came by the hospital to interview me."

"What did they say?"

"That it was an accident. The deputy who investigated — incidentally, it was the same deputy who investigated my car accident — examined the toothbrush and concluded that the problem was caused by a loose wire."

"Where does the sheriff get those guys?"

"And gals."

"Right."

"Beats me, Jack. It's all made me realize that the police are not here to protect us. They're here to file reports once crimes have been committed. They get irritable if you talk to them about doing something before a crime happens. In truth, they are not in the crime prevention business."

"That's as true a statement as I've ever heard. I hope you are going to take steps to protect yourself."

"You can count on that."

"Good — the reason I called was to let you know that I talked to my sources about your situation."

"Did you use my name?"

"Sure — saw no reason not to."

"OK. I don't mind. You know best in these matters. What did they say?"

"Whoever is trying to do you in is not a local professional. It's got to be someone with a personal grudge. Or someone from out of town."

"That your friends' opinion?"

"Yes."

"And yours as well?"

"Yes. Do you have any patients who have a grudge against you?"

"Not that I know of. Oh, there are a few who might, but they are all in mental institutions. The only red flag I've come across involves a patient who has had two attempts on her life."

"Really! Do you think they might be connected?"

"I don't see how."

"What are you going to do?"

"Jack, I don't know what I can do except to wait for them to make another move. Did your sources tell you that they would let you know if they came across anything?"

"They did."

"Do you trust them?"

"I believe them when they say they would know if it's a professional job. I think I can trust them to let me know if they learn that it's a professional from out of town, or if they hear anything on the street."

"You can't ask for more than that."

29

Oscar hated summertime stakeouts. Mainly because Memphis heat was so oppressive that it could blister the paint right off of a car. If he left his car engine running for too long, to keep the air conditioner on, the engine could overheat and shut down. If he turned the engine off and rolled down all the windows, the temperature could balloon up to 120 degrees inside the car.

At the moment, the engine was running and cool air was circulating throughout the car. He looked at his hands. They were parched from the unrelenting rays of the sun. Tiny drops of blood formed on his knuckles. He wiped them with a handkerchief, but bright-red droplets quickly reformed. He was one miserable son of a bitch. Not only were his hands causing him grief, his hemorrhoids were flaring up again and it was hard for him to sit in a position that did not cause his ass to ache. When the hemorrhoids strangulated, which happened every few weeks, it generated a knife-like pain that shot through his body like an electrical jolt. He longed for the days of his youth, when he didn't have to worry about his hands or his ass.

Finally, when he couldn't stand it any longer, he got out of his car and walked over to Doe's front door and pushed the doorbell. Doe was shocked to see him at the door since he'd told her she would never know he was around.

"I've got a problem," he said, showing her his hands.

"My God!" she exclaimed. "What happened?"

Realizing that he'd frightened her," he said, "I'm sorry—didn't mean to alarm you. I have a problem with my hands chapping. When that happens they start bleeding. Do you have any cream or lotions that I could use?"

"You mean like cold cream?"

"That would be fine."

She invited him into the hallway and closed the door so that all the cool air wouldn't escape. Then she went into the bathroom and returned with a jar of cold cream. "Use this—it works great on chapped hands."

"If you unfasten that top, I can scoop out a dab."

"Oh, no," she insisted. "Take the jar. You may need it again."

"Thanks. Thanks a lot."

He turned to go out the door, but then paused to say, "I'm just down the street if you need me. I'm on the job. Nothing for you to worry about."

"I feel so much safer with you looking after me."

"My pleasure, Ms. Peterson."

Doe watched him amble down the street, walking in a shuffling motion that caused him to sway from side to side. Then she shut the door and went about her business, confident that she had nothing to worry about.

Oscar sidled into his car and started the engine. He flipped on the air conditioner and turned the fan on high. He set the vents so that the air blew directly onto his face. He looked at his hands. Liver spots. Knarled and bloody knuckles. Skin so dry it had a crusty appearance.

He opened the jar of cold cream and lifted it to his nose. Odorless. At least he wouldn't smell like someone's grandmother. He dipped his fingers into the jar and scooped out enough cold cream to smear onto both hands. It instantly had a soothing effect.

He leaned back and gazed at Doe's townhouse. Maybe this would be the day he caught the son of a bitch who was terrorizing his client. He would like nothing better than to collar the low life. Men who abuse women make all men look bad. Just thinking about it sent his hand absently down to his waist to touch his .38-caliber pistol. The department had moved on to 9mm automatics, but he still liked the feel of a snub-nosed revolver.

Oscar noticed a tingling sensation in his mouth. He raked the tip of his tongue against the roof of his mouth to see if that would stop it. Then he started experiencing numbness in his right hand. His pulse quickened. Instinctively he knew that something was wrong.

As he pondered whether he should leave his post and go to the hospital, the numbness spread throughout his entire body. He attempted to shift the transmission to drive, but both arms were paralyzed. Breathing became labored. His entire body was shutting down—and he realized that. He tried to scream for help.

Nothing happened. The scream rattled around inside his head like a stone in a tin can. He could hear it. He knew no one else could.

A passerby waved. Oscar could move his eyes from side to side, but that was the only muscle function he had left. The passerby looked offended that he didn't return the wave. Oscar called out for help a hundred times but nothing happened. He wondered if all death was like that. Was everyone clear-headed to the end? Did everyone go out of this world screaming inside their head for help?

About ten minutes after the first tingle, breathing became difficult. The small amount of air that made its way into his lungs was insufficient. He gasped for air, but only inside his head since his skeleton muscles would not respond.

A brittle coldness flowed through his entire body.

So this is what death feels like he thought.

Beyond his windshield, the sky was a brilliant blue. Not a cloud in sight. He savored every detail, right up until the instant that everything went black.

30

Doe just happened to look from her window when she saw smoke billowing from Oscar's car. She called 911 and rushed from her townhouse out into the street. A small crowd was gathered around the car, but no one made an effort to rescue Oscar. She wasn't sure that he was even in the car. The black smoke was so thick that it was impossible to see if anyone was inside.

"Is there a man in there?" she screamed.

A woman in the crowd looked at her with a blank expression on her face. "Yeah, there's a man in there. I saw him."

Doe leaned over, trying to see past the smoke. It was impossible to tell if there was anyone in the car. It was an inferno.

"How do you know there's a man in there?"

"Because I saw him before the smoke got so bad."

"We've got to help him!" screamed out Doe.

She ran toward the car, covering her nose and mouth with her hand. She reached out for the door handle and winced with pain as she withdrew her hand. The handle was red hot. She retreated to the sidewalk across the street, where the crowd gawked and pointed at the car.

The fire truck siren filled the air with a sense of urgency. The moment the truck arrived, men and women wearing protective gear with oxygen tanks attached, leapt from the truck with axes in hand and dashed over to the car. One of the firefighters broke out the window with an axe and then stepped back for a moment as a billowing gust of smoke escaped and rose skyward.

Then the firefighter stepped forward and reached into the car, grabbing Oscar by the scruff of the neck, dragging him from the car seat onto the pavement and then over to the truck, where a paramedic took one quick look at him and said, "There's nothing we can do for him."

As Oscar was being examined, other firefighters knocked down the fire with foam extinguishers. It was all over within minutes.

Doe looked at Oscar with disbelief. His entire body was charred. There was no face. No Hands. No feet. Just a mass of charred tissue that resembled a log that had been pulled from a

140

fire. She looked on in horror, tears flowing down her cheeks. The fire officer approached her and said, "Haven't we met before?"

"Yes," she answered without taking her eyes off of Oscar's body. "When my car caught on fire, you put it out."

"That's right," he said. "I knew I had seen you before."

The fireman turned and looked around the scene. The crowd was quickly dissipating. Within minutes, Doe was the only remaining spectator.

"Did you know this man?"

"Yes I did."

"How did this happen?"

"I don't know," she said looking at him for the first time. "He worked for me. He was a private investigator. He was watching my house."

"Really," said the fire officer, his eyes widening. "That's an odd coincidence, isn't it?"

Doe looked at him as if he had lost his mind. She was angry. Her fists were clinched. Her jaw muscles pulsated.

"You thought my fire was an accident. Do you think this fire was an accident?"

"Yes, as a matter of fact I do. From the looks of things, he was sitting in the car with the engine running to stay cool. Dropped off to sleep. The carbon monoxide fumes took over and kept him from waking up. It's one hundred degrees right now. If you leave a car engine running in this heat, it will overheat to the point where a gas line expands and ruptures and spills gas and before you know it you've got a raging fire."

"You don't think he was murdered?"

"That's possible. If he was shot or something like that, the coroner will be able to see that. But that's not what happened here. We see this sort of fire every day during the summer months."

Doe glared at him. Her impulse was to scratch his bloody eyes out. Instead, taking Dr. Mann's advice, she took a deep breath and imagined a red balloon rising from her angry thoughts into the blue sky. As she navigated that fantasy, a police officer walked up and stood next to the fire officer.

"She a witness?" asked the police officer.

The fire officer nodded.

"Lady, I'm going to need a statement from you," said the police officer. He removed a note pad from his back pocket and clicked a Bic pen to indicate his readiness to begin. With that, the fire officer tipped his helmet at Doe and said, "Have a nice day." Then he rejoined the other firefighters, his work there done.

The police officer took down Doe's name and address. Then he asked her if she knew the man in the car. When she told him Oscar's name, he grimaced. "He was a cop. Do you have any reason to suspect foul play?"

"No," she lied, not wishing to revisit her suspicions.

The police officer took down all the details and then wished her a nice day. She looked at him as he walked away, wondering how many times a day he went through that same routine. She never realized how matter of fact death was. When she returned to her townhouse, she was shaking. The secure world that she'd created had evaporated in a whiff of smoke.

She no longer felt safe. What should she do next? Where should she turn? She double locked her front door and then checked her back door to make sure it was locked. Then she rechecked her front door.

She sat in the living room for a long while, wild thoughts flying through her head. The world no longer made sense to her, if it ever did. Oscar's death brought back old fears that went back to her childhood. Who was she? Really? Why was she having all these problems? None of the people she worked with had problems. Why her?

She called Trent on his cell, but he didn't answer. It frustrated her that she never was able to reach him when she needed him. He put way too much effort into his work. How much better it would be, she thought, to date a man who did not have a job. Someone who could be there for her twenty-four-hours-a-day. She made good money. She didn't care whether her boyfriend made money or not. She made a mental note to be on the lookout for an unemployed man with a big heart. And a great bod.

Flutie was the only person she really could count on to be there when she needed her. Doe called her at the café, knowing that she would be there.

"Are you busy?" she asked.

"Not really," she answered, though she was elbow deep in pastry dough and cradling the telephone on her shoulder. Whatever her faults in other areas, she was the ultimate loyal friend. "What's up?"

Doe told her about the fire, breaking down into tears before she finished the story.

"Are they sure he's dead?" asked Flutie.

"I was there! He was burned to a crisp! Who's going to protect me now?"

"Have you called Trent?"

"Yes. His phone is turned off. You know how busy he is."

"I think the first thing you should do is call Dr. Mann's office and get an appointment to see him. He'll understand."

Flutie finished with the pastry dough and signaled for an assistant to take over. Then she walked to the back door to sign an invoice for the delivery of fresh produce. The entire time she spoke to Doe, she moved about the café, smelling fruit, pointing to a table of people who were frantically trying to get the attention of a waitress.

Bedlam. Chaos with a chocolate aftertaste. Flutie liked it that way.

"You're right. My regular appointment is not until next week. I'm sure he'll see me, though."

"Be sure and tell the receptionist about the fire."

"I will."

"If you need me, you know where I'll be."

"Thanks."

31

Preston was on a delicate mission. The federal government would think unkindly of him using Mack 222 to solve a mystery involving his personal life, yet that was exactly what he was doing. He'd always been a risk taker.

You've heard of panic rooms? Fortified bunkers within a home that can withstand anything a devious mind could devise to throw against them, short of a direct nuclear attack. Preston's penthouse computer room was such a place, though it *was* built to withstand a nuclear attack by virtue of the fact that the entire room could be lowered from the penthouse into a sub-basement.

Each time he used the computer, he felt like the Wizard of Oz, hiding behind a curtain, pulling levels, pressing buttons, creating an illusionary world. If people only knew that the government had created an alternate universe in which every citizen of the planet was duplicated though millions of data bytes, they surely would rise up and revolt. It was a world in which no one ever died since each person's alternate existence was timeless, sustained by minute flashes of magnetic energy.

Once Preston was within the sacrosanct chamber of Mack 222, he again entered the names Yao Bai and Yao Ta. He spoke the words as he typed them into the computer, the mere speaking of them bringing back painful memories. Yao Bai was a strikingly beautiful Chinese woman who spoke flawless English. He met her at the United States consulate in Shanghai, where he was assigned as a computer tech. She smiled at him. He smiled back. She had a flowery scent that he still remembered all these years later.

The consulate building itself was steeped in romance. An early Twentieth Century mansion, located in the French Concession of the city on Huai Hai Zhong Road, the stately mansion was once owned by the finance minister of the Quing Dynasty, a man who also was one of China's most prominent entrepreneurs. The old house smelled of wealth and lovers' vows and late-night intrigues in which secrets lurked behind each closed door. It was the perfect place to fall in love.

It was forbidden for American embassy personnel to date Chinese employees, mainly for security reasons, but also because officialdom felt that such relationships had no upside whatsoever. So Preston and Yao Bai kept their romance a secret. Inside the consulate, they only made eye contact if they were alone. Otherwise, they walked past each other without speaking, each hesitant to look into the other's eyes for fear of breaking into an involuntary smile. Even so, they followed their hearts, knowing full well that it could result in him being sent back to America and her being sent back to work the fields outside the city. It was a high stakes romance.

Outside the consulate, they crated a new world of their own making. She moved out of her family's house and into a furnished apartment, where they met each evening and made love and talked until the sun rose once again. The tables and chairs in the apartment were square-shaped and poorly made, but the canopy bed was exquisite. It was made of bamboo and scented rose wood and it surrounded them with artful carvings that depicted ancient Chinese traditions.

Preston had many girlfriends before going to China, but none that understood him like Bai. She smiled whenever he spoke and she voiced sympathy to every problem that he faced in life. When they made love, she touched him not only in a sexual way, but in a spiritual way, so that his heart was always full, even when he was not in her presence. As the days went by, he realized that what he wanted most in life was to see her sweet face when he went to bed at night and then again upon rising the next morning.

Bai was wise beyond her years, but she was not experienced when it came to relationships. Preston was her first lover and there was much she did not understand about sex and how men and woman communicate with each other. To her, all Americans were strange and exotic. She listened with patience when they spoke, but she did not always understand the nuances of their conversation, just as she saw that they did not always understand when she spoke of matters unfamiliar to them.

"Why do Americans speak so loudly," she once asked Preston.

"I didn't realize that we did."

"Oh, yes. Very loud. Sometimes very angry."

Preston was perplexed. The other people in the office didn't seem loud to him.

"Is that why your people speak so quietly?"

"My people don't speak quietly."

"Yes, you do—you speak so quietly that we sometimes think that you are afraid."

"Chinese people are afraid of nothing."

"Really?"

"Sometimes we think that you are like bulls that walk through a field destroying all the plants."

"We are a nation of builders, not destroyers."

"That's what you think."

Preston thought it was cute the way she got angry with him. Her eyes blazed. She wrapped her arms, one around the other. She took tiny steps so that three of hers would equal one of his. There was something about her anger that made her feet buzz along like a wind-up toy automobile. He laughed. She answered his laughter with clipped sentences, the meaning of which he never fully understood.

When they made love, she had a special way of caressing him all over. Fragrant kisses on his face, his hands, his fingers, his knees, his back, the top of his head. She massaged his feet and she pressed her body against his, warming him on a cool night, her weight no more than a feather as she caressed him in ways he'd never thought possible.

Over several months, their relationship blossomed. He could not imagine life without her. She felt the same way. Although she tried, she was unable to keep the relationship a secret from her family. One day her father sternly told her that she had shamed the family by having a relationship with a foreigner. The only solution, he argued, was for them to get married.

Several times she attempted to bring up the subject of marriage, but each time there was something about Preston's mood on that day that made her back away. He was often angry at the people he worked with. Sometimes he brought that anger home with him and that was all he could talk about. She wanted to talk about the two of them. He wanted to talk about the people in the office that were too dumb to understand his work.

One day the decision of whether to talk about marriage was taken out of her hands by providence. She fretted about it from the time they got home, until they finished dinner and she remained in her chair long past the time she usually cleared the table.

"What's wrong?" asked Preston, seeing that something was on her mind.

"We need to talk."

The effect of those words is the same in China as in America. He sighed, fearing the worst. "What's on your mind?"

"Do you love me?"

"Of course, I love you."

"I love you."

"I know you do. Where are you going with this?"

She took a deep breath. She gazed into his eyes, prepared for the worst. Her words came out slowly, and then gained speed like a rock rolling downhill.

"Something has happened."

"What? What are you talking about?"

"Everything has changed."

"In what way? I'm afraid I don't understand where you are going with this."

"We are going to have a baby."

At first he froze. Not sure what to say. What *does* a man say in a situation like that? What do women consider appropriate? "Thank you! That's wonderful!" What in God's name is a man supposed to say? Unsure of himself, he returned her gaze, unblinking, a huge grin suddenly covering his face.

"Oh, Preston!" she explained, lunging into his arms.

He kissed her on the mouth and said, "We have to get married — our child can't be born a bastard."

"What if I don't make you happy?"

"You already make me happy. You always will make me happy."

For days afterward, she walked on clouds.

As Preston made arrangements with the consulate, she met with her family to plan the marriage ceremony. Her father was happy that she was getting married, but he was unhappy that so many important steps had been overlooked. By tradition, Chinese

147

couples are set on a path of marriage by a matchmaker who woos the woman on the man's behalf and obtains an agreement from her to marry the man. An engagement ceremony is performed, after which betrothal gifts are presented to the woman's family.

Bai skipped those important steps, which meant that she and Preston proceeded directly to the marriage ceremony itself. Before that took place, Bai and Preston met with an embassy official and announced their plans to marry. They were presented with a marriageabilty certificate by the consulate, which meant that the marriage would be recognized by American authorities, an important step in Bai receiving an American visa to travel to the United States.

At the marriage ceremony itself, administered by a respected member of Bai's family, the couple stood side by side and made the customary three bows — the first to honor the ancestors of each person, the second to honor Bai's family, and the third to honor each other. At the end of the ceremony, there was a banquet at which each member of her family made a toast that wished the couple a long and happy life.

Preston's head swirled with precious memories of that long-ago event. Bai had looked radiant, dressed in a silken gown. It was what happened in the months after their marriage ceremony that brought tears to his eyes. Bai's pregnancy was uneventful, as was the birth, which brought forth a brown-eyed girl they named Yao Ta.

For the first two months, life was wonderful. Bai quit her job at the consulate to take care of Ta, and Preston spent his work days daydreaming about going home to his family. It was unusually hot that summer. The intense heat made everyone difficult to get along with and arguments were a frequent occurrence. Making matters worst was an infestation of mosquitoes that swarmed throughout the city.

One day Bai came down with a high fever. Preston stayed home from work to nurse her and take care of baby Ta. Within days, her fever escalated and her eyes turned a bright yellow. The Chinese doctor she'd used since childhood assured Preston that she would throw off the fever in a matter of days. All she needed was the right mixture of herbs. When that didn't happen, Preston asked the physician assigned to the consulate to examine her. By

148

that time, she was coughing up black vomit, sometimes spraying it all the way across the room. Once he'd examined her, the physician was very pessimistic.

"Have you ever heard of yellow fever?" asked the physician.

"I remember it from my history books. Is that what she has?"

The physician nodded gravely.

"Can you give her something to make her well?"

The physician looked down at his shoes and shook his head. "Not really. There is no cure for yellow fever. Antibiotics don't work. Nothing works."

Preston felt as if he'd been kicked in the gut. He sat in silence for a while. Then he asked, "How much time does she have?"

"One week at the most."

The physician's words sucked the life out of him. The two men stood there for a while, neither man speaking.

Finally, the physician said, "If there is anything I can do, please let me know."

"You can save her life."

The physician shook his head.

"I cannot perform miracles. I wish I could."

The physician reached out and gently patted Preston on the shoulder. Then he walked out of the room, leaving Preston with his thoughts.

Bai lingered two days before she died.

Preston was devastated. He asked her family if they would take care of the baby, but they refused without explaining why. He spoke to his boss at the consulate about taking her back to America so that his family could take care of her but his boss told him that he would be better off putting her up for adoption there in China.

"That baby'll be much better off here," said his boss. "Believe me. You can't provide her with the kind of life that she needs."

"I just don't know."

"The paperwork for taking her to America is unbelievable. It could take a couple of years. Who's going to take care of her during that time? Also, you've got to think about your career. You've got a bright future. You're the best I've ever seen when it comes to computers. Do you want to throw all that away? Who's got your daughter right now?"

149

"A neighbor lady has her."

"You better go home and see after her and think about our conversation. If you decide to put her up for adoption, I know some people who can help you."

Preston went home and held Ta for two days. She looked just like her mother. It broke his heart to look into her face. At the end of the second day, he took Ta over to the lady next door and went into the consulate to talk to his boss.

"I want to put her up for adoption," he said.

"You're doing the right thing."

His boss's comment was a phrase that had echoed in his thoughts for more than a quarter century. He wondered if he'd ever in his life done the right thing. Now that he was at the end of his life, he vowed to finally do the right thing. Before it was too late.

32

Faith paced back and forth next to her front door.

Thoughts raced through her head like lizards scurrying across hot pavement. She sighed. She rubbed her temples with her fingertips. She took deep breaths and closed her eyes.

What if something goes wrong, she thought.

Once she heard the knock, her hand shot out to the doorknob, so that she was opening the door before the knock had even been completed, the resonance of it vibrating against her fingertips.

Eddie had a face like a pit bull. You didn't have to ask anyone if he was mean, you could tell that just by looking him in the face. When she first met him, she thought he must have had one hell of a childhood, judging by his face. She hoped he would spare her the details.

"Come in," she said meekly.

Eddie walked past her, his shoulder brushing her aside. He went over to the other side of her living room and leaned against the window. He looked her over from head to toe. "I was hoping you'd be wearing something a little more revealing. Considering how you're a porn queen and all."

"I was never a porn queen. I was in a few videos, but that was years ago. I don't do things like that anymore."

"You know what they say. You're everything you've ever been. You can't run from your past. It's who you are."

Oh, God! she thought. *Please don't tell me about your childhood.* She tossed his comment off with, "People change."

"Not much they don't."

"I have changed."

"Sure," he said, smirking. "That's why you owe my people so much money. Because you've changed. Right?"

Faith folded her arms and moved over to the far side of the room.

"You aren't as smart as you think you are," Eddie said menacingly. "Don't you understand that when you owe money you have to accommodate those you owe the money to?"

"I ran up those tabs when I was using."

"So you aren't using anymore. Big deal. You still owe the money."

"I know."

"Do you?"

"Of course, But just because I owe your people money, that doesn't mean you have the right to be abusive to me."

Eddie slowly walked across the room and stood in her face.

"What kind of fuckin' fantasy world do you live in? Your ass is mine if I want it. Don't you understand that?"

"You'll get your money."

"Today?"

"No."

"When?"

"Soon. I'll be coming into some money."

"So what do you have for me today?"

Faith reached into a drawer and pulled out an envelope. She handed it to him, practically dropping it into his hand as if it were a hot plate.

Eddie looked through the envelope, counting the money.

"Two thousand dollars," he said derisively. "You owe two hundred thousand and you offer two fuckin' thousand dollars?"

"It's the best I can do right now."

Eddie shook his head, his displeasure clearly evident. The vein on the side of his head pulsated, visible through the sweat that beaded around his eyes. Faith glanced down at his trousers and saw that he had an erection. Her heart sank.

"Tell you what I'll do," he said. "I'll accept this pissy down payment, just as long as you add on some interest."

"That's all I have."

"It ain't *all* you have."

Eddie reached out and started unbuttoning her blouse. She didn't resist. Once he'd unfastened all the buttons, he pulled her blouse open, exposing her breasts. He reached out with both hands and cupped them, squeezing and releasing them, over and over, obsessively glaring at them as if they were characters in a video game. She turned her head and looked to the side, the way she'd heard men do when a doctor grabs their balls and asks them to cough. She was dead inside. Had been for a long time.

33

Preston retrieved the information he'd gathered on his last search. When Ta was adopted by an Arkansas couple, they'd changed her name to Doe, giving her their last name, Peterson. He spoke the name aloud. He felt an instant kinship with her adoptive parents. The name Doe fitted her so perfectly, as it would have fit her mother. He closed his eyes and visualized her face. These days his memories were more vivid than his reality.

Once he knew her name, it was easy to locate her in Memphis. He was still within the window for working on Mack 222 without an alarm going out, so he logged off and went to his on internet provider so that he could do a more mundane search on Google. He was surprised that her name came up hundreds of times, usually accompanied by photographs. He was stunned when he saw her. She had her mother's eyes and smile. She was so beautiful that he was amazed that she carried his DNA.

What have I done to that girl? he thought. *How could I ever abandon a part of myself. Her face is a living memory of the love I felt for her mother.*

He downloaded several photographs and read all the information on her that he could find. The worst that he came across were references to her moodiness. He couldn't help but smile. Chip off the old block and all that. He found no references to children, nor did he come across anything that indicated she'd ever been married. He taped her photographs to the shelf next to his computer and gazed at them for a long while.

Images flooded his memories.

Bai at sunset, with the warm rays of the setting sun creating an enveloping halo around her. The radiant glow on her face as she held Ta in her arms. The grace with which she walked. The gentleness with which she touched him.

He could see all that in Doe's face, in her posture, the way she held herself. She was much taller than Bai, five-ten according to her bio, but her mother clearly lived within her.

They can vaccinate us against disease he thought *why can't they vaccinate us against self-destructive, hurtful decisions?*

Once he had his fill of public information about his daughter, he logged back onto Mack 222 to see if the agency had stored any of her telephone conversations. They had. Hundreds. The trigger words were **smoke, fire, exploded, dead,** and **kill.**

Doe's telephone files were listed by name, telephone number, and date. He chose one at random: Doe Peterson (901-555-2121) to Trent Boggs (901-555-0068). He activated play (taping on this conversation, as with all others, did not begin until a trigger word was detected. When he heard her voice for the first time it so reminded him of Bai that it took his breath away.

". . . **smoke** I ran outside and went up the street to see what'd happened. I saw right away that it was Oscar's car . . ."

Trent interrupted. "Who is Oscar?"

"I meant to tell you about that. Oscar was the private eye that I hired . . ."

"Private eye! Why would you hire a private eye?"

"You know, because of my car catching on **fire** and . . ."

"Why didn't you tell me you'd hired a PI?"

"He asked me not to. Not just you. He asked me not to tell anyone."

Silence.

"Are you there, Trent?"

"Yeah, I'm here. Was he watching you when we did things together?"

"Yes, he was always there."

"Damn you, Doe! That could have been very bad for my business!"

"But you sell insurance!"

Another pause.

"Are you angry at me, Trent?"

"No, no, not at all. So finish telling me about Oscar."

"Like I said, I went outside when I saw the smoke. It was Oscar's car, all right. It was totally on **fire**. Black **smoke** everywhere. Outside the car. Inside the car. It was just awful. When the fire department got there, they put out the fire and pulled Oscar out of the car, though it wasn't Oscar anymore—it was just a big hunk of charcoal. You couldn't even see his face.

154

When the police got there, they interviewed me about the fire and I told them everything I knew."

"Did you mention my name?"

"No, why would I mention your name?"

"I don't know. Sometimes they ask about boyfriends and things like that."

"Your name never came up. I don't understand. Why would anyone want to **kill** Oscar? He was a really nice man. Do you think that the people who want to hurt me went after Oscar to get him out of the way? I would hate to think that I was responsible for his death, if you know what I mean."

"I don't think so. If the person who is harassing you, wanted to **kill** you, I think they already would have done so. They would have worked around the PI."

Doe sighed.

"You're probably right. You know more about those things than I do."

"Why do you say that?"

"Because you're a man, and those are things that men think about—**killing** people. Personally, I don't like to think about such things. I rather think about you being inside . . ."

Preston stopped the recording.

Some things a father shouldn't hear.

He paused, fighting the urge to do what he knew he was going to do anyway. *Some things no one should hear.* He pressed delete, sending the entire telephone conversation to its cyber grave.

The penalty for deleting an agency file was severe, but at this stage of his life, he didn't care. He returned to the directory, where an audio file caught his attention: Harry Blackberry (901-555-0000*) to Trent Boggs (901-555-0068). He didn't know what the asterisk signified, but he knew it was an earmark of some kind. The trigger words were **Doe Peterson, Dr. Rivers Mann, fire, hairdryer, explode** and **bomb**.

The recording began:

" . . . **Doe Peterson**?"

"Yes sir, I know her. I know her rather well. She's my girlfriend."

"I didn't realize that. So I don't have to tell you that she's been having some problems . . ."

155

"Yes sir, if you mean the problem she had with her car and then the **hairdryer**."

"What about the **hairdryer**?"

"It sort of **explod**ed on her. Almost caught her house on fire."

"Really."

"Yeah. The fire department said it was an accident. Something wrong with the wiring."

"Is that true?"

"I have no reason to think it's not."

"How are you and the girl getting along?"

"Great. She's quite the looker. A model. I'm a lucky guy."

"So you're not having any problems with her?"

"None. We're tight."

"Do you think it could be someone who wants to get back at you?"

"No, I don't. If they wanted me, I think they'd come after me."

"You're probably right. Unless they're fucking with your head. What do you know about her therapist, **Dr. Rivers Mann**?"

There was a short pause, one that did not escape the caller's attention.

"I think she's been seeing him for a week or so."

"What do you think about him?"

"He seems to be doing a lot of good with **Doe**."

"So you have no problems with him?"

"No, not at all."

"Did you know he's been having the same type of problems that Doe's been having?"

"Doe's mentioned a couple of things."

"You haven't heard anything on the street about him, have you?"

"No, I haven't. Sir, I hope you don't mind if I ask, but is he a friend of yours?"

"No, but he's a friend of a friend, if you know what I mean."

"I understand."

"I want you to let me know if you hear anything. Will you do that for me?"

"Yes sir, you know I will."

"Fine — I'll see you at the meeting in a couple of days."

"Yes sir."

156

Preston closed the file. There was no need for him to delete it. He didn't like the sound of that conversation. Trent didn't sound like a standup kind of guy. He knew a shady operator when he heard one. He shook his head.

Why do women go for the bad boys?

Preston looked at the egg timer he'd put over his desk. He'd set it for fifteen minutes. He only had a few minutes left. He used that time to tap into the FBI's files. There were only a few pages of information on Trent Boggs, but there were hundreds of pages about Harry Blackberry and his brother Joseph. Mostly it consisted on memorandum from field staff in Memphis to their supervisor at headquarters. Wiretap transcriptions. Newspaper clippings. Names of associates.

The Blackberry brothers were major crime figures in Memphis. There was no doubt that they controlled most of the topless bars and adult bookstores in the city, but they also were suspected of bringing drugs in from Central America aboard a private parcel carrier and then distributing the drugs across the South from a small town airport across the state line in Mississippi.

One memo from the field staff noted: "When it comes to titty bars and escort services, they run the cleanest operations we've ever seen. That's probably because they're both lawyers. Operating a titty bar or an escort service is not against federal law, so we can't touch them. The city council has given them a green light, probably because they contribute heavily to the re-election campaigns of the incumbents. The girls get busted from time to time for allowing touching in the clubs, nothing major. Nothing that sorority girls at the university don't do every night of the week. The escort girls get busted by an overzealous cop from time to time for prostitution, but the girls pay small fines and the Blackberry brothers stay above it all."

The information about Trent Boggs was mostly the sort of biographical information you'd read about someone in the obit section of a newspaper. There were a couple of news stories about him. In one, he was interviewed for a feature about local insurance agencies. In another, he was written up as a participant at a heart fund gala, with special attention given to his date, Doe Peterson, a local model the reporter saluted as "the new face of Memphis." There was only one memo from the Memphis field

157

staff. It detailed a surveillance operation that mentioned Trent Boggs as a person of interest.

The egg timer buzzed, startling Preston, who quickly logged out of Mark 222. *Damn, I bet they caught me this time.* Within seconds, the telephone rang. It was Agent Cefalu who told Preston that he was on his way up.

Preston wrote out a name and address on a memo pad and locked up his computer room. He was just approaching the front door, when the doorbell sounded. He threw open the door, surprising Agent Cefalu.

"Damn—you must have been standing next to the door."

"I made it to the door a second or two before you did."

"So what's your excuse this time?"

"Same as last. I was running a periodic test."

"Sure."

"That's my story and I'm sticking to it."

"Fine. I don't care, you know that."

Agent Cefalu turned to leave, but Preston stopped him.

"Come in for a minute, won't you?"

"Sure I've got nothing better to do."

Preston closed the door and led him into the living room. He poured him a scotch and water and offered him a Cuban cigar, which he declined "for patriotic reasons." Then he got straight to the point. "I need you to do me a favor."

"Is it anything I'll get fired over? Or maybe arrested?"

"To be honest, it could go either way."

"Then you know my answer."

"I take that to be a yes."

"Of course."

Preston laughed. Agent Cefalu was the only friend he had left.

"Before you scare the hell out of me with your favor, tell me this: How is your health?"

"I've got swelling in both ankles. My gut protrudes like I've just had a case of beer. Now they tell me I got something they call portal hypertension. They say the blood vessels in my throat could rupture at any time. Nasty business this disease."

Agent Cefalu shook his head. He had come to love Preston as if he were his brother. The thought of losing him made him sick to his stomach. The older you get, the fewer friends you have. When it gets to the point where you're the last man standing, it's like, what's the point? He pulled himself together and said, "I'm sorry to hear that. Is there anything I can do?"

"As a matter of fact there is."

"OK."

Preston handed him a piece of paper upon which he had written a name and an address. He said nothing. Just watched As he read it.

Agent Cefalu looked at the piece of paper, puzzled. "What do you want me to do with this?"

"I want you to find her and let me know if she needs my help."

Agent Cefalu starred at the piece of paper.

"Forgive me for asking, Preston, but you've got a name, address and telephone number here — if there's something you want to know, why don't you just call her yourself?"

"Because she doesn't know who I am."

"But you know who she is?"

Preston nodded.

"This doesn't make sense."

"Does that mean you won't do it?"

"Of course, I'm going to do it. But I'd like to know what my liability is here."

"Doing this favor for me could cost you your job. Maybe even your life."

"Preston, I'll do whatever you ask, you know that. But don't you think you should at least let me know who this woman is?"

"I'm going to tell you more than you need to know — to put your mind at rest."

Agent looked at him expectantly.

"Doe Peterson is my daughter — and I have reason to think that she's in danger. Someone wants her dead. "

Agent Cefalu let out a long, low whistle.

"I don't think I ever told you before, but I was married once in China."

"I didn't know you ever were in China."

"My wife died. I put our child up for adoption." He shook his head, a blend of disgust and self-loathing. "Biggest mistake I ever made."

"So you want to correct that mistake now?"

"You can't correct a mistake like that. What I can do—pardon me, what *you* can do—is protect my daughter. It's what I should have been doing all these years."

"It's never too late to do the right thing," said Agent Cefalu.

"Sometimes it is."

34

"Damn," she said, plopping down into the chair directly across from Rivers. Her eyes were swollen. Her nose was red. Her complexion was splotchy. She felt like hell and she looked like it. "It'll be days before I can work again."

Rivers nudged the box of tissues over closer to her. Like a bird pecking into a feeder, she reached out and withdrew a tissue. Blew her nose. Reached for another tissue. Wiped her nose. Reached for another tissue. Dabbed her eyes.

When she completed that ritual, Rivers said, "I'm not going to tell you that the things that have happened to you lately are part of a rational universe, because they're not. I can't imagine watching someone I know burn to death. You have a right to be upset. You have a right to cry as much as you like."

"It just makes me so damned angry!" she bellowed, her voice carrying past the office and into the waiting room, where an anxious patient looked up from her magazine and gazed with uncertainty at the receptionist, who whispered, "She's got issues."

"Oscar was a nice man. At least, he was a nice man when he was around me. He didn't deserve to die."

"What did the police tell you?"

"They said he was sitting in the car with the motor running and dropped off to sleep and the car got so hot it caught on fire," she said, a look of incredulity on her face. "Can you believe that? *Everything* bad that happens to me, they say it's an accident. You tell me, Dr. Mann—is that even possible? Is it possible for one human being to have so many bad things happen to them?"

Rivers paused, wondering if he should inject himself into her therapy. He decided it would be appropriate to answer a direct question she asked him, even if she did pose the question in rhetorical terms.

"To be honest, it is possible for someone to have a rash of bad things happen to them," he said.

Surprised, she said, "I don't know anyone who's had experiences like mine."

161

"Yes, you do," he said. "Me—for the past couple of weeks, my life has paralleled yours."

"What do you mean?"

"Someone deliberately forced me off the road into a ditch. My car caught fire and exploded. And my toothbrush almost electrocuted me."

"Are you serious?"

Rivers nodded.

"Do you think it's because of me?"

"Why would someone go after me because of you? That doesn't make sense."

"None of it makes sense."

"Not from our perspective. But it obviously makes sense from someone else's perspective."

"So you don't think I'm crazy?"

"If you're crazy, then I'm crazy, too. No, I don't think you're crazy. And I don't think you're being paranoid. A true paranoid would not have police reports to back up their statements."

"Thank you for that."

"I am concerned about you, though. Did you hire another PI to replace the one who died?"

"Not yet. I was going to do that, but my boyfriend said he would look out for me, or ask his friends to watch my house."

"Are you comfortable with that?"

"To be honest, I would be more comfortable with another private investigator keeping an eye on me, but I told my boyfriend I'd give him a chance."

"You want to please him, right?"

"Don't you usually want to please the people you love?"

"Absolutely. But you have to know when to look out for your own self interest. Being in love doesn't offer protection against being hurt."

Doe smiled. "They say that I'm famous for looking out for my own self interest."

Rivers laughed, but he was thinking *I wish I had a nickel for every woman that came into this office saying the same thing, actually believing it, when the truth is that many women, far too many women, seem incapable of saying no to men that other men can clearly see are out to take advantage of them.*

162

"At our previous session, you told me that you believed that men were either good or bad, never in between."

"That's right."

"Since then has your boyfriend—I think you said his name was Trent—showed you any behavior that was what you felt was between those two extremes?"

Doe thought a minute. "I don't think so. He loves me as much as I love him."

"How do you know that? Has he told you so?"

"He doesn't have to tell me. I know how he feels by the way he treats me, by the way he looks at me. Women know those things about a man."

"Do you ever tell him that you love him?"

"Yes, of course."

"And what does he say?"

"What do you mean?"

"When you tell him that you love him, does he say it back?"

"He's not that kind of a man. He doesn't express his feelings easily. But, like I said, he doesn't have to tell me. The men who have told me that they loved me, never did love me. They just said it to get in my pants. To be honest, I don't trust men who say they love me."

"Do you think that's because you don't feel you are worth loving?"

Doe looked shocked. "Is that what you think? That I'm not worth loving?"

"Not at all. I'm certain that you've been loved for the right reasons many times in your life. Certainly, your mother and father love you."

"They do love me. Very much. And I love them. But there are people that don't love me that should love me."

"Like whom?"

Doe was hesitant. It was as if she thought that if she waited him out she wouldn't have to answer. Rivers didn't bite. He sat in silence, looking at her with a steely gaze, as she looked down at her hands.

Finally, when she no longer could stand the silence, she said, "I don't understand why my birth father gave me up for adoption. He must have really hated me to do that."

163

"So you feel your life won't be complete until your birth father tells you that he loves you."

"I didn't say that."

"But that's what you mean. What if your birth father is no longer living? What if you have to live the rest of your life without hearing him say that?"

"I don't think it's all that big an issue with me."

"I do."

"Why do you say that?"

"Because it is a big issue with all adopted children. I think it will affect your life until you deal with it in a constructive way."

"Why do you say that?"

"Because I can see how it affects your relationships with men. You are afraid to trust a man you loves you because you are afraid of the pain that would follow the termination of that love. You feel emotionally safer with men who don't love you. Men who mistreat you. Men who promise you nothing. That way they can't disappoint you."

Doe sat in silence for a long while, thinking.

Rivers gave her the space to sort things out for herself.

Finally, she said, "If a man loved his daughter, why would he give her away?"

Rivers was thinking *she's beginning to get it.*

"He may have thought it would be best for her. He may have received bad information. He may have thought he could not provide her with a good life. There are any number of reasons why parents give children up for adoption. I've never once encountered a situation in which the birth parent thought, 'I don't think this baby is loveable, so I'm going to give her away.' It just doesn't work that way. When birth parents give up a child, they have good reasons in their own mind. Don't get me wrong. I'm not saying those reasons are always good for the child. But they are almost always rationalized as good reasons."

"Is it possible that my birth dad loved me so much that he sacrificed a life with me so that I would have a better life?"

"Certainly that is possible."

"I would like to think so. That would make him sort of a hero."

"I'm sure he wouldn't see himself that way. I'm sure he feels a lot of pain when he thinks about you. He's at an age now where your absence will be felt more intensely because of his awareness of his own mortality."

"I've always felt so alone . . . if I thought for one minute that my birth dad ever thought about me, that would make me feel not so much alone."

"You have grieved for the loss of your birth father ever since you learned you were adopted. I think its time for you to move on to the next level in the grieving process. Adopted children often go through the same stages that a person goes through when they discover that they are going to die. The first is denial, when you insist that you are not adopted. The second is anger, when you discover that you are adopted and you feel angry that your birth parents would abandon you. The third is bargaining, when you promise to become a better person if only your birth parents will reclaim you. The fourth is depression, when you simply quit caring about your life and you make bad relationship choices because you don't think you are worthy of a good relationship. The final stage is acceptance, when you position yourself for healthy responses to the future. I think you've moved through the early stages and are now working your way through the depression stage."

"I really haven't had any good relationships with men."

"I know."

"And you think that has something to do with my attitude toward my being adopted?"

"Yes—and when you get to the point where you can accept that I think you will move on to acceptance and a happier life."

"You make it sound so simple."

"Trust me, it's not. But you are headed in the right direction, I'm convinced of that. My job is to help you read the road signs."

"Oh, Dr. Mann, you don't know how good that makes me feel. You believe in me, don't you?"

"I do."

35

Shelly nervously licked her lips as she walked from the parking garage, up to Trent's apartment. Her throat was dry. Heart pounded. Thirty minutes earlier she was putting the finishing touches on a root canal. Totally in charge of the situation. She imagined the patient's heart was probably pounding. Now it was her turn. She didn't like being in that position.

When she got to the apartment door, she hesitated. How had she ever gotten herself in this position? She'd never once been unfaithful to Rivers. Not until she met Trent. What was there about him that made her drop her guard?

Whatever it was, it was inconsequential compared to seeing Rivers stretched out on the bathroom floor, not breathing. She'd never loved anyone but Rivers. She didn't love Trent. She didn't even like Trent. Why had she risked the relationship with the man she loved to pursue something she didn't even understand? Was she capable of self-destructing over sex? Was she that stupid? Just thinking about it gave her chills.

She knocked on the door, lightly, so that other residents would not hear. She wished she were invisible.

Moments later the door swung open. Trent greeted her with a huge smile and reached out for her hand, drawing her into the apartment and into his arms. He kissed her on the mouth, even as he reached out and pushed the door shut. She allowed him to have the kiss, perhaps enjoying it a little bit more than she should under the circumstances.

"I've been looking forward to this all week," he said.

She broke away from the embrace and walked across the room to the window, dropping her purse into a chair. She gazed out the window. The street was deserted. No cars. No one walking on the sidewalk. Trent walked up behind her, putting his arms around her, pressing his body next to hers. He kissed her on the neck and chills raced all over her body.

"I love having lunch with you." he said. "No, let me correct that. I love having you for lunch. You are a delicious fuck."

This is so wrong she thought. *Why does it feel so right?*

She turned and put her arms around his neck. They kissed passionately, her breath quickening, and he ran his hands up and down her back, and across her hips.

"Are you wearing underwear?" he whispered.

"Yes," she answered.

"What color?"

"Black."

"My favorite color."

He led her into the bedroom, a tight grip on her hand. She followed passively, wondering why she was so weak around him. She sat on the edge of the bed and he released her hand. She crossed her legs, looking very much like someone in the waiting room at a doctor's office waiting for her name to be called. As she watched, he removed his shirt and tossed into to the floor.

He unbuckled his belt and unzipped his trousers, slipping them down his legs, leaving them on the floor where they fell. He was not wearing shoes and socks, so that left only his jockey shorts. He removed them slowly, watching her eyes follow his every move, a broad smile creeping across his face. He stood in front of her, only inches from her face. His penis stood at attention.

"Now, it's your turn to strip," he said.

Instead, she said, "We need to talk."

Trent was stunned.

"You want to talk at a time like this? Can't you see how excited I am?"

Shelly chose not to answer his questions.

"Why don't you sit down over here next to me?"

She patted her hand against the sheet.

Suddenly, he felt embarrassed – and angry.

"What's going on here?" he demanded, his voice rising.

"Sit down, please."

He felt humiliated, not at all what Shelly wanted him to feel. He pressed against her, expecting her to respond. She didn't. Instead, she pushed him away and said, "Why don't you just sit down so that we can talk?"

He was damned if he was going to sit down naked, so he reached down and picked up his jockey shorts and slipped them back on. Then he sat down, his anger clearly growing. Shelly was surprised to see him so angry. She'd never seen him any way except eager to please her. Now he looked like he wanted to rip her head off. He was beginning to frighten her.

"OK, you want to talk—talk!"

In her eyes, he was becoming a petulant child, pouty lips and all. "I've been thinking about us a lot lately and I've come to the conclusion that we should stop seeing each other. It's not good for either of us. It would be better if we just saw each other around town."

"Around town! You mean seeing each other is not good for that son of a bitch husband of yours!"

"That's not what I'm saying at all."

"Listen. All you need to know is that I love you. I care about you more than I've ever cared about a woman."

"What about your girlfriend? Don't you care about her?"

"I don't love her. Not like I love you."

"Well, that's beside the point, anyway. I want us to be friends. That's all."

Trent jumped to his feet. He started pacing, from one end of the room to the other. His feet slapped down hard against the carpet. He walked past a lamp and struck it with his fist, sending it crashing to the floor.

"Trent!" exclaimed Shelly. "Get control of yourself!"

"I thought you loved me!" he shouted, his eyes ablaze.

"I never said that!"

"You never said that! If you don't love me, why were you cheating on your husband to fuck me?"

Shelly suddenly felt very ashamed. She wanted to leave that instant, but she was afraid to get up off the bed, afraid he would strike her. So she sat.

"It's that fucking husband of yours! He's filled your head with that psycho babble of his. I hate that son of a bitch. He's screwing with your mind. Can't you see that?"

"He's not like that. If you really want a reason, I guess it's because I've decided I want to adopt a child. I realize now that Rivers would make a wonderful father. That's what I want most in life. A family!"

"I can give you a family! If you would give me a chance, I could do that!"

Shelly rose to her feet. Trent stormed over to the bed and pushed her back down, hard. "Don't push me!" she said, careful not to raise her voice.

"That's what you're doing to me. You're pushing me!"

"I am not. I'm being honest with you. We've had some great times. I'll never forget you. But I've got to move on."

She rose to her feet again and started for the door. He didn't try to push her again, but he walked in circles around her, swinging his arms in a threatening manner, totally out of control. When she got to the front door, she turned and said, "Bye, Trent—take care of yourself."

Then she opened the door and stepped out into the hallway.

Without saying a word, he slammed the door shut behind her.

As she hurried down the hallway, frightened by his display of anger, thinking *you really don't know someone until you see them angry* she heard glass breaking inside the apartment. Not until she got into her car and drove out of the parking garage did she feel safe.

What should I tell Rivers? she thought.

Nothing, an inner voice responded, shutting down any further thoughts in that vein. It was at that moment that she realized what a gigantic mistake she'd made. She felt so ashamed. She had no explanation for her behavior.

On top of the shame she felt over the relationship, she'd just had one of the most disturbing experiences of her life and she couldn't tell the one person with whom she wanted to share it, the man she loved.

36

The Commodore Hotel had one of the best dining rooms in the city. Restaurant guides almost always gave it a five-star rating. One of the restaurant's hallmarks was the two private dining rooms it offered to small groups.

Though the incident with Shelly had happened earlier in the day, Trent was still hot under the collar when he entered the private dining room in which Harry and Joseph Blackberry sat with their business associates.

There was a chair midway down the table (the Blackberry brothers anchored both ends of the table), so Trent sat there, hoping not to attract any attention. Not many people scared him. This was one group that did.

"Trent, you look a little out of sorts," observed Harry Blackberry.

Trent looked in his direction, trying his best to look pleasant.

"No sir," he said. "I'm doing just fine."

Harry nodded, letting him know that while he accepted his explanation, he didn't believe it. One of many reasons why Trent's gut was always tight when he was in the presence of the Blackberry brothers. *They're fuckin' mindreaders!*

Harry tapped his knife against his glass to get the attention of the other diners. "Gentlemen, I want you to meet my guest, Trent Boggs."

He gestured in Trent's general direction.

"He has done many good things for us here in Memphis."

Trent smiled and nodded, but inside he was cringing. Attention from these men was the last thing he wanted. True, he was affiliated with the Blackberry brothers, but only at a very low level. He did just enough business with the brothers to feel protected, but not enough to feel threatened. He knew next to nothing about how the organization operated and that suited him fine. The less he knew, the better.

Trent wanted nothing more than to fade into the background but he soon realized that Harry Blackberry had not completed his introduction.

"Trent, I want to introduce our other guests to you," Harry Blackberry said. He motioned to the man on his left. "This is Alfonso Gaia, a representative from New York. The man sitting next to him is Buddy Greco from Chicago. And you know our team members from here in Memphis—Henry, Armond, Philip and Boone. That stout fellow on your left is Eddie, from Vegas, and next to him is Leon, from Seattle."

Each time a man's name was mentioned, he nodded at Trent, a signal of his acceptance.

Once the introductions were complete Eddie turned to Trent and offered his hand in the way of a greeting. Trent thought it was the biggest, hardest hand he'd ever shaken. When Eddie squeezed his hand, he counterattacked by using his left hand to firmly grasp Eddie's upper arm. It was a way to demonstrate dominance. Knowing that he'd been out-played, Eddie released his handshake.

"Welcome to Memphis," said Trent, a slight smile on his lips.

"Yeah, whatever," he responded.

After dinner, Harry Blackberry again solicited the attention of the other diners. "Gentlemen, I've invited Trent here today because he's having a problem I want you to know about. His lovely girlfriend, Doe Peterson, and her therapist, Dr. Rivers Mann, have been going through a rough patch lately. I want to make it clear to each of you gentlemen that Trent's problems are Joseph's and my problems."

Trent never knew that he was such a prolific sweater. The back of his shirt suddenly became soaked. His worst fear was that it was a cruel joke directed at him. The longer Harry spoke, the smaller Trent felt.

Finally, Harry said, "I would like for each of you gentleman to communicate with each of your . . . er, sources . . . and confirm that Trent's friends have not been earmarked for special attention. Can you gentlemen find it within your hearts to do this favor for me?"

A murmur of approval washed over the table. The diners respected the way the Blackberry brothers had a knack for laying down the law without really seeming to be forceful about it. The brothers were the subtle princes of intimidation. They could do more with a whisper than the average man could with a violent rant.

Seeing all the diners nodding, Harry said, "Thank you—now let's have coffee and dessert."

As the waiter made the rounds, Eddie turned to Trent and said, "Buddy, you ever have any problems you can't solve, you let me know. I specialize in trade outs."

"What do you mean?"

"I do you a favor that I can't be connected to. You do me a favor that you can't be connected to. It all comes out in the wash."

Trent nodded, wondering if he really was cut out for this kind of work. Maybe. Maybe not.

37

Rivers sat up in bed. He couldn't breathe and he couldn't hear his own screams, for the fright was so overpowering in its hold that it smothered everything that was outside of himself. He felt as if he were collapsing inward. His heart raced. His face was covered with sweat. He thought he was dying.

Shelly was lying next to him when the screams began. She sat up and put her arms around him, saying over and over again, "It's all right. It's all right, baby. I'm here."

Rivers looked at her wildly. She pulled him down to the bed, cradling him in her arms. With a voice filled with compassion, she said, "Just relax. It's over now. You're safe."

Rivers closed his eyes, his breathing still heavy. They lay together in a fetal embrace for the remainder of the night. After a while Rivers dropped off to sleep. When he awoke, it was morning and the bed covers were pulled back. Shelly was gone and he was alone in the bed.

After his initial surprise dissipated, he became aware of the water running in the shower. He relaxed and took a deep breath. Those nightmares, when they came, always left him feeling bruised and battered. Afterward, his body always ached all over. Like he'd been punched by a prize fighter with lead fists.

When the water stopped, he could hear Shelly drying off in the bathroom. He wondered if he ever would be comfortable in that bathroom again. She emerged with a towel wrapped around her waist. She smiled when she saw that he was awake. She sat down on the bed next to him.

"I'm sorry about last night," Rivers said.

Shelly kissed him gently on the mouth. She sat back up and her eyes wandered around the room. There was something different about her dresser.

"I've always had nightmares, but this was the first one about a toothbrush," he said. "I hope it doesn't become a regular visitor."

She hugged him and said, "I'm sure it will pass."

She looked him in the eyes and brushed his hair away from his forehead.

"Have I told you lately that I love you?" She was thinking *how do I make up my indiscretions to this dear man?*

"You did before your shower. But terms of endearment are equally nice after a shower."

"Well, I do . . . love you, that is. Please don't ever forget that."

They kissed again. Then she got up and walked over to her dresser. Something about it was bothering her.

"Rivers, have you been to my dresser to get anything?"

"No, don't think so."

"That's what I thought."

She rearranged several items on top of her dresser.

"Someone's been moving my things."

She pulled out the top drawer, where she kept her stockings, sports socks, and scarves. She rummaged through the drawer. Everything seemed in order. Then she opened the second drawer, where she kept her panties. They were all color separated and neatly stacked, one on top of another.

"Come look at this," she said.

You wouldn't think that seeing your panties stacked neatly in a pile would be unnerving, but if you've never, not even once, stacked your panties in any type of order, then it would be disturbing, to say the least.

Rivers peered over into the drawer.

"I've never seen any of your drawers look like that."

"I would never stack my panties like that. Are you sure you didn't do it, sort of as a joke, and then forgot about it?"

Rivers grinned.

"I'm a lot of things, honey. But I'm not a panty stacker."

"I didn't think so"

Rivers spotted a pair of lacy black panties and pointed at them.

"Why don't you wear those today?"

"Are you listening to me, Rivers?"

"Yes, you're upset about your panties. All I'm saying is that you should wear those today."

"Someone has gone through my dresser drawers."

"Well, it wasn't me! If it was me, you'd have found that lacy pair on your pillow when you got out of the shower."

"Then who was it?"

"I don't know, honey. Maybe you walked in your sleep. Maybe you did it while I was in the hospital. Were you anxious that night?"

"Of course I was anxious."

"Sleepwalking is an explanation."

"But I haven't done that since I was a child."

"Stress sometimes brings repressed behavior to the surface. Perhaps you were so stressed that you rearranged your drawers to create a sense of order in your life."

Shelly looked at him and shook her head.

"I would marry a shrink!"

"It's an explanation, that's all."

"It's beginning to look like we have rational explanations for everything that has happened to us lately. You going into the ditch. Your car blowing up. The toothbrush. Now, it's my panties. The scientist part of me, the part of me that busted my ass in dental school, tells me that's all bullshit."

"But?"

"The part of me that has to live in the real world tells me that it's possible that I did it in my sleep."

"There you have it."

Shelly whipped the towel away from her hips, bringing a smile to Rivers' face. "OK, toss me those damn panties that you're obsessing over."

Yes yes yes! he thought. He wadded them up into a ball and threw them at her. The panties landed softly in her hand and she slipped them on as he watched. Sometimes — and this was one of those times — he thought that the sexiest moments between men and women were not the contrived moments that preceded lovemaking, but the ordinary moments, such as slipping on panties or stockings or a bra. In his eyes, Shelly would have looked sexy doing most anything. But she never looked sexier than during those unguarded moments when she wasn't trying to be sexy. She stood up straight and put her hands on her hips.

"Show's over! How about putting on the coffee?"

Rivers saluted her. "Yes 'ma'am."

While she finished dressing, he went downstairs and put the coffee on. He sat in a kitchen chair and listened to her walking around upstairs. Funny. After all these years, he could recognize her footsteps. At least he thought he could.

When Shelly returned to the kitchen, she was dressed in her dental scrubs. Rivers gazed at her dreamily, wondering if she was still wearing the lacy black panties. "Why are you wearing your scrubs today? I thought you usually changed at the office?"

"No special reason. Just wanted to be different today."

She peered into the refrigerator and then looked into a cabinet.

"What do you want for breakfast?"

"Whatever sounds good to you," he answered, trying to hold his concentration.

"How about pancakes?"

"I love pancakes. Especially . . ." His voice trailed off.

"Especially what?"

"Especially when they're prepared by a woman wearing lacy black panties."

She looked away and grinned.

"You'll never know that for certain, will you?"

"There are ways to find out."

"Oh, really."

"Really."

She took a box of pancake mix from the cabinet and a jug of milk from the fridge and, with her back turned to Rivers, mixed the ingredients in a large bowl, elbows pumping as she stirred.

"Anything I can do to help?" he asked.

She turned and said, "No, I'll be fine. You can sit there and watch."

From the back, her hips had a slight pear shape, but her buttocks were firm and round. He wondered what he had ever done to deserve a woman like that. Pancakes don't have an overpoweringly strong attraction while cooking, but watching someone cook them can be an absolute treat.

As she poured the batter onto the griddle and then flipped and turned them, her body twisted and turned and shook in a thousand different ways. It was the most erotic sight he had seen in at least ten minutes. He walked over to the stove, wrapped his arms around her, and hugged her from behind.

She turned her head back and kissed him. It was then that he saw the batter on the tip of her nose. He started to tell her about it, but then he thought better of it. He liked the way it looked. It was a good look for her.

After breakfast, they pushed back their chairs and had second cups of coffee. Shelly seemed unusually inquisitive. She fired one question after another. Mostly, she wanted to know about the women in his life. None of the relationships had lasted more than a few months. Nothing bad happened to end the relationships; they just sort trickled away.

"You never fell head over heels in love?" Shelly asked.

"Never," he said. "Not until I met you. Now it's your turn."

"No, I'm not playing."

"Oh, no," he laughed. "It would be a terrible violation of etiquette for you not to take a turn yourself. You would be banned from polite Memphis society."

"Okay, so what do you want to know?"

"How many times have you fallen in love?"

"I don't know how to answer that. When I was ten I fell in love with the little boy next door. He was twelve."

"Have you fallen in love with anyone else since you met me?"

"I can honestly say the answer is no."

She leaned over and kissed him, thankful that she was old enough now to understand the difference between love and lust. She was also old enough to know that love sometimes requires you to parse your answers to spare the feelings of the one you love.

"You always know what to say."

"Thank you, honey."

She gazed at Rivers, reveling in the love that she felt for him. How would she ever come to terms with her betrayal? How would she ever be able to live with herself? Slowly she was beginning to realize that the true test of a marriage was its ability to withstand grandiose urges to purge the air of secrets.

38

Agent Cefalu knew that it was about ten degrees cooler in Memphis, but when he got off the plane he was hit by a wall of heat unlike anything he'd ever experienced in Vegas. He took a cab to the Commodore Hotel, a nightmarish ride as it turned out, not just because of the hot plastic seats that stuck to his trousers, or the near misses at several intersections because of speeding motorists who ran red lights, but because of the eighteen-wheeler ahead of his cab that ran over a jogger, scattering his brains across the pavement.

The cabbie, whose day job was as a paramedic, pulled over to help the man, but there was nothing he could do, other than help pick up the pieces of his brain and he was not so inclined. The police handcuffed the truck driver and tossed him into the back of a squad car, one irate cop proclaiming loud enough for everyone to hear that he was being charged with vehicular homicide, adding "and if you don't like that, dude, just call your congressman."

The cabbie said very little the rest of the way to the hotel.

Agent Cefalu tipped him, not just for the cab ride, but for stopping at the accident. Certainly that was worth something. Most people would balk at stepping around a stranger's brains.

"Thanks, man," said the cabbie. "Hope that accident don't put a bad taste in your mouth for Memphis."

"Whenever I sense my thoughts drifting that way, I'll think of Elvis."

"That's what I always do."

Once Agent Cefalu checked into the hotel, he kicked off his shoes and put his pistol on the nightstand. Then he called Preston on his cell.

"Just wanted to let you know I'm here."

"Good. Once you check out her address, just keep an eye out for her until I know more."

"No problem. You don't want me to talk to her?"

"No. Just look out for her. She's had a run of bad luck lately. Someone wants to kill her."

"I see."

"I'll be in touch."

Agent Cefalu turned off his cell and stretched out on the bed. There was an air vent directly above him and cold air blew onto his face. It felt good.

After a short nap, he got up and left the hotel. Doe's address was in the information packet Preston gave him, so he purchased a city map at the front desk and rented a white, four-door Impala and hit the streets. He'd never been to Memphis, but he was well aware of the city's reputation as a music center and as a major gathering place for organized crime.

Doe's mid-town address was not difficult to find, only a fifteen minute drive from the hotel. He drove up and down the street and then parked about half a block away from the townhouse. He rolled the windows down and sat in the stifling heat for almost an hour before he saw anything. Every ten minutes or so, he started the car so that he could soak up coolness from the air conditioner.

When the townhouse door opened, he saw a young woman with dark hair lock the door and get into a car parked on the street. He looked at the photograph that Preston gave him. It was difficult to tell if the woman on the street resembled the woman in the photograph—Preston's photograph showed a model with Asian features in a bridal layout in a magazine spread—but the resemblance seemed close enough for the two women to be one and the same.

After she pulled away from the curb, he pulled out behind her.

39

Before Doe arrived, Trent sat in his favorite chair, brooding, staring at the photograph of Shelly he had stolen from her house and carried in his back pocket ever since. He was convinced that he loved Shelly more than any woman he'd ever known. Why had she turned her back on him? How can everything with a woman be perfect one minute and disastrous the next minute?

He got up and went into the bedroom closet, just off the bathroom, where he had a dresser in which he kept his most important things. He opened the top drawer, which contained items that once belonged to Shelly. Three or four pairs of panties. A sweater. An empty beer can she'd sipped on while in bed with him. A medical ID that had her name and photograph on it. A crumpled cigarette she'd once smoked after sex.

He removed the photograph from his back pocket and placed it in the drawer, face up, so that he would immediately see it the next time he opened the drawer. How was it possible to want to kill a woman at the same instant you wanted to make love to her? It didn't make sense to him.

He heard a knock on the door. For an instance, he entertained a fantasy that it was Shelly, there to apologize and makes things right with him. Then he heard Doe's voice and forgot about the photograph.

"Trent . . . Trent, are you home?"

He swung open the door. Doe looked radiant, a big smile on her face.

"Where were you?" she asked. "I was about to give up on you."

"I must not have heard you the first time," he explained. "I was in the bedroom."

Doe stepped inside the apartment and embraced him, kissing him with her eyes tightly closed, heart fluttering. Eyes wide open, he reached over behind her to close the door. He liked having sex with her more than he liked kissing her. He never craved her kisses the way he craved Shelly's kisses.

She walked across the room and looked out the window.

"I think I'm being followed," she said, looking up and down the street.

"Why do you say that?"

"It's just a creepy feeling I've got."

"Do you see anything outside?"

"No. There's no traffic."

"Was it a particular car that you noticed?"

"No . . . yes . . . oh, I'm not sure. It seems like every time I looked in the mirror I saw the same white car."

"What did it do when you turned into the garage?"

"I don't know."

"It didn't turn in behind you?"

"No, I'm sure it didn't."

"And you don't see it out on the street?"

"No."

"It's probably just your imagination. Especially after what happened with that PI, I can see why you'd be nervous."

She wrapped her arms around him, pulled herself into him, tight. "You'd never let anything happen to me, would you?"

"No . . . never."

She looked around the room. The light was dim. It had a stodgy, shadowy, depressing look to it.

"Let's go somewhere else," she said. "Someplace fun."

He ran his hands up her back, caressing her. He kissed her on the neck, nibbled on her ear.

"Wouldn't you rather stay here and play? Wouldn't that be fun?"

"To be honest, I'm too jumpy for sex. I'm feel like I'm going to jump out of my skin."

"I think sex would have a calming effect."

"Yeah, well maybe it would calm you down. But it would have me climbing the walls."

"You've never told me no before."

"Dr. Mann told me that I wouldn't get angry so often if I stood up for myself more often. He told me not to do anything I didn't want to do."

"He did?"

"Yes, it's part of my therapy."

Trent backed away. He knew it was no use. It would be a mistake to trash Dr. Mann. "I don't want to argue. Let's just go to lunch."

"Thank you," said Doe, turning toward the bedroom. "First, I'm going to freshen up."

*   *   *

The car that emerged from the parking garage was not the one that Doe had driven into the garage — and there was a man behind the wheel. Agent Cefalu clearly saw Doe sitting in the passenger seat, smiling broadly.

He pulled out into traffic behind them.

The stake-out was never his favorite surveillance tool. He much preferred to eavesdrop on conversations. He trusted his ears more than he did his eyes. He always said that he didn't know of a single major bust that ever was accomplished as a result of a stake-out.

If you give them time, people always rat themselves out by saying more than they should, or by being careless with their money. That old saying, follow the money is absolutely true. Nine times out of ten, if you catch someone in the act of committing a crime, it won't be because you followed them from a stake-out — it'll be because you overheard something you weren't supposed to overhear on a phone or Internet tap, or you followed a money trail that took you straight to the goods.

Agent Cefalu was at a disadvantage because he was in a strange city and he had no idea where he was going. If he got separated from them at a traffic light, he couldn't think several steps ahead because he didn't know what was ahead. All the streets looked alike. All the buildings looked alike. Gray or brown blocks of concrete, one stacked on top of the other.

Once or twice he almost lost them in traffic. But each time he came close to losing them, he ran the stoplight, like everyone else was doing, and managed to catch up with them and stay within three or four car lengths.

The humidity was suffocating, even with air-conditioning.

Each time he slammed on brakes to avoid hitting a car sailing through a stoplight, it made his head throb.

*   *   *

As they drove across mid-town in the direction of downtown, Trent was unusually quiet, almost sullen, something inside him festering. There was an invisible wall between them. Doe could sense that something was wrong.

Was it because she didn't want to have sex? Men are so sensitive about the "no" word when it comes to sex. Why are they always insulted if the woman is not in a mood for sex?

"You're being awfully quiet today," she said.

Trent looked straight ahead, saying nothing.

"Aren't you going to answer me?"

Finally, he looked at her, a fleeting glance, then back to the road.

"Oh, I'm sorry — I didn't realize that was a question."

Doe tensed, her fingers gripping the arm rest.

"Of course, it was a question."

"Whatever."

Doe felt her heart racing. Why was he giving her a hard time? She was the one being stalked. It was her hair dryer that caught fire, not his.

Tears flowed. She dabbed them with tissue she removed from her purse.

"What's the matter now?" asked Trent, the irritation showing in his voice.

"Nothing."

They drove on in silence.

"What do I do now?" he asked.

"Nothing."

40

Tony Apple hung back, allowing the white Impala to stay a good distance ahead of him. It was obvious that the car was following Doe and Trent, though he doubted that they realized it.

Whoever is behind that wheel is a real pro he thought *not at all like that hick in the silver Altima.*

For the life of him, he couldn't figure out what a PI would be doing with cold cream, especially *that* particular jar of cold cream. He'd walked by the car after they put out the fire and carried off the body, and he saw the jar on what was once the front seat. *That fuckin' jar is indestructible.*

Tony was fed up with Memphis. The city was too hot for human habitation. The streets were dirty. The buildings were either too old or too new. A health freak, he didn't know that people still chewed tobacco, but they did in Memphis, spitting it onto the sidewalks and in the parking lots, right where people could step into it. Every time he went into a restaurant, or a store, or movie theater, he felt compelled to wash his hands after touching anything.

He followed them all the way downtown. He was concerned about the white Impala, but only because he didn't know who the hell was driving it. When he'd signed on for this job, it was for a friend—and he thought it'd be a simple hit, nothing more. A chance to make some easy money. But it was much more than that now. His reputation was on the line.

Tony watched as Doe and her escort pulled into a garage. The Impala pulled over and parked on the street just past the entrance to the garage. Tony drove past the Impala, stealing a glance into the car, seeing a middle-aged man who had a look of professionalism about him, and then he pulled over and parked further up the street. He got out and put money in the meter, just as the man in the Impala got out and put money in his meter.

While that was happening, Doe and her escort walked out of the garage and crossed the street. They paused to look into the window of a restaurant, pointing at something inside, but then they turned and walked away, apparently not happy with what they saw. They walked down a side street, with the man in the Impala following, but pretending to window shop as he walked.

I'm not that stupid thought Tony.

Instead of following them, he went the opposite direction, walking down a parallel street on the other side of the block. If his target didn't duck into a building along the way, he could pick up their trail at the end of the block.

If they did duck into a building, they wouldn't be difficult to locate. He walked quickly, stepping around suspicious spots on the sidewalk, ignoring the desperate pleas of a homeless man wearing a garbage bag on his head.

At one point, he paused to look at his shoes. Most men his age wore sports shoes. Not Tony. He preferred expensive leather shoes. His shoes looked clean, but he hated to think about what was stuck to the soles.

As he rounded the corner, turning left, he saw Doe and her escort cross the street, continuing south. At the end of the next block was Beale Street, the heart of the city's entertainment district. White Impala Man stayed about a half block behind them. Very slick the way he anticipated their movements, turning away each time they looked in his direction.

Doe became animated as they approached a restaurant named Models. They paused outside to look at a window display, one that Tony subsequently discovered contained photographs of Doe, arranged in a very flattering presentation. Then they went inside and were escorted to a table.

White Impala Man followed them into the restaurant and was seated at a corner table, across the room from where Doe and her escort were given a better table. Tony also was given a corner table, where his back was to the wall, a placement he always requested.

Doe seemed to be in a bad mood. Her escort pointed to a wall of pictures and said something to her about them, but she refused to look. Instead, she stared down at her hands and said something that made him throw up his arms, a universal symbol of frustration. Tony wondered what they were fighting about. If they had a big fight and broke up, it would give him the opportunity he needed to catch her alone. He crossed his fingers.

Tony thought the cold cream was ingenious. He didn't know what went wrong, but he was confident that it wasn't his fault. Shit happens. Now he had to come up with an even better idea. Killing someone is not as easy as you'd think. Especially if you have to make it look like an accident or suicide or freakish.

White Impala Man seemed impervious to Tony's interest in Doe. He ordered lunch, chatted affably with the waitress, and settled back into his chair with a frosted beer bottle. The way he was acting, Tony figured he had to be a bodyguard that Doe hired to replace the dead PI. Every time the door opened, White Impala Man's eyes shot to the door, checking the situation out.

Tony watched him out of the corner of his eye, knowing that before he could get to Doe he might have to take him out. He wanted to learn as much about him as he could, particularly his reaction time, something he witnessed every time the kitchen door slammed open and shut. White Impala Man was fast, he knew that much for certain. It was knowledge that might save his life.

After two hours, the only people left in the restaurant were Doe and her escort, a couple seated at a table near them, White Impala Man, and, of course, himself. He was bored to tears. The waitress returned numerous times to ask if he wanted his check. The answer was always no. She walked away in a huff. Her shift was almost over and she wanted her tip.

Finally, Doe and her escort got up from the table and left the restaurant. Tony waited for White Impala Man to fall in behind them. Then he tossed enough money on the table for his lunch and a nice tip and he joined the parade.

Once he was out in the open, he called Faith on his cell.

"Are you done?" she asked.

"Not yet. I've tried, but stuff has happened."

"What kind of stuff."

"I don't want to say over the phone, but I promise it was unavoidable."

"Just get it done. Time is running out."

"I will. I promise. It's not as easy as you think."

"Just remember, it can't look like murder."

"Do you think I'm stupid?"

"Not at all. I'm just reminding you of our conversation."

"You worry too much."

"If you were me, you'd be worried, too. I've got a lot to lose if you screw up."

"So do I. Don't worry about it."

41

Rivers could see that she was fuming as soon as she entered his office. She sat down hard in the chair across from his desk. Tossed her purse into another chair, ignoring it when it bounced out of the chair and onto the floor, spilling its contents onto the carpet. Tossed her hair back away from her face. Waved her hands in the air as she gestured.

"I've had enough!" she said, exasperated.

"Enough what?"

"Trent Boggs. He's so inconsiderate!"

"So you've had a fight?"

"I don't know what it was we had."

"Did you break up?"

"No."

"But you're angry?"

"Most definitely."

"If you're not sure why you're angry, let's find the point where you first started feeling angry."

"I was feeling fine when I arrived at his apartment. I wasn't angry at anyone. I needed support, that's all."

"Obviously, something happened."

"Everything started out fine. I got there and we kissed. I was eager to take him to this new place for lunch. But all he wanted to do was make love. There's nothing wrong with that, but I was excited about something else at the time. We didn't have sex, but we did mess around for a few minutes. Before we left, I went to the bathroom to check my makeup. On my way back to the living room, I passed his dresser. A drawer was opened. I glanced inside and saw a picture of a woman in a bikini. An older woman. A real slut. I'm not sure why, but I took the picture and stuffed it into my purse. I had every intention of confronting him with it, but then as we left the apartment I decided not to."

"Why didn't you want to make him angry?"

"He's got a really bad temper. I didn't want him to make him think I didn't trust him."

"Do you trust him?"

"Not really. Would you trust a man who kept pictures of women in bikinis in his dresser drawer?"

"What do you think that picture means?"

"I think it means he's sleeping with someone else."

"Do you have an understanding with him that neither of you will sleep with other people?"

"That's kind of understood, isn't it? I mean, if a woman is sleeping with a man on a regular basis, does she flat-out have to ask him not to sleep with other women? Aren't some things in life understood?"

Rivers nodded. "It never hurts to tell your partner what your expectations are. Relationships are all about communication."

"Some things you shouldn't have to say. They should be understood."

"Doe, I hate to tell you this, but most men are very specific when it comes to their expectations in a relationship. Women should be, too."

"What do you mean?"

"If a man doesn't want you to sleep with other men, he will say so. If you do not tell him that it is unacceptable for him to sleep with other women, he will assume that it is not an issue with you and he will sleep with other women, if he gets the chance. Has he ever asked you not to sleep with other men?"

"No."

"Then I can guarantee you that he feels he has the right to sleep with other women."

"Think so?"

"Guaranteed. You have to tell men what you want. You have to be very specific. Men aren't good at picking up subtle clues. You have to tell them outright. Don't make them guess."

"Perhaps I was afraid to ask him not to sleep with other women. Afraid he would say no and I would have to break up with him."

"So instead of telling him that you found the picture and you were upset because you thought it meant he was sleeping with other women, you cried and told him you didn't know why you were crying, and he got angry because he knew damned well you knew why you were angry — is that correct?"

Doe nodded.

"It makes sense the way you tell it."

"Are you afraid that if you challenge him about the picture, he will end up choosing her over you?"

"That's just it. She's much older than I am. She's not as pretty as I am. But if he picked her over me, I would be devastated."

"What did you do with the picture?"

"It's in my purse."

She got up and knelt down and gathered up the things that'd fallen from her purse. When she found the picture, she reached up and slapped it down on the desk in front of Rivers.

"There's the slut," she said, still on her knees.

Rivers was stunned when he looked at the photograph.

Heart pounding. It was one he'd taken of Shelly while they were on vacation in the Bahamas. In her most revealing bikini. Smiling. Half sloshed on margaritas. A million thoughts raced through his mind. How did that photograph get in Trent Boggs's dresser drawer? Why did he have it?

He shuffled through those thoughts with the quickness of a dealer in a poker game. Never once did he consider the possibility that his wife would have an affair with a man like Trent Boggs.

"Well . . . say something," said Doe, after she'd returned to her chair. "I didn't show it to you so that you could ogle it. You men are all alike."

"I'm sorry," he said. "I was trying to figure out where it was taken."

"What difference does that make? She's a slut, right?"

Rivers wanted to scream out, hell no, she's no slut, she's my wife, but that only would have complicated matters, besides making him look foolish. The cardinal rule for therapists is to keep their private life separate from their professional relationship with the patient, even on those occasions when honesty would be beneficial to both therapist and patient.

Instead of telling her what was on his mind, he said, "All you've got here is proof of a photograph. You don't know what kind of relationship they have, if any. Don't be so fast to jump to conclusions. There may be a good reason for this photograph being in his dresser drawer. Perhaps he found it on the street. Perhaps he stole it."

"Stole it!" she exclaimed. "Why would he steal of picture of a woman in a bikini? Do you think he stole it so that he could masturbate when he looked at it?"

That sentiment sent chills racing up Rivers's arms.

"No, I don't think so."

"Men do that, don't they?"

"Yes, but I'm just trying to show you that there are possibilities other than him being in a relationship."

"You don't know Trent very well. He's a real ladies man. If he's got a picture of a woman in his dresser drawer, you can damned well bet he's screwing her."

"I refuse to believe that!"

Doe looked confused, thinking it odd that he would overreact to *her* problem. "Why would you refuse to believe it?"

"Because it doesn't make sense."

Doe leaned forward and reached across the desk for the photograph, but Rivers picked it up and held it away from her. He said, "Why don't I hold onto this for my files."

"Why would you need that picture?"

"For collateral documentation."

"I don't know what that means, but I'm beginning to think that maybe you've got a thing for this woman, too. I admit it. I don't understand men. This woman that I've never met, never even heard of, is coming not only between Trent and me, but also between you and me. How crazy is that?"

Rivers smiled to defuse the situation.

"Doe, I promise you that this picture is not going to factor into our doctor-patient relationship. And, to be honest, I very seriously doubt that it has anything to do with your relationship with Trent."

"I don't know how you can be so sure."

"Trust me. This picture is not a threat to your relationship."

"You're sure?"

"I'm sure."

After Doe left the office, Rivers sat in silence for a long time, looking at the photograph. It brought back a flood of memories. He'd probably dated a couple of dozen women before he met Shelly, but within ten minutes of meeting her he knew that he

191

wanted to spend the rest of his life with her. It's funny how people can connect in that way. Makes no sense.

On the day that photograph was taken, they celebrated their fifth wedding anniversary. Champagne. Dinner at a fine restaurant. Then back to their room. He undressed her just inside the door and she dared him to run naked up and down the hallway with her. He refused, but she did it anyway, running from their room to the fire escape at the other end of the corridor and then back again, laughing the entire way. The images of that day were chiseled into his memory.

The thought of a thug like Trent Boggs having Shelly's photograph in his dresser made his skin crawl.

42

Preston's health was rapidly deteriorating. Each morning he looked in the mirror and saw less of himself and more of someone he almost didn't recognize. Because of the swelling in his legs, he found walking increasingly more difficult. He wondered how soon he would need the wheel chair that he already had purchased and stored in the spare bedroom.

Most people like Las Vegas at night, when the multi-colored lights blink and flash and sparkle, creating a fantasy world in which the next big thing is always at the lights beckoning from next door. Preston didn't much care for Las Vegas at night. He liked the city best early in the morning, when the remaining lights has the least impact. Early in the morning, the traffic signals were more noticeable, with their "walk" and "don't walk" commands dominating the strip.

Still wearing his robe, a ratty terry-cloth artifact that he'd had for twenty years, he walked from window to window, thankful that he saw no one on the streets other than the drivers of the slowly moving trucks that diligently swept the streets clean of broken glass and dreams. Sometimes he wondered if humanity might be a determent to the planet's evolution.

Never in his wildest dreams did he ever imagine that his life would end in Las Vegas. Lately, he'd been thinking a lot about China. He missed the sights and sounds, the bright colors and fleeting scents. China would be a fine place to die. He would like that very much. He fantasized about lying next to Bai for all eternity. Unfortunately, that would not be possible: He still had work to do.

When he had his fill of Las Vegas streets, he poured himself a cup of hot coffee and retreated to his computer room. He set the egg timer for ten minutes and logged into Mack 222. Now that he knew where he wanted to go within the program, bookmarks instantly moved him along to his destination.

Doe Peterson and related activity had picked up considerably overnight. There were phone calls and emails to and from Doe, from Dr. Rivers Mann to Jack McCain and Shelly Mann, from

Trent Boggs, from Harry Blackberry to Joseph Blackberry, from an unknown caller to Faith Holiday, from Harry Blackberry to an unknown at a Las Vegas number.

The item that intrigued him the most was a telephone call from Harry Blackberry to Joseph Blackberry. Everyone in Vegas knew the Blackberry brothers, if only by name. The brothers were to Memphis what Bugsy Siegel was to Las Vegas in the old days. Why would they mention Doe Peterson's name?

Preston hesitated a moment and then activated *play* on the Blackberry telephone conversation, unconcerned about being able to ID which speaker was Harry or Joseph:

". . . his girlfriend is named **Doe Peterson**."

"What do you know about her?"

"Next to nothing. She was adopted by a family in Arkansas. Has a good reputation as a model."

"Is she connected?"

"Not to us."

"Anyone who might not like us?"

"The best I can tell she's just a pretty face."

"That's **Trent**'s biggest weakness."

"Mine, too," laughed one speaker.

"Yeah, me, too."

"We've got to find out who doesn't like the girl. Trent says he can handle it, but he's in over his head."

"Yeah."

"The girl's causing us a lot of trouble. There's only one degree of separation between her and us. That makes me uncomfortable."

"I never thought about it that way."

"Now's the time."

The conversation ended abruptly, without either man saying "bye."

Preston looked at the egg timer. Three minutes gone by. He pulled up an email from kingedward3 to darkfruit01. He ran a quick server check and learned that darkfruit01 was a Memphis address and kingedward3 was a Las Vegas address. Nothing surprising about that. He read the email:

Dear Mr. Harry,

I checked out Doe Peterson. The word on the street is that someone here in Vegas doesn't like her. I couldn't find out what the problem is, but from the best I can tell, it has nothing to do with your friend Trent. I doubt he knows how unpopular she is. When I find out who doesn't like her, I'll let you know. I'll be delivering your Christmas present on Friday. Where should we meet?

Eddie

Blackberry01 replied:

Dear Eddie,
Thank you for the information and for the early Christmas present. It is gratifying to have friends who think so far ahead. The entire family will be gathered for dinner in the Heritage Room at the Magnolia Casino, across the state line in Mississippi. Why don't you join us there?

Harry

The egg timer still had time to go. He quickly entered "edit" and revised the email to read:

Dear Eddie,
Thank you for the information and for the early Christmas present. I am sure that everyone here will get a big *bang* out of it. It is gratifying to have friends who think so far ahead. The entire family will be gathered for dinner in the heritage Room at the Magnolia Casino, across the state line in Mississippi. Why don't you join us there? You can help us wrap our present for the *President*. I'm sure he will get as big a *bang* from our gift as the family will get from your gift.

Harry

195

Once he completed the edit, he hit "delete original, save edit" and slugged it "Level 1 Priority," a designation that he knew would redirect the email to FBI headquarters in Washington, the way he'd designed the system. It was a devious thing for him to do, highly illegal, but at this point he didn't give a damn.

He logged off with thirty seconds to go on the egg timer and sat back in his chair, his heart racing. Someone in Vegas wanted to kill Doe. Why? Was it directed toward him? That seemed very unlikely, but still possible. Outside of bureaucrats in China, only three people knew that he had a Chinese-born daughter—himself, Agent Cefalu, and his daughter from his second marriage.

The more he thought about it, the more it bothered him. Maybe this was a way for the CIA to erase his history once he was gone. Maybe he was being cleansed from the Agency.

Preston called Agent Cefalu on his cell.

"You on the job?" Preston asked. He never identified himself when he called Agent Cefalu. He didn't have to since his voice was well known to the agent.

"As we speak."

"Anything to report?"

"Yeah, I've tailed her and a guy that I checked out from his vehicle registration, a fellow named Trent Boggs. Bad actor. Low level hood with ties to the Blackberry brothers. You got anything new?"

"I do. There's a hit out on her that originated in Vegas."

"Wow. Any details?"

"Not yet. You see anything suspicious?"

"There's a guy tailing my car and the car that Doe's riding in. You have any reason to think that the guy she's with is a danger to her."

"He's not someone I'd want for a son-in-law, but I don't see him as a central player in all this."

"So should I stick with Doe, or switch over to the guy tailing us. Could be he's the one who's a problem."

"That's a tough choice for me to make from this distance."

"I can stay with her and try to intercept him if he makes a move. Or I can gamble on him being the shooter and tail him if he breaks away."

Preston paused, considering the option.

"My gut tells me that he's the one you need to keep an eye on."

"I agree."

"I'm counting on you, Cefalu."

"I know."

"Don't let me down."

"I won't."

When Preston turned off the phone, his robe was soaked with sweat. There was a bitter taste on his lips. He wiped his hand across his mouth and saw bright-red blood on his hand. Not a good sign, not at all.

43

Rivers and Jack McCain sat huddled at a rear table at the Mud Pie Café, eyes intense, voices lowered.

"Why would Doe Peterson's boyfriend have a picture of Shelly in his dresser drawer?"

"I don't think you should jump to conclusions."

"Well, I've got to jump somewhere. A conclusion seems like as nice a place as any."

"The way I see it there are three possibilities. You or Shelly lost the picture and he found it. It was stolen by the person who broke into your house and tampered with your toothbrush. Or, and this is the one I'd pay least attention to, he and Shelly are having an affair."

"What are the odds that Shelly would have an affair with Doe Peterson's boyfriend?"

"Not very good. That's why I said I'd discount that option if I were you. Besides the logic involved, Shelly loves you. She'd never have an affair with anyone, much less a guy from the wrong side of the tracks. She's never impressed me as the bad-boy type."

"I'm sure you're right. Since I don't buy the odds of that picture being lost and found by that guy, I've got to consider the possibility that he's the person who broke into our house."

"That doesn't make sense, Rivers."

"None of this makes sense."

Their conversation trickled off to a sustained pause, a fortunate turn of events since the waitress arrived with two jumbo-sized pieces of chocolate pie and a pot of dark coffee. Both men sat with their hands in their laps, eyeing the pie as it jiggled down in front of them.

"Anything else?" asked the waitress.

The men shook their heads in unison.

If it seems odd that they would suddenly drop a passionate conversation to delve into chocolate pie, it's obvious that the quality of the pie has not been factored into the equation. Chocolate pie, when properly prepared with a two-inch white meringue and served at room temperature, is about as close to culinary perfection as it is possible to achieve. The men's eyes looked like slots that'd rolled up triple sevens.

Conversation is the first casualty of chocolate pie. Rivers and Jack sat like tribal chieftains as their forks clanked against the china, slicing, lifting, savoring, avoiding eye contact since it might be misconstrued as an invitation for conversation. Both men finished at the exact same moment, their pie-stained forks dropping to the table like weapons discarded on the field of battle.

Jack bemoaned the fact that he would have to return to the newspaper and write something clever.

"That's better than listening to the coulrophobic waiting for me back at the office."

Chocolate pie sometimes makes men bitter.

"What's that?" asked Jack.

"Fear of clowns."

"We've got those in Memphis?"

"You bet."

They were still savoring the aftertaste of the pie, when Doe and Trent entered the restaurant and sat at a table across the room.

"Unbelievable," intoned John, when he spotted them.

Rivers's eyes widened. "Is that Doe's boyfriend?"

"I'd say yes."

Rivers looked at Jack in disbelief.

"Let me get this straight—Doe's boyfriend is the same guy that had lunch with Shelly?"

Jack didn't respond. His eyes were glued first on Doe and Trent, who shared a brief kiss before they were seated, and then to the gentleman with the shaved head who came in behind them and sat at a nearby table.

Rivers continued, "I feel like I'm walking around inside someone else's dream. I'm pretty sure that Shelly doesn't know Doe, but I know for certain that she knows Doe's boyfriend."

"He *is* an insurance agent. Maybe he underwrites your homeowner policy?"

"I don't think so. The insurance is part of my mortgage premium. It was with one of the major insurers."

"Maybe he's a rep for the major. Or maybe he handles your car insurance."

"That's a possibility. Shelly takes care of that."

"Well, there you have it. Don't look for trouble where none exists."

As they talked, Jack was drawn to an older man who entered the restaurant alone and sat several tables away from where Doe was seated. All his instincts told him that the man was a cop. Not a street cop. Maybe a fed.

Jack watched both men. They were careful not to look at each other. They were equally careful to look at Doe and Trent when they were looking at each other and not looking around the room.

"I've got to be honest with you," Jack said. "Something is going on here. And I don't think Shelly is the issue."

"What do you mean?"

"Look at that man over there, the one with the shaved head."

"OK."

"Now look at that older man sitting across the room."

"OK."

"Unless there was something in the pie that shouldn't be there, I'm thinking the fellow with the shaved head is a hood, and the older gentleman is a cop."

"I can see why you'd think that. What's your point?"

"They're both tailing Doe and her boyfriend."

"Think so?"

"I'm positive."

"Doe thinks someone is trying to kill her."

"And you think someone is trying to kill you."

"Right. Do you think the two are related?"

"Doe, may not know it, but she's in something over her head."

"And you think I'm getting the spillover?"

Jack nodded.

"Buddy, I'd say you're knee deep in trouble."

"That's what I'm afraid of."

44

Before she left town, Doe didn't tell a soul what she had in mind, except Flutie, but she knew she wouldn't say anything. If she couldn't trust Flutie, she couldn't trust anyone—at least that's the way she saw it.

Doe's absolute trust in her annoyed Flutie sometimes, mainly because she felt Doe was too trusting of other people.

"You can't trust anyone!" Flutie insisted. "Not even me! Don't ever forget that!"

"Don't be silly," Doe responded. "Of course I can trust you."

"That's why you have so many heartbreaks. If you don't believe me, ask Dr. Mann. I'm sure he's figured that out by now."

That was very much on her mind when she crossed the Mississippi River Bridge into Arkansas. Perhaps she *was* too trusting. Right now she trusted Flutie. She trusted her parents. She trusted Dr. Mann. And she trusted Trent.

Perhaps her trust network was too large. She wrestled with the idea, that whole thing about trust, but what kept coming back to her over and over again was the realization that she didn't trust the person she should trust the most, *herself.*

As she exited the bridge, Tony was midway across, keeping his white panel truck well within the speed limit, and Agent Cefalu was approaching the entrance on the Memphis side in his Impala. Agent Cefalu got Preston on his cell. "Your friend is headed into Arkansas, with the subject behind her."

"She must be going to see her adoptive parents."

"That makes sense. I'm going to turn her loose and keep my eye on the subject."

"Don't let him get away."

"I won't."

Doe didn't have a perfect childhood, especially in the early years when it became apparent that she wasn't going to easily bond with her adoptive parents, but as the years went by, she came to appreciate them—and, yes, love them as if they were her birth parents.

As she drove through the Arkansas countryside, she had flashbacks to her youth. She was the only child of Asian ancestry in her school. Some children gravitated to her because of that; others were repelled by her differences, sometimes to the point of ridiculing her appearance. A time or two she was called a gook. At an early age, she decided that she was going to be *someone* when she grew up, someone important who'd make everyone envious.

By the time she arrived at her parents' cabin, she was in tears.

Isn't it silly she thought *that we can be so affected by our thoughts?*

That's one reason why she didn't like to think so much. It usually made her cry.

Doe saw the front door open before she even came to a full stop, just giving her time to wipe her eyes and put on a big smile. As her mother and then her father wrapped her in their arms, she felt the fear she'd been living with for the past couple of weeks slip away with the ease of a garment being tossed onto a chair. She loved that about them. The curative powers that they possessed and didn't know that they possessed. They were special people.

"What a nice surprise!" exclaimed her mother.

"I had some free time."

"Have you been crying?" asked her mother.

"No ma'am," she lied.

Doe walked between her mother and father, an arm around each waist, her strides morphing into childlike skips as she beamed all the way to the cabin door, home at long last.

"Would you like something to eat?" asked her mother.

"No thank you."

"Or something to drink?" asked her father. "We've got orange or grape juice, or soda, or iced tea. Whatever you want."

"Thank you, but I'm fine."

45

Agent Cefalu watched the white panel truck ahead of him drive past the cabin and then pull off the road into some high grass. As he went by the truck, he noticed that the subject, who had a shaved head, had a very serious expression on his face. He got a better look in his rear-view mirror when the man, dressed in camouflaged sports gear, got out of the car carrying two large canvas bags. The man hurried across the road and disappeared into the high grass.

Agent Cefalu drove about a quarter mile past the truck and pulled well off the road. He waited fifteen minutes and then headed out through the high grass at a forty degree angle so that he would intersect the subject's path at the point where he entered the woods. He felt foolish tramping through the woods in a light-gray business suit and expensive Italian shoes, but he didn't have a change of clothes in his car.

To his surprise, he encountered a river. It was a typical Arkansas stream, shallow water that flowed over a bed of broken rocks. He paused long enough to remove his Italian shoes and socks. Then he splashed across the stream, holding his shoes high in the air, grimacing with each step because of the icy water.

When he reached the tree line, he stopped to listen for movement. Leaves rustled in the treetops. Otherwise the woods were silent. He tied his shoelaces together and looped the shoes around his neck. Then he pressed on, moving slowly and quietly on bare feet, assuming that the subject would veer sharply to the left so that he could approach the cabin from the rear. Using his cell, he anonymously called the local sheriff's office to tip them off about a suspected intruder at the cabin. They said they'd send a deputy out right away.

Something about his surroundings gave him the creeps. He couldn't help but think about that novel, *Deliverance*. He hoped that he would not encounter any good ole boys that looked like they'd been in the woods too long.

Soon the sky faded into moonless darkness. He forged ahead, briars and evergreen branches scrapping against his hands, tearing his trousers in several places. He made a mental note to send Preston a bill for the trousers.

In the distance, he saw a flickering light. A campfire. He approached with caution, still barefoot, pausing after each step, careful not to step on dry twigs that would reveal his position, listening. He saw the subject on his feet, pacing around the campfire, talking to himself.

"How in the hell do you kill someone and make it not look like murder?"

The subject kicked a pine cone into the dark.

"People expect too fucking much."

The subject circled the fire several times and then sat on a tree stump. He began to sing an old soul ballad, his voice plaintive and riddled with regret: "Sitting on the dock of the bay . . ."

He stopped singing, swallowed hard, and then grimaced. From a knapsack he removed a coil of grass rope. Slowly, with great care, he fashioned the rope into a perfect noose. He held it up, admiring it, but then he frowned and quickly unraveled the noose, perhaps feeling that it was too perfect. This time he reshaped the rope into a more amateurish noose.

Agent Cefalu knew damned well what he had in mind.

46

Inside the cabin, Doe sat in the den with her parents, watching television.

"How long are you going to stay?" asked her mother.

"I need to go back in the morning. I just wanted a break, you know?"

"Stay as long as you like. You know we are always happy to see you."

"I know."

Her mother reached over and hugged her.

"I was your age once. I remember how frustrated I got when everything didn't go my way. Trust me—what seems important today is hardly ever important next week. Things have a way of working themselves out."

Doe desperately wanted to tell her parents that she thought someone wanted to kill her, but she really didn't have the heart to turn their peaceful world upside down. The incident at the cabin, when she last visited, had been explained away by deputies as nothing to worry about and her parents quickly put the incident out of mind. They'd lived their entire lives minding their own business, being a friend to everyone, and it was inconceivable to them that anyone would want to harm them or their daughter.

"Before I forget," her father began, "I put some things in a box for you to take back with you."

"What kinds of things?"

"Mostly canned goods. Laundry powder. Paper towels. Things you need."

"Dad, you don't have to do that."

"Yes, I do."

Doe felt guilty because she knew they lived on Social Security and her annual income was ten times more than theirs. They couldn't afford to put together care packages for her. Even so, she had no choice but to accept it since they would find a refusal highly insulting. The things you do for your parents.

"Thank you so much," she said.

They had just turned in for the night, when there came a knock at the door. By the time Doe got to the living room, her father and mother already were there, her father holding a shotgun.

"Who is it?" her father asked.

"Sheriff's office," said the visitor.

Benjamin Peterson turned on the porch light and pulled the curtain aside to peer into the night. He saw a man in uniform. He opened the door and asked, "What's the problem?"

"Mr. Peterson we got a call that you had an intruder."

Benjamin and Anna looked at each, perplexed. Then they looked at Doe, who shook her head. Said Benjamin, "That call didn't come from us."

"Must have been a crank call," said the deputy. "We get them all the time." He turned away, talking over his shoulder, "You folks have a good evening, you hear."

"Thank you officer," said Anna.

Benjamin closed the door and grinned. "You just never know, do you?"

47

Agent Cefalu hunkered down and leaned against a tree, watching the subject move about his campsite. The criminal mind fascinated him. This guy was in the final stages of carrying out a murder staged to resemble a suicide and he was totally absorbed with the neatness of his campsite.

The fire had to be just so, the wood stacked like a pyramid. He apparently thought there was too much ground clutter around the fire because he torn off a branch from an evergreen and used it like a broom to sweep the clutter away from his campsite. Obsessive-compulsives don't make good killers because they have a difficult time leaving the crime scene. They go back again and again to make sure they didn't dropped something incriminating. Or they go back to rearrange the body. Or they go back to straighten up the house, pick up overturned lamps, wipe their fingerprints off the doorknobs. Their obsessions are endless. They worry so much about making mistakes that they are destined to do what they fear the most.

At first, there was very little smoke from the campfire, but as the subject continued to toss ground clutter onto the fire, the smoke plumes grew denser. The subject stared at the fire, perhaps thinking that the smoke plumes would taper off, but when they didn't he kicked dirt onto the fire and extinguished it.

Suddenly, the only light filtering through the trees came downward from the moon. The subject's silhouette moved about in the clearing, left to right, right to left, but Agent Cefalu could only guess at his activities.

As the night wore on, Agent Cefalu drifted off to sleep. He dreamed of following a white van that fell off the end of the world. When he awoke, he was in pain, his hands going to his neck, slowly understanding that there was a rope pulled tight around his neck, forcing the back of his head into tree bark.

Couldn't breathe. *The son of a bitch is trying to strangle me!*

48

Doe felt renewed after her visit with her parents. That's why she went to see them. Renewal was something she always could count on. She was on the road back to Memphis, only a few miles from the Mississippi River Bridge when her cell rang. The call was from her mother.

"Dear, I just wanted to let you know that a friend of yours stopped by the house. He said he'd get in touch with you later."

"Who was it?"

"Didn't really give his name. But he seemed real nice."

"Did he say what he wanted?"

"No, dear."

"Thanks Mom."

A few minutes later, her cell rang again. She looked at the caller ID. The call was from J. Cefalu and the number had a Las Vegas prefix. She hesitated before answering, but with all the strange things happening in her life, she was afraid not to take the call in case it was important.

"Hello."

"Doe Peterson?"

"Yes."

"This is Agent J. Cefalu with the Secret Service and it's urgent that I meet with you as soon as possible."

"Why would you want to talk to me?"

"I've been called in to investigate the death of a private investigator named Oscar Ross. Your name came up as one of his clients. I believe he was working for you on the day he passed away. Is that correct?"

"Yes. Yes, he was working for me. It was a horrible accident."

"We're pretty sure it wasn't an accident."

"Why do you say that?"

"This may seem like an odd question, but did you by any chance give Mr. Ross a jar of cold cream on the day he died?"

Doe was taken aback.

"Why would you ask a thing like that?"

"We think the jar contained a tactile poison that was meant for you."

Doe didn't say anything for a moment. First, she felt a surge of guilt that Oscar might have died because of her. Then she felt that type of fear that snatches your breath away and tugs at your gut, twisting until it hurts.

Finally, she asked, "What do you want me to do?"

"I would like to meet with you at a secure location. Do you know the Charlton Hotel in east Memphis?"

"I do."

"Meet me there tomorrow night at 7 o'clock in the glass elevator. Just get on at the lobby level and go to the top floor. Keep going up and down until I introduce myself."

"How will I know it's you?"

"I'll have Secret Service ID."

"OK, I'll meet you there."

"One other thing. It's important that you come alone. We don't know who we can trust."

"I will."

When Doe turned off her cell, her hands were shaking.

49

The office was regulation government issue: metallic chairs with beige cushions, a low-gloss wooden desk, metal filing cabinets, a photograph of the president on the wall next to a FBI emblem.

Five men and one woman stood around the desk as an older man leaned back in his chair, hands clasped behind his head. There was a smile on his face that ran counter to the seriousness of the meeting, but no one dared comment on that because the boss was . . . well, the boss, and no one ever got a promotion by asking the boss why he had in inappropriate smile on his face.

A printout of the email that Preston had doctored was face-up on the desk.

"This is not the way we wanted it to come down," said the boss. "But our job is to react to good fortune, in whatever form it arrives."

One of the agents shook his head.

"I guess my only problem is that I've had my eye on the Blackberry brothers for a good ten years and I've never known them to make a mistake like this. It doesn't make sense."

The boss kicked his feet up on the desk and in his most paternal voice said, "Boys, if it's one thing that I've learned in this business it's that the bad guys always make a fatal mistake. Some take longer than others. No one gets away with anything in this country, at least not forever."

The agent with reservations nodded.

"You're right, of course."

The female agent said, "Do you think they'll put up a fight?"

"Hard to tell. Might."

50

Frankly, Preston wasn't all that used to worrying about other people. But he was concerned about Doe. Couldn't get her out of his head. As a result, he found it difficult not to log into Mack 222 every hour to check the telephone log. As long as he logged off within ten minutes, he was in the clear.

Once he logged in, the first thing he saw was a telephone conversation between Agent Cefalu and Doe Peterson, with Cefalu placing the call. His first response was anger. Cefalu wasn't supposed to contact Doe under any circumstances. His second response was concern that perhaps Doe was in trouble of some kind. He clicked on *play* and listened. Right away he knew that the caller wasn't Cefalu. The caller was a much younger man. He listened to the conversation three times and then logged off the system. He wasted no time in calling Cefalu on his cell.

"Hello," someone answered—a male voice.

"Who's speaking please?"

"What number are you calling?"

"I'm calling . . . " He gave him the telephone number.

"You've got the right number. Who'd you like to talk to?"

"Is Cefalu there?"

"This is Cefalu."

Certainly, it *was not* Cefalu.

Preston hesitated a moment. Then he said, making it up as he went along, "I wasn't sure it was you. I just wanted to let you know that your voucher was approved."

"What voucher is that?"

Preston gave him credit for gravitas. He obviously wasn't afraid of being discovered.

Preston answered, "The one for your trip to New York."

"Oh, that's good. Anything else?"

"No, that's it."

"Thanks."

Preston turned off his cell and stared at his computer. What were his options? He couldn't contact Secret Service because

Cefalu's mission was unauthorized. Where the hell was Cefalu? He was still pondering his options when the visitor's buzzer sounded off. He clicked on the viewer and saw that his visitor was Faith Holiday.

"Come on up," he said, and then touched the button that released the elevator so that it would stop at the penthouse. He was in no mood to deal with this today, but he really had no choice. Family might not be worth a damn, but they are still family.

Preston opened the door and walked into the hallway to wait for the elevator door to open. Faith stepped off the elevator and saw Preston looking her way. She didn't smile. She didn't wave. She didn't acknowledge that he was even there. Neither did he smile or wave. His stern demeanor told her that he wasn't happy to see her.

"Come in," he said, when she reached the door.

She walked past him without saying a word and stopped just inside the door. He watched her walk across the room to a corner chair. He disliked her walk. It was one part swagger and one part insolence. She cared about no one but herself and it showed in the way she handled herself. He sat in a chair near the window.

"How you feeling?" she asked.

"I've felt better."

"What do the doctors say?"

"I've pretty much given up on them."

"Oh."

There was a long pause as the two of them gazed out the window, their thoughts lost in the clouds. Finally, he said, "You must need money."

She nodded. "I've got a deal going, but it hasn't paid off yet."

"How much do you need?"

"How much can I get?"

"I've only got about eight thousand in cash here."

"If that's an offer, I accept."

Without a word he got up and went into the bedroom and returned with a handful of money, which he dropped into her lap. She slowly gathered the money and put it into her purse. She wanted to say something, but she couldn't quite get the words out. She sensed it might be their last visit.

Finally, she got to her feet and looked him directly in the face for the first time. Her eyes were wet with tears, but her body language remained combative. She said, "I'm sorry."

"About what?"

"That I'm a disappointment to you."

"That works both ways."

"As I look back, it's like we never had a chance."

"Life offers us roads to take. We have to take responsibility for the choices we make—and live with those choices. God knows, I have."

Faith started for the door. "I'll let myself out."

Preston got up and watched her walk away, emotions surging.

Suddenly, she stopped and turned. She walked back across the room and stood in front of him. "Do you mind if I hug you?"

He reached out and embraced her, fighting back the tears.

The kiss on his cheek was cool and quick.

51

Harry Blackberry liked to keep his distance from those associated with his organization. But since he was only as strong as his weakest link, there were times when he was forced to deal with some associates on their level.

Trent was ill at ease when he entered his office. There was a Picasso on the wall behind the desk, and the furnishings were dark and rich, lots of leather and brass, what you'd expect to see in a bank president's office. No expense was spared. He squirmed when he sat in the chair opposite the desk. Trent was a big deal on the street, but here he was nothing.

"What can I do for you, Mr. Blackberry?"

"I just thought we should talk."

"Sure." He shifted his weight from one side of the chair to the other.

"Are you happy with the amount of work you do for us?"

Trent nodded. "But you know how it is. More is always better. Not that I'm complaining."

"I understand."

"Is that why you wanted to talk to me? Has someone complained about my work?"

"Not at all," said Harry. "I've got a very serious matter to discuss with you. It has become obvious to certain people, including us, that someone has a problem with your girlfriend, Doe, and her psychologist, Dr. Mann. It's no one in our organization and we've been unsuccessful locating the source. I'm hoping you can help with that because, emotional attachments aside, it is in no one's interest for anything bad to happen to either of those people."

"I know. I've been really concerned about Doe. Do you think the two incidents are linked?"

"You mean, your girlfriend and the shrink?"

"Yes."

"I can't imagine that they are not linked. Why do you ask? Do you have any reason to think that they are not related?"

214

"No, I don't have evidence about anything. I'll just be glad when it's over with and she's safe."

"Amen to that. Something like this could be hurtful to us in a lot of ways."

"I understand."

Harry got up and reached out to shake hands with Trent.

"I want you to let me know if you hear anything. Don't try to do anything on your own. Understand?"

"Yes sir."

Trent was almost at the door when Harry said, "We're having a little get-together Friday in the Heritage Room at the Magnolia Casino. Why don't you make plans to attend. There'll be some people there I'd like you to meet."

"Yes sir."

52

Rivers and Shelly packed a picnic lunch and made their way down the steep bluff to the boathouse where they kept their boat moored. It was in a still-water inlet, away from the direct currents of the river.

After they loaded the picnic lunch, Rivers selected the fishing gear that they needed and put it in the boat, along with a specially rigged bow that he used to hunt catfish — and they left without much conversation.

Shelly thought that he was unusually quiet, even for a lazy Saturday morning, but he seemed annoyed when she asked him why he was being so quiet, so she only asked once. She made a mental note to ask Rivers, in his capacity as a psychologist, to explain why men hate to be asked questions.

Rivers eased the boat out of the inlet and then gunned the throttle once he was in the open river, a refreshing spray bathing his face. Their destination was Bear Claw, a large island that was unique because of a clear-water, spring-fed lake that occupied about one-third of the land area. Because of its isolated location, about five miles from Memphis, midway between Tennessee and Arkansas, it had few visitors, despite its reputation as a great place to fish and swim.

"This was a good idea," shouted Shelly as they skimmed across the water. "I needed a break."

"I think we both did," answered Rivers, his eyes riveted on the water ahead.

Truthfully, he liked the forest better than he liked the river. For one thing, the forest stayed in one place and did not re-arrange itself in the blink of an eye. He also liked the fact that when he stood on solid ground he did not have to worry about what was beneath this feet, at least not the way he did on the river. The woods represented the male of the species, to his way of thinking, while the river represented the female.

To navigate a river, you practically have to make love to it. You have to be attentive and considerate of its many moods. Not so in the woods, where you fight for each step you take, whether by cunning stealth or brute force—and a willingness to give as good as you take—you are challenged to overcome its natural opposition to your will.

Time passed quickly on the river, aided somewhat by the unspoken tension between Rivers and Shelly. Things needed to be said. Rivers wondered exactly what he should say. Shelly wondered how much she should say. Few things in a relationship are more stressful than shared, unspoken thoughts. They wear away love's protective armor, like dripping water.

Rivers and Shelly both were relieved when the island approached. Two of the island's four sides were covered with sandy beaches. As they expected, there were no other boats in sight. Rivers beached the boat and they both leaped out to drag it far enough onto the beach so that it would not drift away. They quietly gathered their picnic lunch, fishing and hunting gear and headed straight to the lake on a well-traveled trail.

Since they were familiar with the island, they knew exactly where they wanted to go—a cleared area that had a ridge of stone that backed up against the lake, creating a picturesque spot to set up camp. Shelly liked it because there were no insects on the sun-baked rock and because there was an overlook that provided her with a splendid diving platform.

Once they arrived, Shelly stripped down to her bikini and walked over to the overlook. Unlike the river, which was muddy and polluted with floating debris, the water in the lake was clear and cool, unspoiled by the whims of man.

When it came to swimming, she had only one rule: don't dive until you first get your hair wet. She came down off the rock and walked around to the side, where she could enter the water in less spectacular fashion on a rocky slope.

"Looks great, doesn't it?" she said, smiling.

Rivers smiled back.

"I think I'm going over to the west bank to do some fishing. I'll go swimming with you later."

"Have fun," she said.

He waved and walked away with his bow and arrows.

As he was leaving, she walked carefully across the stones, careful so that she wouldn't cut her feet on the jagged edges. The slope was gradual for about twenty feet, then it dropped off suddenly, a shear cliff that fell about one hundred feet to the lakebed. The water was cold and made her skin tingle, a sensation that she relished. Visibility was good, but not great. The refracted light from the surface presented her with a shadowy world that had a pristine quality to it. She was surprised at the extent of rock formation she found beneath the surface. The soothing water was like a salve to her skin.

There was no trail to where Rivers wanted to go, so he had to forge his own pathway. He went quietly among the trees, walking around the thick underbrush that appeared from time to time.

At the bottom of a slope, he stopped and leaned into a tree. He had seen or heard nothing since leaving Shelly. Suddenly, he heard something unexpected. He tensed, slipping an arrow into his bow.

At first, he did not know where it was—it was only a single, light snap of a fallen branch—then he listened very hard and figured out that it had come from directly behind him, probably on the other side of the tree. He whirled around the tree, bringing his bow up into shooting position, just in time to see a cottontail rabbit disappear into a thicket halfway up the slope.

Rivers unstrung the arrow and pushed on through the woods until he reached the sandy beach on the west side of the island. Then he turned south and followed the beach until he could turn east onto the south side of the island, where ragged dirt and clay banks replaced the sand. That was where he was most likely to find catfish feeding or nestled into the bank.

Bow fishing for catfish was much more difficult than bow fishing for other fish, primarily because river water was always so dark and muddy, concealing whatever lurked beneath the surface. What made it possible at all for catfish to be hunted under those circumstances was their enormous size. Fifty pound catfish were not uncommon and sometimes they grew as large as one hundred pounds. Monsters that size can be identified by their shadowy forms and the ripples their dorsal fins make as they constantly move to stay in position.

As he walked along the riverbank, gazing down into the water, searching for catfish, Rivers thought about Shelly. In all their years of marriage, he'd never once asked her if she'd had an affair. That is not an easy question to ask a partner who has shared so much of your life.

If he asked that question—and she said no—it would irreparably damage their relationship because she would view the question as an assault on their marriage. If he asked that question—and she said yes—where would he go from there? Would he ask her for a divorce? Is it possible to live with a woman who has deceived you?

It made him sick to his stomach to even think about that possibility. But the psychologist in him made him ask, what if *she* wanted a divorce and the affair was her way of forcing the issue? It was clear to him that he could not win with either answer. Not to ask the question would be to retreat into a world that soon would become unbearably tense. The unknown is sometimes more difficult to manage than the known.

The best way to handle it, he decided, would be to show her the photograph, which he had in his back pocket, and laugh about it. Maybe say that it was obviously the most valuable item in the house since it was the only item stolen by whoever sabotaged his toothbrush. See if she laughed, too.

He settled comfortably into that thought and it brought him relief for about five minutes, when he wondered if there was any way possible that Shelly was having an affair with this guy Trent Boggs and together they might have devised a plan to murder him, making it look like an accident.

That was possible, wasn't it?

He no sooner thought it, than he started muttering to himself, "No, no, no . . . you're going off the deep end now." *Even psychologists have their moments of insanity* he thought, then added *especially psychologists.*

53

Shelly felt like a different person in the water. Like when she changed from cut-off jeans and a tube top into an elegant black, low-cut dress. Water had that same effect on her. It made her feel more attractive, slimmer, taller, funnier. Impossible to explain, yet very real.

She swam for long stretches at a time. Floated on her back, looking up into a pastel sky. Dove deep into the water, holding her breath until she thought she'd explode, bursting back into fresh air like a gigantic air bubble.

Throughout it all she thought about Rivers. About how much he meant to her. After thinking it over, she knew she had to tell him about the affair. How can a woman who loves her husband keep something like that a secret?

The problem was not so much telling him as it was explaining it to him. Then what? Would he immediately ask for a divorce? Would he pack this things and move out of the house? Would he suggest they undergo counseling? No, not that—she was certain he wouldn't want counseling since the low success rate for marital counseling was something he'd written papers about for the journals.

She decided to see if she could reach rock bottom, so she took a deep breath and swam downward, the water growing darker and darker with each kick of her feet. She ran out of air long before she reached the bottom. As she swam up toward the light, she saw something directly above her. A large object. It seemed to be floating without a tether.

When she got closer, she realized that it was a human. It was floating face down, arms extended. The upper part of the body was dressed in what looked like a T-shirt of some kind. The lower body had on shorts or a swimsuit. She looked for a face, but the head was turned sideways in the water.

She broke the surface of the water about six feet from the body and swam toward it, fearful of what she would see. Bodies that have been in the water for long periods of time are often grotesquely disfigured.

She reached out for the hand that was floating closest to her, but before her fingers could grasp it, the hand rose up out of the water and lunged for her, grabbing her tightly around the wrist. The body rolled in the water and before she knew what had happened she felt an arm around her neck and a hand on her wrist. She was drawn, back first, against the body, which she now understood was not a body at all, but rather a living human being. She tired to break free, but the grasp was simply too strong.

The two of them churned about in the water, until the arm around her neck tightened to where she thought she would lose consciousness, at which point she stopped struggling and allowed herself to be taken to the river bank.

She was flung face-down onto the sandy beach.

Then she was flipped over on her back, at which point she saw the face of her attacker for the first time.

"Trent!" she exclaimed.

His wet hair hung down to his shoulders. The Grateful Dead T-shirt he wore was distorted by the water. He tried to kiss her, but she pushed him away.

"What are you doing?" she insisted.

She tried to get up, but he straddled her and leaned over, pressing his hands against her, holding her down.

"Let me up! Right now!"

He made a low shushing sound with his lips. He gazed into her eyes, but she could not get a reading for what he was thinking. All she knew was that it could not possibly be good.

"Get off of me! Rivers is here!"

His voice sliced into her like a knife.

"I love you, Shelly," he said, his eyes clearly love struck. "You're going to have to choose between me and Rivers."

"I'll do no such thing!"

"You have no choice."

"Then I choose Rivers. Let me up! Now!"

He reached into a nearby canvas bag and withdrew several leather strips that he used to tie her wrists together. She offered no resistance; she was depleted of all energy. She felt like a rag doll. He was able to move her arms about as if they were stuffed with cotton.

Once he had her hands bound, he tied her ankles together.

"Let's talk," she said. "Let's talk about what you're doing."

No response. He sat on a nearby rock and stared at her. The sight of a beautiful woman in a bikini with her hands and ankles tied was something he knew would stick with him for all eternity. Totally helpless. Totally submissive to his wishes. Why had he never thought of that before? The sight of her in a state of submission took his breath away.

Finally, he said, "What is there to talk about?"

"Let's start with, how did you find me? What are you going to do to me? Have you lost your mind? Questions like that."

"You made your choice. You have no right to ask me questions."

"I did make a choice, but that doesn't mean we shouldn't talk."

"Well, to answer your first question, I've been watching your house from my boat. When I saw you coming down the bluff, I went downriver and waited for you to leave."

"I never saw you."

"You weren't supposed to see me. I hung back about a half mile. Then followed you to the island."

"But why, Trent? Why are you doing this?"

"Have you ever wanted something so badly that you knew you couldn't live without it?"

She thought, *yeah, my husband* but she answered, "No. Not that way."

"That's a shame. You're missing a lot."

"There's something I've got to ask you."

"What's that?"

"Was it you that broke into our house and went through my dresser?"

Trent grinned.

"And did you do something to Rivers' toothbrush to make it shock him?"

"Guilty on all counts."

"Rivers never did anything to hurt you. Why would you want to hurt him?"

"That's obvious, isn't it? With him out of the way, you will need me."

Did he say 'will?' she thought. *Not 'would.'*

222

"Trent, no matter what happens to Rivers, I would never need you."

Trent got up from the rock and walked over to where she lay twisted into a knot. He glared at her a moment. He reached into the canvas bag and pulled out a pair of jeans, which he quickly changed into. Then he withdrew a revolver from the canvas bag and stuck it into his waistband.

"What are you going to do with that gun?" demanded Shelly. "Have you lost your fucking mind?"

"I'm just a man in love," he said, a smirk on his face.

Then he walked away without explanation.

"Trent!" she called out, tears running down her cheeks. "Nothing you do would ever make me want you. Do you hear me? Do you hear me?"

54

Rivers almost stepped on a cottonmouth lazily stretched out on a sunny patch of ground. He walked around the snake, surprised that it did nothing more threatening than flick its tongue.

As he walked along the water's edge, his eyes were glued to the lapping waves that momentarily grew stronger with the passing of each barge and then subsided, only to begin again with the next barge.

There were three aluminum arrows attached to a brace on his bow. He withdrew one of the arrows, attached the guide wire from the spool on the bow, and notched the arrow shaft onto the bowstring, holding it in place so that it could be fired quickly if necessary.

Finally, after walking more than one hundred yards, he came across what he was looking for. A ripple that ran counter to the waves brushing against the bank. An ominous dark shadow. He moved quietly to the edge of the bank and took aim with his bow. He released the arrow with a *swoosh* that quickened his pulse. He watched the arrow as it hit the water and burrowed about five feet before striking the target.

The giant fish, which Rivers estimated to weight about fifty pounds, rose close enough to the surface to allow him to see that his arrow had struck just behind the fish's massive head. He saw its mouth open and its eerie eyes and the thrash of the dorsal fin. Once it fell back into the water, the fish slipped out of sight in the muddy water, only to come charging back to the surface moments later, its angry head breaking free of the water, its mouth chopping wildly at something it couldn't even see much less grasp.

When the fish broke for open water, Rivers fed it line from the spool on his bow, but the fish didn't go far before it turned around and propelled back to shore, causing Rivers to drop the bow to the ground so that he could reel the line back with his bare hands. The fish went through that maneuver several times, with Rivers relaxing the line and then tightening the line, to the point where his palms and index fingers began to bleed.

He slid down the bank to the water's edge, picking up a three-foot tree branch as he scruffed along the rocky terrain, feet slipping, to better position himself. This time, when the fish came back to shore, he pulled hard on the line with his left hand, while holding the tree branch over his head, ready to strike.

As soon as the fish burst through the water, chomping its oversized mouth, about a foot in diameter, Rivers slammed the tree branch down against the fish head, striking with such force that the fish instantly went limp. He quickly pulled it onto the shore and hit it again to be certain. Then he fell back against the sloping ground, his chest heaving. The fish was a magnificent specimen of prehistoric river life, with whiskers almost two-feet in length.

After catching his breath, he dragged the fish up the slope to the bank and then retrieved his bow and remaining two arrows. He attempted to remove the arrow in the fish, but it was embedded too deeply, so he left it where it was, glinting in the sunlight like a miniature harpoon.

Suddenly, something caught his eye in his peripheral vision.

Movement to his right. He looked back through the trees and saw someone walking in his direction. Was it Shelly? He strained to shape a recognizable face from the fleeting shadows that obscured the person's features. Wasn't Shelly in her bikini when he last saw her? Whoever this was had on jeans, he was pretty sure of that.

As the person got closer, Rivers was able to make out facial features. It was the man he'd seen in the Mud Pie Café with Shelly.

Trent Boggs.

55

The first thing that Agent Cefalu saw when he opened his eyes was darkness. At first, he wasn't sure he was even alive. His last waking memory was of being strangled. Was it possible he'd survived? Or was he dead—and was his mind playing tricks on him as his brain cells shut down?

He felt a sudden pain in the back of his neck. No, he was alive all right. Dead men don't hurt. He was pretty sure of that. It took awhile, but he managed to free himself from the rope.

Then he remembered. He was being strangled when he blacked out. His first instinct was to reach for his pistol. It was missing. So were his cell and his Secret Service ID. He walked over to the clearing, where he had watched him build a fire. The fire was cold and the campsite had been vacated. He got a sick feeling in the pit of his stomach. He'd been outsmarted by a punk.

He walked back through the woods to the point where he'd first entered and he crossed the river and made his way through the tall grass to his car. He checked out the tires. They were fine. Luckily, the man hadn't taken his car keys. He put the key in the ignition. It cranked on the first turnover. He wondered why he hadn't disabled his car. Probably because he turned around and went back the way he'd come and didn't see his car.

He pulled his car off into the tall grass and turned around and headed back to the house where Doe had stopped. Her car was gone. The white van was nowhere to be seen. He got out of his car and knocked on the front door.

Mrs. Peterson opened the door, a big smile on her face.

"Hello, I'm a friend of Doe's. Has she gone back to Memphis yet?"

Mrs. Peterson eyed him suspiciously.

"She told me that she was going to spend the night here and I hoped to catch her before she left." He wanted to ask if anything unusual had happened last night, but he didn't want to make her any more suspicious than she already was.

"Thank you," he said, turning. "Have a nice day."

"When I talk to her, I'll tell you stopped by."

"Thanks."

Agent Cefalu drove to the nearest town and pulled over at a payphone to call Preston. It was a wretched phone booth, covered with graffiti and dried fluids, some of which looked like blood. He was relieved when he heard a familiar voice at the other end of the line. He wasted no time getting to the point.

"I've got some bad news. I'm still in Arkansas, but I lost the man I was tailing. Doe Peterson has gone back to Memphis and I'm headed there now."

"Where are you calling from?"

"Payphone."

"Why aren't you using your cell?"

Agent Cefalu paused.

"Well . . . to tell you the truth, I was keeping the subject under surveillance when I dropped off to sleep. When I woke, he was choking me and I passed out. By the time I came to, he was gone, along with my gun, my ID and my cell. I just spoke to the girl's mother and she said she'd returned to Memphis. So apparently nothing happened last night. I have no idea where either of them are, though I assume he's still following her."

"He's got you cell," said Preston matter of factly.

"How do you know?"

"Because I intercepted a call he made to her using your phone."

"Really. Why did he call her?"

"He pretended to be you."

Agent Cefalu didn't sigh, he was much too professional to do that, but Preston could feel him freeze at the other end of the line. That was every federal agent's nightmare. After a moment, he said, "What did he want from her?"

"He told her that he Secret Service was aware of the threats against her and he wanted to meet with her at 7 p.m. at the Carlton Hotel to go over the details of the case with her."

"He's going to kill her and try to blame it on me."

"No, he's not going to kill her. You are going to stop him from doing that."

"Yes, of course."

"Where are they supposed to meet at the hotel?"

"From what I understand it has one of those exterior glass enclosed elevators. He told her to ride the elevator until he met up with her."

"The son of a bitch."

"I'm counting on you, Cefalu."

"Don't worry. I won't let anything happen to her. I promise."

After he turned off his phone, Preston sat for a long time, looking out at the Vegas skyline. *This is all a learning experience for me* he thought. *Not just the part about locating my daughter. Becoming a father to someone I don't even know. A stranger. That's hard enough. But also the part about giving up my life. We walk through life thinking that we understand what life is all about. Trust me, we don't. I don't figure I'm much different than other people. I've always thought about death in the back of my mind, but always in the context of it being like a dental appointment, something to be dreaded, but also something that I will somehow get through. That's not true. Death is not like a dental appointment. Death is the one thing in life that you can't get through. It is the end of everything that you know.*

Preston watched the people on the street below. How he envied them. They would carry on with their twisted, corrupt lives long after his body had turned to dust. Someone else would live in the penthouse. Someone with a totally different perspective on life. Someone with different secrets.

After killing a glass of scotch and then doubling over in pain, Preston went into the computer room and logged onto Mack 222. He'd gotten in the habit of checking the world's messages, like someone who compulsively checks his voicemail every thirty minutes or so. It was a bit much, and he knew that, but he really didn't give a damn. Right off, he saw something that made his heart race.

There was a phone call from **Agent Cefalu** to **Faith Holiday.**

Preston listened in, realizing instantly that the man's voice did not belong to Agent Cefalu. He recognized the voice. It was the same voice that called Doe to set up a meeting at the Carlton Hotel. Why would the man who stole Cefalu's cell have reason to call Faith Holiday?

" . . . **killed an agent** that got in the way. I've got his **gun** and his phone and his ID. Listen, this has turned out to be bigger than you told me it would be. I'm going to need more money. That's all there is to it."

"Fine. Whatever you want. Did you make the agent's death look like an accident?"

Long pause. "To tell you the truth, it wasn't possible to do that. He followed me. It was either him or me. Didn't have time to make it look like something else."

"That's bad. Do you think he can be linked to the girl?"

"Not a chance," he said, knowing full well that it was a lie.

"That's good. You know you have to make the girl's **death** look like an accident for sure?"

"Oh, yeah. No problem. Got to go. Just saw her drive up. Check with you later."

Preston logged off Mack 222, a sick feeling in his stomach. He rushed into the bathroom just in time to empty his guts into the toilet bowl. The entire time he was throwing up, he thought *If I save one, do I save the other . . . and if I lose one, do I lose the other?*

56

When Doe arrived at the Carlton Hotel parking lot, she was hesitant to get out of her car. There was a lot of activity in and around the hotel, but she didn't know who she could trust. She saw a young couple drive up in a pickup truck and she got out and walked close behind them into the hotel lobby.

The desk clerk, a young man with a punk haircut, smiled at her and shouted, halfway across the room, "Can I help you with anything?"

Doe didn't return the shout. Instead, she walked over to the desk and told him that she was there to meet someone.

"I know you," said the desk clerk.

Doe looked at him, trying to place his face.

"Oh, I don't mean personally. I've seen your pictures. I've got some of them taped on my wall at home."

"That's nice."

"My favorite is the one of you in a red swimsuit on the boat."

"I like that one, too."

"It's super cool."

"Thank you for offering to help," she said, walking away.

"Let me know if you need anything," he shouted after her.

Doe cringed. She positively loved modeling. She was not shy about showing her body. Her problem was not with the modeling, but with the finished product. She could not bear the thought of someone actually looking at her photographs, especially the ones that showed her body. The desk clerk made her acutely aware of that. She wondered exactly what he did while he looked at her pictures. Maybe she didn't really want to know. She looked around the lobby. She didn't see anyone who looked like a Secret Service agent, though she wasn't really all that sure what one would look like.

She looked at her watch. Six forty-five. She was fifteen minutes early.

After a few minutes, she realized that the desk clerk was staring at her. She moved to another chair so that her back was turned to the front desk. She watched people come and go. Couples with families. Couples with lust. Men in dark suits who looked like business executives. Women moving about in pairs or threesomes. Hotel staff, most of them black or Hispanic. She saw no other women who were obviously single. She hoped someone didn't mistake her for a hooker. She cringed as she watched people go by.

When did everyone get so fat?

Doe didn't often feel sorry for herself, but she did now. *Why do things like this happen to me and not other people?* She wondered if there might be something seriously wrong with her. Something that made her a target for bad things. Her sessions with Dr. Mann had made her feel better about herself. But she couldn't help but feel that there was a hole in her soul somewhere, a defect of some kind.

She loved her parents dearly, yet she couldn't embrace them without feeling a deep sadness for what she'd lost in life, even though she didn't know what that loss was. It didn't make sense to her, which is why her life didn't make sense to her. For a long time, she thought that her modeling success would fill in that hole, but it never did, never even came close.

Doe sighed. She despised waiting, not because her time was more important than anyone else's, but because it forced her to think about things she'd rather not think about.

Hours seemed to go by, but each time she looked at her watch, she realized that the hours passed in one-minute increments. Five to seven. Four to seven. Three to seven. Two to seven. Careful not to look in the direction of the front desk, she walked across the lobby to the elevator and pushed the up button.

A middle-aged couple appeared behind her from nowhere.

When the door opened, the elevator was empty. She got into the elevator, followed by the couple. She pushed the button for the twentieth floor. They pushed the button for the sixth floor. The elevator bumped up one floor to the mezzanine. The door opened.

Into the elevator walked television celebrity Bud Phillips and his lovely wife, Candace. Phillips lived in Memphis but flew to Los Angeles every two weeks to tape segments of his popular game show, *Spinning Wheel*. Candace clutched a toy poodle in her

231

arms. Phillips looked at the elevator panel and saw that the light already was on for floor twenty.

The elevator went to the sixth floor and stopped. The middle-aged couple got off and the door closed. Philips looked at Doe and smiled. She wondered if she should ask him about job opportunities on his show, but then thought better of it. She wondered if he thought she was pretty enough to be a host on his show.

Up purred the elevator.

Breaking the silence, Candace said, "It's so quiet, I can't stand it!"

Bud looked at his wife and said nothing.

Candace looked at the poodle and said, speaking in tortured baby talk, "Now you be *goooood* while I'm gone. Don't do anything I wouldn't do."

The elevator reached the twentieth floor and Bud held the door open for his wife, who walked past him without a word. Still holding the door, he looked at Doe and said, "After you."

"I'm going back down," said Doe. "I forgot something."

Bud stepped out of the elevator and allowed the door to close.

As soon as the door closed, Doe pushed the lobby button. Once it started moving, she turned to look out the rear of the elevator. The sun was low in the sky, about an hour from sunset, and it cast a reddish hue onto the high-rise buildings on the horizon. Doe didn't feel entirely comfortable in the elevator. She knew it was safe, but she couldn't help but feel as if she was standing on a precipice. The parking lot looked so very far away.

The elevator went all the way down to the lobby before it stopped again. A man with a briefcase entered first, followed by a man with a shaved head, who stepped to the rear of the elevator without saying a word or selecting a floor.

The man with the briefcase pushed button six and gazed at the floor as the elevator purred upward.

Bing!

The man stepped out of the elevator and the door closed behind him.

"Miss Peterson?" asked the man at the rear of the elevator.

Doe smiled and offered her hand.

"You must be Agent Cefalu."

232

"Yes," he said, nodding.

"Could I see your identification, please?"

"Certainly." He showed her the badge, but folded the ID so that she could not see the photograph.

57

Rivers crouched down behind a tree, watching. Trent's right hand swung with a greater arc than his left hand. Was it because he had a pistol or an ax in the right hand, giving it greater weight?

What in the hell is going on here? he thought.

He had no answers, but he had a clear reading of the man's threatening body language. When a man aims to kill you, there's a certain walk he has as he approaches, a deliberate stride that's unmistakable in its intent. Film directors have made a fortune off that walk. You'd know it if you saw it.

Rivers had seen enough. He grabbed his bow and retreated along the bank. Tree branches slapped hard against his face, with a total disregard for the urgency of his mission, leaving small cuts and bruises on his cheeks and forehead. Every few steps he turned back to look at his pursuer. His clothing was drenched, his shirt sticking to his chest. There was primeval wildness in his eyes, something of greater impact than color or pupil size. He looked like a man possessed.

Rivers ran as fast as he could through the thick brush, wondering if the man had spotted him yet. Question asked. Question answered. A gunshot rang out. Rivers had no idea how close the bullet came to hitting him. He kept running, his feet striking the ground with loud smacks that kept him rolling forward to an uncertain future.

There was a second gunshot.

He felt nothing. He hoped he wasn't hit. He'd counseled war veterans who'd been shot, but continued on with their mission, unaware of their wound. He hoped he wasn't one of those people.

Up ahead, he saw a rise capped off with a flat rock. That was where he'd make his last stand. For some reason, he found his footing slippery, as if he'd been running through water. He clawed and scratched his way to the top of the rise and lay on his stomach so that he could look down on the path he knew the intruder would have to take. He couldn't see him yet, but he knew he would be there soon. He removed his second arrow from the brace and threaded it and lay his bow flat against the rock, ready to be fired.

When Trent came into view, he was surprised that he was moving along in a slow jog, not running full out. He was right about his right hand. It contained a gun. He knew he had no choice. He sighted his arrow at Trent's chest and released it. Somewhere along the way, it was deflected by a tree branch, sending it veering off to the left.

Trent saw the arrow miss and he looked up at the rock, spotting Rivers. He grinned and pressed on, casting off an air on invincibility.

Rivers threaded his third—and final—arrow onto his bowstring. As he did so, Trent stopped and raised his pistol and pointed it at Rivers. He fired. The bullet slammed into the rock less than a yard away from its target. He fired a second time. This time the bullet was so close that it sprayed crushed stone onto Rivers' face.

Thankful for a stationary target, Rivers pulled back his bow, sighted his arrow and released it, the string rubbing painfully against the tender skin on his forearm. He watched with amazement as the arrow struck Trent in the center of his chest, causing him to drop to his knees, look up at him with amazement, and then topple over onto his side.

Rivers pulled himself up and noticed that his leg was covered with blood. He pulled out his knife and cut away his pants leg and saw that one of Trent's bullets had passed through the fleshy past of his calf. There was an entry wound and an exit wound. It bled, but not profusely, so he felt confident that he was in no immediate danger.

When he reached Trent, he took his pulse to see if he still was alive. He wasn't sure if he had a pulse or not. His arrow had struck the upper right quadrant of his chest, probably severing a major artery. There was something grotesque about the way the arrow complimented the Grateful Dead T-shirt, as if it were part of the design.

That's my shirt he thought. *Did he steal that, too?*

Once he checked Trent, his thoughts immediately went to Shelly. Had he killed her? Did she know his intentions? Was she a coconspirator to his murder? His emotions were a complex blend of concern and anger.

Taking his bow with him, he retraced his steps, running as fast as he could manage with an injured leg. Shelly loomed in his thoughts like a giant balloon being tossed about by the wind. One he couldn't imagine living without.

58

Doe looked at the Secret Service badge and nodded her approval.

"What do we do next?"

Tony reached over and pushed twenty.

"There is a conference room on the twentieth where we can have some privacy without being seen."

"Fine." Agent Cefalu was younger than she thought he would be, but he seemed very competent. She was already feeling better about her situation. She took a deep breath and felt her shoulders relax. Even so, she wondered if she should have told Dr. Mann about the meeting.

"This is a fine city you have here," he said.

"Thanks," she said, and then laughed. "It is a fine city, but I'm afraid that I had nothing to do with it."

"You live here — and that certainly adds to the overall beauty of the city."

Doe blushed, something she didn't do often. Probably because he was a representative of the federal government and she felt intimidated. He wasn't at all what she expected. She imagined a Secret Service agent to be more distinguished, and to have . . . well, more hair. She noticed his earring.

"I didn't know government workers could wear earrings," she said. "Is that something new?"

Tony's hand instinctively went to his ear.

"Oh, this — it helps when I go undercover. Most people think the same way you do."

"I didn't mean anything by it. It looks fine to me."

"I understand."

Bing!

Twentieth floor. Tony politely held the door open for her and then followed her into the hallway.

"Which way?" she asked.

"Over here," he said.

The entire floor had only two suites. At the end of the hallway was a luxuriously furnished conference room that resembled a smoking room in a gentleman's club. The furnishings were plush and the lighting was subdued. The walls were punctuated with several oversized paintings of Southern scenes such as riverboats, cotton fields, and stately mansions with expansive verandas.

Tony led her into the room and closed the door.

"Just sit anywhere," he said.

Doe looked around the room. If she sat on the sofa he might sit next to her and she didn't want that. She chose a chair adjacent to the sofa. As she settled into the chair, he walked over to a glass door that opened onto a balcony. He seemed a little nervous. He turned around and pointed across the room, "There's a bar over there. Would you care for something to drink?"

"I don't think so."

Tony went over to the bar and poured himself a drink. Doe thought that was odd. Were Secret Service agents supposed to drink on the job? He found a couple of ice cubes to put in his drink. Then he sat on the couch. He seemed mildly annoyed about something.

"So what happens next?" asked Doe with trusting innocence.

Tony sipped his drink, looking at her over the glass rim.

"We're close to making an arrest," he said, wiping his mouth with his sleeve. "The important thing is to protect you, without tipping off the suspect."

"So you have a suspect in mind?"

Tony nodded.

"Who is it—someone I know?"

"I would tell you if I could."

"But who would want to kill me?"

"You'd be surprised." He reached into his coat pocket and pulled out a set of folded papers. He unfolded the papers and put them on the table next to Doe, along with a pen. "I need for you to sign these papers so that we can get a search warrant to enter the suspect's apartment."

"What is this?" she asked, picking up the papers and reading the cover sheet marked *Affidavit*. The paper, written in legalese, referred to the cold cream that she'd given to Oscar Ross. Second and third sheets were more of the same legalese. The fourth sheet, which contained the line for her signature, was a typed suicide note. Tony figured she'd never read that far—and she didn't.

After reading the first and second pages, she flipped to the fourth page and signed it without reading it. She handed it to Tony, along with the pen.

"Thank you, Miss Peterson. I wish more citizens were like you."

Tony looked up and saw a rapidly changing sky.

"Oh, look," he said, coming to his feet. "What an impressive sunset."

He went to the balcony door and opened it and stepped outside. Over his shoulder, he said, "You've got to see this."

Doe walked over to the door and stepped onto the balcony. The sunset was breathtaking, brilliant fingers of red and gold light embracing the city.

"It *is* beautiful," she said.

Tony moved next to her. She was surprised to feel his hands on her arms. She was about to step away, when she felt his fingers tighten around her biceps, both arms. She turned to look at him and saw a different expression on his face. Before she could speak, he lifted her up off her feet, pushing hard, attempting to leverage her over the rail.

She dug her fingers into the rail and kicked back, hard, her heels striking him in the gut. He tumbled back, tripping over a potted plant, hitting the floor. She dashed from the balcony and ran back through the room, overturning lamps and chairs. By the time Tony got to his feet, she already was at the door.

Once she was outside the apartment, she entered the exit staircase, her high-heeled shoes smacking hard against the concrete steps as she ran as fast as she could, bouncing, holding onto the metal rail to keep her balance. When she reached the thirteenth level, she heard the door slam open on the twentieth floor, erasing any doubt about whether he was pursuing her.

She hoped she wouldn't fall. Everything about her was either concrete or steel. By the eighteenth floor she was taking the steps two and three at a time, feeling herself fall forward but holding onto the railing so tightly that the forward motion of the body never went past the point where she'd lose her balance. In the background, she heard the *thump thump thump* of his footsteps.

After five flights, she exited onto the fifteenth floor and ran straight to the elevator. She hit the down button. Her heart pounded. She looked over at the exit door. Then back to the elevator door. Turning her head at one second intervals. Finally, she heard the exit door slam open at the same instant that she heard the elevator *bing!*

She didn't bother to look again. She stepped onto the elevator and hit the lobby button, holding her breath that the door would close before he could stop it. There was a man already on the elevator. Middle aged. His eyes brightened when he saw her, but she was too terrified to notice.

Then the door started closing. She saw his shadow on the opposite wall as he ran to catch the door. He was too late. The door closed shut and the elevator started down. The man standing behind her said nothing.

The elevator only dropped one floor before it stopped again. This time it was for a man and a woman with three children, all of them under eight years of age.

"Come on," said the man to the children. "We don't have all day. "You're going to make us late."

A little girl about five dropped one of her toys. She leaned over to pick it up, but her tiny fingers were unable to lift it from the floor. One of the other children started crying, protesting getting onto the elevator.

"It's all right," said the mother. "It won't hurt you."

She looked at Doe and said, "He's afraid because of the glass."

Oh, please hurry up thought Doe.

The woman picked up the toy and gave it to the little girl. Then she reached over and grasped the little boy's hand. There was a third child, but the man didn't attempt to rein him in, choosing instead to hold the door open. To the woman's dismay, Doe stepped out into the hallway and grabbed the third child's hand, pulling her, a little too hard perhaps, into the elevator.

"I don't think that was necessary," said the woman, glaring at Doe.

"Sorry — I was just trying to help."

Once all the children were on the elevator, the man stepped away from the door, allowing it to close. The woman talked to him constantly about the children, but he maintained an expressionless look on his face. Didn't even bother to say, "Yes, dear." Just looked at her with a blank stare.

The elevator bumped down another floor and stopped.

This time, when the door opened, Tony was standing there, a wild look on his face. First he glared at Doe, who stood frozen in place. Then he looked at the man behind her, a look of shocked surprise on his face. His hand shot into his coat pocket and emerged with a pistol that he pointed at the middle-aged man.

The woman screamed.

"Ohmygodohmygodohmygod."

The children screamed, and the man backed into the corner.

Before Tony could fire the pistol, perhaps slowed for a split second by the screams of the children, the middle-aged man lunged forward and grabbed Tony's arm, attempting to disarm him. Tony fell forward and the door closed behind him.

The two men went around and around the elevator as the men slammed each other into the glass walls. Back and forth. The pistol fired, shattering one of the elevator walls, eliciting screams from both Doe and the woman with the children. The father of the children did nothing to help. Just stood there in shock.

Doe glanced outside, seeing nothing but dark sky. She wanted to help the middle aged man but she didn't know what to do. After a particularly violent shove back and forth, the men fell to the floor of the elevator.

There was another gunshot.

Everyone froze. The elevator bumped to a stop at the lobby floor. *Bing!*

No one attempted to leave. Instead, they watched the middle-aged man slowly get up from the floor and look at the blood on his shirt. Tony lay lifeless at his feet. The man turned to Doe and said, "Miss Peterson, I'm the real Agent Cefalu. Everything is all right now."

Doe breathed for the first time in fifteen floors.

59

When Rivers first ran into the clearing and saw Shelly stretched out on the sand with her hands and legs tied—and seeing no movement—he feared the worst and he approached her with great apprehension.

Her head was turned away, so he could not see her face.

"Shelly," he whispered.

To his surprise, she whipped her head around so that she could see him, her eyes swollen with tears, her beautiful blonde hair turned dirty yellow.

"Rivers! Thank God! I heard the shots . . . and I thought . . ."

Her voice trailed off to a plaintive sigh.

As she spoke, Rivers was already on his knees, using his knife to cut away the leather strips that bound her wrists and ankles.

Once she was freed, she flung her arms around his neck, squeezing him so hard that he toppled over, with her attached. They lay in the sand for a moment, with her kissing every inch of his face, and his hands racing across her back, her arms and her thighs. After a moment, Shelly pulled away from his face, breathless, gazing into his eyes.

"When I heard the shots, I was so sure . . ."

"I've got a leg wound, but . . ."

"Where?"

"Right here," he said pointing to his leg.

She sat up and examined the wound.

"Went clean through. Just a flesh wound. We'll put antiseptic on it when we get back. You should be just fine. Didn't you get a tetanus last year?"

"Yes, I think so. Before we went on that trip."

He gazed into her eyes, for the first time allowing his fear to show.

"He tried to kill me. I just knew he'd killed you."

"Where is he now?"

She looked away at the tree line, her eyes wrinkled in fear.

"He's dead," said Rivers. "I killed him with an arrow."

Shelly hugged him again, burying her face into his shoulder.

"There's something I've got to tell you."

"No, no you don't."

He knew at that instant that he would forgive her. Hearing the details of her infidelity would only make forgiveness more difficult. What she did hurt him deeply, but the alternative to forgiveness—living his life without her—would create a pain so deep he didn't even want to contemplate it, not for a minute.

"You don't know what it is."

"Yes, I do."

He reached into his back pocket and pulled out the photograph.

"What is this?"

"My patient, Doe Peterson, found it in her boyfriend's dresser."

"But I don't understand. How did my picture get in her boyfriend's dresser?"

"Her boyfriend was Trent Boggs."

"Oh, my God!" said Shelly, her hands shooting to her mouth. "But where did he get the picture? I certainly didn't give it to him."

"He must have stolen it from the house."

Shelly's eyes brightened.

"Before he left me here tied up, he told me that he was the one who broke into our house and rigged your toothbrush."

"I figured as much."

Rivers and Shelly lay on the beach for a while, saying nothing. Holding each other. Each silently reaffirming to themselves that their love was stronger than any threat to that love.

Finally, Rivers sat up and said, "We've got to go back. I've got to call the police."

"Didn't you bring a cell?"

"I forgot."

The sun set moments before they shoved off from the island. On the boat ride back down river, Shelly stood next to Rivers, her arm around his waist. Above the roar of the motor, she shouted, "I hope you know that what I did will never happen again."

Rivers smiled at her. "I know."

Most of the ride back was in darkness, with the moonlight bouncing off the rough water. The wind blew from the south, rolling the waves back into whitecaps as the river ran counter to the wind. The boat rose and sank with each swell, bouncing them up and then down like an amusement park ride.

When they spotted their inlet and turned into calmer water, they saw a light moving down the bluff toward the dock.

"Oh, no," said Shelly. "What now?"

Rivers cut the throttle and steered the boat into the dock. He secured the boat and they got out of the boat to meet their unexpected visitor. The light flashed across their eyes and then moved off to the side.

"Hope I didn't frighten you," said a voice that Rivers instantly recognized.

Jack McCain walked out onto the dock and gave Shelly a cursory hug and shook hands with Rivers. From the looks on their faces, he knew that something was wrong. "Are you folks OK?"

"It's a long story," said Rivers. "But—yes—we're fine."

Jack looked at Rivers' blood-caked leg. "What's with that?"

"He got shot," said Shelly, putting her arm around his waist.

Jack stared at him, waiting for an explanation.

"It's a long story, Jack. A man tried to kill me. I shot him with my bow. I need to go inside and call the police and tell them what happened."

"I don't know what to say," said Jack. "What is this all about?"

"I'll tell you all about it later. To tell you the truth, I'm damn glad to see you. You've had more experience with the police than I have. I may need your help."

"Whatever I can do, you've got it."

Jack saw that both of them were a little wobbly on their feet, so he walked between them, an arm around each waist, keeping them steady as they ascended the bluff. Once they got inside the house and Rivers called the police, they sat on the back porch and popped the caps on several beers, staring out into the night sky as they waited for the first hint of a police siren.

Rivers looked at Jack, a curious expression on his face. "What, may I ask, were you doing on our dock at this time of the night?"

Jack smiled. "Thought you needed to know about something that will be in tomorrow's newspaper."

"What's that?"

"That patient of yours, Doe Peterson—she's been through hell."

Rivers' relaxed mood suddenly changed.

"What's wrong," he said, concern on his face.

"Remember all those problems you told me that she was having? Turns out she wasn't imagining that someone wanted to kill her. A professional hitman was after her."

"Is she all right?"

"She's fine. But the hitman is not doing so well. He tried to kill her at the Carlton Hotel, but before he could a Secret Service agent nailed him."

"Are you serious?" asked Shelly.

"And you're sure she's OK?"

"She's upset as hell, but who wouldn't be. Otherwise, she's fine."

Rivers looked at Shelly. "I probably need to call her tonight. Certainly, she will need to talk to me in the morning."

"Do you think this has a connection to Trent?" asked Shelly.

"I know Trent," said Jack. "What does this have to do with him?"

"Believe me, you don't want to know."

60

Faith Holiday was sitting in a movie theater, when a man entered the row behind her and sat slightly to her right. It was a classic movie theater, where both classic and newer cult films were shown twenty-four hours a day.

On this day, the Paul Verhoeven film, *Showgirls*, starring Elizabeth Berkley and Gina Gershon, was showing in consecutive runs. She was engrossed in the scene in which Nomi Malone, a wannabe showgirl from the boondocks, gets a job as a hyperactive, somewhat obsessive lap dancer at the Cheetah Club, where she meets Cristal Connors, a superstar showgirl with lesbian fantasies who has come slumming to the Cheetah Club to check out the talent.

Faith never noticed that a man sat behind her. They were the only two people in the theater. If she had turned around, she would've recognized the man. Eddie, broken knuckles and all — the stuff of hardcore nightmares.

Faith had seen *Showgirls* twenty-six times. She identified with Nomi more than she was willing to admit, even to herself. When she got her money, she planned to finance a movie similar to *Showgirls*, only her movie would be autobiographical. She munched on popcorn and sipped a supersized soft drink, the air smelling of she didn't know what. Breakfast. She promised herself that she'd eat a decent lunch. Maybe a salad or something.

The man stared at her, his arms folded across his chest. He ignored the movie, even when Nomi got naked and expertly twirled herself about a damp brass pole. If anyone had been watching him at that moment, which they weren't, they would've thought it odd that a man in his prime wasn't interested in naked Nomi. Definite red flag.

Faith made mental notes that she wanted her star to downplay her role, even if it meant coming off as mousey. Being Bette Davis hyper is all right, she decided, but not when you're naked. Naked hyper doesn't work on screen.

Better to be subdued, capitalizing on a woman's natural curves. Breasts were never designed to express anger. Was it her imagination, or were Nomi's breasts mad as hell?

Faith bit her lip. Maybe it's a mistake to be dogmatic about art. A hyperactive naked woman with a meat cleaver might just work, angry breasts or not. She made a mental note not to take herself so seriously.

Faith hated her own body. Her legs were too short. Her boob job had cost plenty and everyone agreed that they were spectacular, but she didn't like the way they felt when she lay on her stomach. Her ass had a nice shape, but it was too wide, or at least it looked too wide in the mirror. No doubt about it. She needed to lose about ten pounds.

There's a difference in having a body that men will die for and one that they will kill for. Most girls out of high school have the former. Only a few women have the latter. She knew she didn't. Sometimes it made her sick to think about it. Once she got her money, she planned to have a complete makeover.

Showgirls tugged at her heart. Not so much for the movie, but for the actress who played Nomi. She identified with that girl. All she wanted was one big break — a fair chance to be somebody.

Tears trickled down her cheeks.

Without saying a word, Eddie pulled his arms apart — each hand containing piano wire wrapped around the palms — and he swiftly lifted the wire over Faith's head and brought his hands down, twisting the wire around her neck. The soft drink and popcorn fell to the floor. Instinctively, her hands shot to her neck, trying to worm her fingers beneath the wire, but it was no use.

Faith twisted in her seat, arching her back slightly, Eddie's tightening grip lifting her slightly out of her seat. Feet tapping frantically against the floor. She made a gurgling sound. Eddie released her and she slumped forward in her seat, a painful little smile stuck on her face. He pulled her head back against the seat and turned it to the side so that a passerby would think she was asleep.

On the screen, Cristal taunted Nomi, demanding a private performance, the background music building with anticipation. One woman sensually licking her lips with a viper-like tongue.

The other scanning the audience with wild eyes, as if she was considering a violent act, her breasts cocked and loaded.

As it turned out, Nomi's angry breasts were the last thing that Faith saw on this planet. Not a bad thing. Not a good thing, either.

Eddie left while the music still played. Only an idiot would wait until the music stopped. He had a plane to catch.

61

The Magnolia Casino was located in Mississippi, across the state line from Memphis. Since Tennessee didn't allow casinos, something about them being a pipeline for laundered drug money, Mississippi was happy to oblige, giving the Magnolia Casino a permit to occupy land that ran flush with the Tennessee state line. Memphians could get from downtown to the casino about as quick as they could get to the other side of town in the opposite direction.

Harry and Joseph Blackberry owned a controlling interest in the casino. Its legitimate income was close to one million dollars a week, but they were able to run three, sometimes four times that amount in drug revenue through the casino. Who was to say the money didn't come from the blackjack tables and the slots? It was a sweet deal for all involved. The Blackberry brothers were untouchable in Mississippi, close friends with both the governor and the U.S. attorney.

The Blackberry brothers lived a life of privilege, protected by a network of Tennessee and Mississippi elected officials to whom they'd supplied extravagant campaign financing for many years. Harry's favorite quip was, "Is this a great country, or what?" Everyone always laughed whenever he said it. When it came to politics, he knew that *everything* was for sale.

The Blackberry brothers like to dine early, around 5 o'clock. On this day, the guests started arriving late in the afternoon, early enough to have a couple of drinks before dinner. The Heritage Room was more than a simple hotel room. It was a suite of rooms, the most prominent of which was a banquet hall, furnished and decorated as if it had been snatched from the stone walls of a medieval castle. Shields, swords, lances, red and royal blue velvet drapes, dark mahogany furnishings polished to a high gloss.

Well dressed women, most of them beautiful in a cheap sort of way, milled about in the sitting room just off the banquet hall. There was talk of children, country clubs, jogging trails, and restaurants. Discussion was open to any subject, except their husbands' various business interests.

In the next room, which was stripped of all furnishings, the men gathered, talking in small groups as workmen brought in box after box and stacked them in the center of the room, neatly so that the edges did not overlap.

Harry and Joseph Blackberry stood near the door, looking every bit like department store managers checking in new inventory. Sometimes they talked about going legit. But the problem with that was that once they went legit, their protection would vanish overnight, and it'd just be a matter of time before a competitor used their past against them. In their line of work, quitting was not an option.

Brown boxes sealed with masking tape. Could have been shoes or purses or jeans. Nothing about the boxes gave any clue that they were filled with marijuana. Harry elbowed Joseph. "Look at that," he said, indicating the boxes. "You never know what's in a box until you open it."

Joseph frowned.

"I don't like it, Harry. This cargo was supposed to be moved out of the Mound Tibido airport."

The cargo had been brought into the country from South America aboard an overnight carrier and then trucked to the Mound Tibido airport, where a leased jet was supposed to pick it up and take it to Las Vegas. Unfortunately, the jet went down in a violent thunderstorm en route to the airport.

Harry explained, "I don't like it either, but we couldn't leave it at the Mound Tibido airport."

Joseph nodded, accepting the situation for what it was, but not liking it.

Harry said, "When we were kids, did you ever dream that we could be as successful as we are?"

"Not in a million years."

Harry leaned forward and looked into the sitting room. Then to Joseph he said, "Have you seen Trent? I need to talk to him."

"I haven't seen him. I can get him on the phone."

Harry nodded. "It'll wait."

Across the room Eddie spotted them and walked over to where they were standing. He looked wrinkled. Hot and out of sorts.

"Just got in," he said. "It was a hell of a flight. Big thunder storms over Oklahoma. Lost a fucking engine. There was some talk of landing on the Interstate in Arkansas, but they made it all the way in to Memphis."

Both brothers nodded and smiled. They were set in their ways and didn't much care for the out-of-towners that intruded in their lives, but they were necessary to do business and there was little that they could do except tolerate them the best they could.

"We were expecting you earlier," said Joseph.

"Sorry about that," said Eddie. "Had a local matter to take care of in Vegas."

"We understand."

Eddie thought of something he wanted to ask, but he hesitated, afraid it would make him look bad. He wanted to ask the Blackberry brothers if they'd ever seen *Showgirls*. On the flight to Memphis he couldn't stop wondering about how the movie ended. That's one of the things that he hated about his job. Too much unfinished business. He'd just rent the movie when he got back home.

"Did you guys ever get that problem solved?"

Joseph asked, "What problem is that?"

"You know, the one where someone had a hit out on somebody."

Harry shook his head. "We're still working on that."

"I never heard anything that would help you out any."

Eddie didn't have a lot of social skills. Not knowing what else to say, he cracked his knuckles, a gesture that made the Blackberry brothers cringe.

When it was announced that dinner was about to be served, everyone felt a sense of relief, even the wives who had long since run out of things to talk about. Harry looked at the man supervising the cargo.

"How much longer?"

"Two more boxes, sir. Then we'll be done."

Harry nodded his approval.

The Blackberry brothers went into the sitting room and gathered their wives, with Eddie stumbling along in their wake, not certain what was expected of him, other than driving the cargo back to Vegas in a rental truck. He didn't especially like being around the Blackberry brothers. They were pretentious. Not his kind of people. His Vegas bosses came from more rugged stock.

The banquet table was wide enough at the end for the Blackberry brothers and their wives to sit side-by-side and present themselves as the dinner hosts. The brothers pulled out chairs for their wives, a gesture so elegant in its presentation that it made Eddie sick to his stomach. The brothers had always reminded him of the neurotic, foppish brothers on the television show *Frasier*. He didn't figure he'd ever get over that. In the old days, bosses were tough, able to defend themselves in a fist fight, not afraid to get their hands dirty.

Eddie sat at the other end of the table and tried to stay out of everyone's way. As far as he knew, he was the only heat-packing guest allowed a chair at the table. On the fringes of the room armed bodyguards for the Blackberry brothers and various guests milled about, trying to stay on top of things. It was boring work, the most challenging aspect of which was presenting a convincing aura of perpetual alertness.

The Blackberry brothers stood in unison and welcomed their guests. Once their remarks were concluded, a swarm of white-jacketed servers descended upon the guests, taking orders for beverages and appetizers.

Some of the younger guests sat timidly with their fingers laced in their laps, but most of the older guests were boisterous and totally at ease as they exchanged stories with those seated around them.

Life was good for the Blackberry brothers.

Suddenly, there was an ear-smashing explosion.

All conversation stopped. Everyone froze where they were. Then there were gunshots, prompting the bodyguards to run toward the sitting room. All the diners, except Eddie, rose, their eyes wild with fright.

Eddie, who understood exactly what was happening, kept his hands in his lap. Whatever was going on, he reasoned was *their* problem, not his.

FBI agents swarmed into the storage room, returning fire from several men with automatic rifles. The *rat-a-tat-tat-tat* bark of the weapons sounded worse than it really was, but two men were taken down by agents before the others in the room dropped their weapons. Someone called for an ambulance.

As agents cuffed the men not taken down, other agents poured into the sitting room, where a bearded bodyguard stood with his hands raised, and then they rushed into the banquet hall, where horrified guests continued to scream and run about the room, some of them with their hands flailing about in the air.

Eddie attempted to raise his arms, but his knotty knuckles bumped against the table in such a way that it appeared that he was lifting a weapon from beneath the tablecloth. An FBI agent fired one shot, striking unlucky Eddie in the center of the forehead. His head kicked back, dangled over the back of the chair.

An FBI agent, wearing an identifying sweater, eyed the gathering and said, "I have warrants for Harry and Joseph Blackberry."

No one stepped forward.

Irritated, the agent said, "Will the Blackberry brothers please step forward?"

A woman in the corner lowered one hand just enough to point to a door across the room. In a whisper, she said, "They're both in there."

The agent signaled for a couple of agents to stand on either side of the door. He stood about ten feet from the door, off to one side. To the gathering, he said, "Does that room have an exit door or a window?"

Someone replied, "No sir. It's a bathroom."

The agent shouted out, "Harry and Joseph Blackberry, this is the FBI. We have you surrounded. Please open the door slowly and come out with your hands in the air."

Inside the bathroom, Harry and Joseph looked at each other with a mixture of horror and disgust. Harry said, "Who the hell tipped them off?"

"I knew it was a mistake to bring that cargo here."

Joseph shook his head.

"What are we going to do now?"

The men sat on toilets that faced each other. Each man had a small caliber pistol in his hand, the kind of weapon women sometimes carry in their purse.

"This is a business, where if you make one mistake you're dead."

"How did we fail?"

"We didn't allow for a plane going down. How many times have we made that run? A thousand. Two thousand. Who would've figured on a plane crash?"

"We should have had backup storage space. We'll do that next time."

"Next time! There is no next time!"

"What do you mean?"

"The feds have enough dope in that storage room to put us away for life."

"If we lose, we'll appeal."

"Sure. But they'll never let us out on bond. They'll say we are a flight risk."

"So what are we going to do?" asked Joseph, a look of fear on his face.

"We had a good run," said Harry, trying to hold his head up with pride. "They can never take that away from us." Harry paused, collecting his thoughts. Finally, he said, "I think you know what we have to do."

Joseph nodded, tears streaming down his cheeks.

"Just tell me what to do."

"I'll point my gun at you. You'll point your gun at me. I'll count to three and we'll put the triggers."

"What if one of us is off on the timing."

"Then the survivor takes his own life."

"OK. Let's do it."

The two men pointed their pistols at each other. Harry's hand was much steadier than his brothers. Before he started counting, Harry said, "I love you, Joseph."

"I love you, too."

One . . . two . . . three.

Outside the bathroom, the agent in charge waited for a response to his demands. There was a gunshot. Then, ten seconds later, there was a second gunshot.

"Let's go!" said the agent in charge to the men on either side of the door. The agent on the left reached across the width of the door and turned the knob, slowly opening the door, while the agent on the right rushed inside.

The Blackberry brothers were visible from outside the bathroom, both sprawled out on the floor. A woman screamed. The Blackberry widows sobbed and comforted each other. Harry's widow called out to no one in particular, "May I call my lawyer?"

62

The deputy sat across the room from Rivers and Shelly, a notepad on her lap. It was the same deputy who investigated Rivers' car accident and the exploding toothbrush.

Rivers couldn't tell by looking at her whether she was embarrassed over her earlier mistakes, but if he'd been a mind reader he'd have known that she wasn't the least bit embarrassed. If a mistake was made on the previous investigations, she was convinced it was because she hadn't been given enough information.

"After you shot Mr. Boggs with an arrow, you left him on the trail. Right?"

"Yes, that's correct," said Rivers.

The deputy shook her head.

"What's wrong?" he asked.

"We found the point of initial impact. The place on the trail where you shot him. There's a big puddle of blood there. But we found the body about two hundred yards away. On the trail that led back to the lake."

"How is that possible?" asked Shelly.

"I don't know," answered the deputy, speaking in a monotone. "Off hand, I'd say it either was because you moved him, or he moved himself."

"I left him right where he fell. He was dead."

"No, he wasn't dead."

"What difference does it make?" asked Shelly. "He's dead now."

The deputy eyed her with bureaucratic disgust.

"It makes a big difference. The law says that if he wasn't dead you had a legal responsibility to administer first aid and then obtain medical care for him. If you didn't, that's a felony offense."

"Felony!" said Rivers. "That's ridiculous. The man was trying to kill me."

"I don't make the laws," she responded. "I just enforce them."

"Does the law say that you have to stop and help people who are trying to kill you?"

The deputy looked puzzled.

"That's a good question," she said. "I'll have to look into that."

"Please do," said Shelly.

The deputy looked about the room, collecting her thoughts.

"I guess, the only question I have left is whether either of you knew Mr. Boggs."

Rivers looked at Shelly.

"I talked to him several times about moving our insurance to his company," Shelly said, looking at Rivers, her eyes begging for forgiveness. "I don't think you knew him at all, did you?"

Rivers shook his head.

"What I don't get," said the deputy, wrinkling her brow, "is what a man who didn't know you would want to kill you. Don't make sense to me."

Rivers glanced at Shelly, who bit her lip. Could she possibly tell the truth? What good would that do, other than satisfy the deputy's curiosity? Shelly did the only thing she could do under the circumstances. She lied.

"I didn't want to say anything, but I've had a problem with him for several weeks. He asked me out and I told him no, that I was married, but he wouldn't take no for an answer and he started stalking me. I think he was the person who sabotaged Rivers' toothbrush and forced him off the road. I think he figured if he could get rid of Rivers, I'd be more receptive to his advances."

"Would you?"

"Would I what?"

"Be more receptive to his advances if your husband was out of the way?"

"Never! Not in a million years!"

The deputy nodded approvingly.

"It's like I always say, there's always something. Now everything makes perfect sense." She closed her note pad and got up. "If I have any more questions, I'll let you know."

"Thank you for everything," said Shelly.

"You bet," said the deputy.

They both walked her to the door and waved to her as she got into her car.

After they closed the door, Shelly put her arm around him and said, "We'll get through this, honey. I promise."

Rivers hugged her back. He knew he would be able to forget, with time.

63

Doe flew to Las Vegas with Agent Cefalu, even though he wouldn't explain why he wanted her to accompany him. He'd saved her life. Why wouldn't she trust him? She was pretty sure that he was who he said he was because when the police arrived at the hotel and asked them both a lot of questions about what'd happened, they treated him with respect and constantly referred to him as Agent Cefalu.

That was good enough for her.

When the plane touched down in Las Vegas, she turned to him and said, "OK, we're here — why did you want me to come?"

"There's someone I want you to meet?"

Doe looked at him suspiciously. She didn't like the way that sounded. Once she went to a party in New York with her photographer and he told her the same thing and introduced her to a notoriously lecherous old man who wasted no time inviting her to his penthouse. She didn't go, of course, but it made her realize that the phrase, "there's someone I want you to meet," almost always has a dirty bottom line.

"Who?" she asked.

"He'll explain when we get there."

"I'm not getting off this plane until you tell me."

Agent Cefalu sighed. Why were young women always so difficult?

"I wish I could tell you everything, but I can't," he explained.

"I at least want a hint."

Agent Cefalu thought *she's so much like her old man it's scary*, but he said, "All I can say is that the person who wants to meet you is a relative."

"A relative?"

Agent Cefalu nodded.

"What kind of relative?"

"Can't say."

"A relative of my adoptive parents?"

"I've already said too much."

Every insecurity Doe had ever felt in her life ganged up on her. She had no doubt that Agent Cefalu would protect her from evildoers. But could he protect her from those who meant her well?

Riddled with self doubt, she followed Agent Cefalu off the plane. Inside the terminal, Doe looked expectantly at each face.

"Not here," said Agent Cefalu.

Doe folded her arms and followed him to the cab, avoiding eye contact as she walked behind him through the crowd.

64

Preston looked out the window with binoculars, his wheelchair pushed flush with the wall. He focused on what he called the airport road. It was the only direct route to his hotel from the airport. He followed each cab headed in his direction, disappointed each time the cab pulled up short and dropped off Hawaiian-shirted tourists in front of a hotel or restaurant.

Preston couldn't remember the last time he'd felt nervous about anything. Or the last time he'd ever felt overlapping emotions of despair and happiness. On this day, he was a nervous wreck, his thoughts alternating between sadness and joy. His body ached as if he'd been pummeled by a heavyweight prizefighter. His health was deteriorating rapidly and he knew he didn't have long to live. Doctors wanted to hospitalize him, but he would have none of that, insisting that how and when he died was his business.

Finally, he saw a cab pass up every hotel and restaurant along the way and continue on to his hotel. The cab pulled up beneath a canopy so that he couldn't see who was inside the car, but he just knew that it was his daughter. He put his binoculars away and rolled over to his entrance door and waited for the buzzer to sound.

Minutes later the intercom buzzed.

"We're here," said Agent Cefalu.

"You know the way," said Preston.

Preston felt unsure of himself. He couldn't decide whether he should wait inside or open the door and roll out into the hallway. *What if she doesn't like me? What if she hates me for abandoning her? What if she's grown into a bitter person?*

He opened the door and rolled into the hallway. His heart raced. His eyes grew moist. His skin tingled. *Dear God, please don't let me die before I meet her!*

The elevator door opened with a resonating *bing!*

Agent Cefalu stepped off first and looked up the hallway, a broad smile on his face. Then she stepped out into the subdued light of the hallway. She paused a moment and then walked toward him, at first keeping step with Agent Cefalu, but then pulling ahead, almost in a run by the time she pulled up just short of the wheelchair, her eyes glistening with tears.

Her hand shot out—slender, graceful, gentle in its promise—and she said, "My name is Doe Peterson."

Preston took her hand, weeping at that point.

"My name is Preston LaGrange . . . and . . . and I'm your father."

Doe pulled her hand away from his and, bending over at the knees, flung her arms around his neck.

"I knew it the moment I saw you."

She knelt beside the wheelchair and took his hand in hers, patting it as if he were a child and she was the mother.

"Are you my guardian angel?"

"Damn right," said Agent Cefalu, who by then had caught up with her.

Agent Cefalu wheeled Preston inside the penthouse with Doe still holding his hand. Once the door was closed, Preston asked, "Do you hate me?"

Doe answered with another hug.

"I have dreamed about you my whole life."

For the next hour, Preston told her everything, the two of them experiencing an astonishing array of emotions that kept them breathless the entire time. Agent Cefalu sat nearby, alternately weeping and grinning as he rode the emotional roller coaster with them.

Finally, Preston glanced at his watch and said, "Cefalu, would you mind going into the guest room and bringing out that item hanging on the door?"

"Sure," he said, and got up and left the room.

Moments later he returned with an elegant black dress and held it up high so that Doe could see it as he approached her.

"Is this for me?" she asked.

"Yes," answered Preston. "There is someplace we've got to go."

"It's beautiful! It looks like a designer gown."

Preston nodded.

65

At the funeral Doe sat between Preston and Agent Cefalu, only six feet away from an open casket that contained a pretty young woman with blonde hair. A young minister stood at a podium off to the side. He was neither happy nor sad. He shuffled through note cards, assembling them in order.

Doe looked around the room. They were the only people in attendance. She wondered if it was unusual in Las Vegas for a funeral to take place inside a casino. She guessed probably not.

An upbeat version of *Amazing Grace* played in the background. The music wasn't what you'd expect to hear in a church. She figured it was probably recorded by the Spinners or the Temptations. Some hip group.

Before the minister started speaking, she leaned over to Preston and whispered, "Who is she?"

Preston hesitated, gathering his nerve. A long moment passed. Then he said, "Your little sister."

Doe looked at him in disbelief. He looked sad, but there were no tears, as there had been when they first met. Was he the father? He'd have to be, wouldn't he? She stared at the woman in the casket. Large bouquets of fragrant white flowers rose up from either side of the coffin. If that was her sister, she bore no resemblance to her. Again, she whispered to Preston, "Are you her father?"

Preston nodded.

"Where is your wife?"

"She passed away quite some time ago."

"Do you have any other children?"

"Only you."

Once the minister began speaking, the three of them sat in silence, each thinking their separate thoughts. Agent Cefalu was thankful for the occasion, primarily because it pained him to see the grief that Faith had brought into Preston's life. She was a troubled woman, but he'd come across a lot of troubled women in his life, and he found it difficult, if not impossible, to feel compassion for any of them. Doe felt mostly confusion. If she felt any grief, it was over her loss. Whoever the woman in the casket was, whatever her faults or shortcomings, she was her only sister, even if she was only a half sister. To an adopted child, a half sister is almost as good as a full sister.

Preston looked at Faith resting peacefully in the casket and he felt a sense of relief that her miserable life was over. Had she moved on to a better place? He sincerely hoped so, but he had his doubts. For so long there'd been only one heart filled with love and hope. God took Faith. Gave him Doe. Yet soon he'd take him away from Doe and there'd still be only one heart filled with love and hope. Where was the justice in that?

On the way to the funeral, Preston wondered how his thoughts would flow once he saw her laid out in the casket. Would he relive Faith's childhood? Her innocence? Would he long for the days when she sat on his knee and looked up at him with respect and admiration, her eyes sparkling with wonderment?

The reality was that the person in the casket seemed like a stranger. He didn't hate her. He didn't love her, either. Not the way a father should. Instead, his thoughts returned to China, even when the minister was droning on about how Faith's life had unfairly been cut short and how much the world had lost by her untimely absence. The single, most indelible image he carried in his heart was the one of Yao Bai with Yao Ta cuddled in her arms. Mother and daughter.

His thoughts drifted back to the times he leaned over and kissed them, first one and then the other, the delicately sweet baby scent lingering with him. He recalled the conversations that he had with Bai about their future together as a family. In youth, dreams are so cheap. So easy to acquire. So difficult to realize.

The memories were vivid. Almost as if he could reach out and touch them. Whispers. Blue skies. Promises. Relics of a past life. It pained him to realize, finally, that the past was like the future—always unattainable in the present. He listened to Doe's breaths, slow and regular. Sitting beside him, it was something real in an unreal world. It didn't exactly make him feel whole again, but neither did it diminish him and he was thankful for that.

Doe envied her father. She longed for memories of their life together, images of the two of them running through the snow or the sun or the water together, but they never existed for her to reach out for.

Just sitting next to him made her heart swell with happiness. She gazed at the casket. Her sister's face was peaceful, almost childlike. The minister still speaking. Dust to dust. Who will take this lost soul? Without thinking, she raised her hand ever so slightly.

66

Preston and Bai walked on a lush hillside, holding hands. A green-scented wind bathed their faces with a whiff of incoming rain. Dark clouds tumbled across the horizon. The valley below teemed with villagers going about the business of life. The future seemed bright, except for the imminent prospect of rain.

Bai said, "If you'd never come to China, I wonder what our lives would be like?"

"I don't want to think about that."

"Do you like living in China?"

"Yes."

"Would you want to stay here forever?"

"No. My heart belongs to America."

Bai swung her left arm around and embraced him.

"And my heart belongs to you."

They stood on a precipice and kissed.

Walking again, she asked, "Will they like me in America?"

"They will love you in America, just as I love you."

Lightning slammed into a tree at the top of the hill. Bai squealed. Hand-in-hand they ran down the hill toward shelter, their feet seemingly running faster than their bodies, as lightning bolts streaked across the sky and thunder roared with unforgiving urgency. Suddenly, her hand slipped from his grip and she was . . . falling . . . away.

Preston awoke from the dream to find Doe seated on one side of his bed and Agent Cefalu on the other side. Doe held onto his hand tightly. She spoke, her voice calm and reassuring: "You were dreaming."

His eyes went from Doe to Agent Cefalu, and then back to Doe.

"It was so real," he said. "So beautiful"

"How do you feel?" asked Doe.

Preston didn't answer. He was thinking, *It's true you can't touch the past. But you can taste it. Smell it. Sense it.*

Finally, Preston said, "Open the window, will you? So I can hear the traffic on the streets."

"Sure," said Doe. She went to a nearby window and lifted it about a foot, allowing the traffic noises to filter into his bedroom.

"How's that?"

"That's fine." His speech was slow, his breathing labored. They wanted him to go to a hospital, but he refused. He wanted to leave on his own terms. The only compromise he was willing to make was to agree to have a nurse in the next room. "But I don't want to have to look at her," he explained. "She can look at me after I'm gone and do the necessary paperwork."

Doe sat back down and grasped his hand again. Their eyes interlocked. Father and daughter. Lost and then found. He tried to smile, but he couldn't quite make it. Death was so exhausting.

"Cefalu will explain everything to you."

"What do you mean?"

"I am leaving you everything."

Doe looked at Agent Cefalu, not sure what to say.

Agent Cefalu nodded.

Preston looked lovingly at Doe and squeezed her hand. Tears streaked down his cheeks.

"Whatever else you think about me, I want you to know that I always loved you."

"I understand that now," she said, her voice barely a whisper. "I'm sorry it took so long for us to find each other."

"Me, too."

He took in a deep breath, the deepest he'd inhaled all day. Then he released it with a rumbling hiss. His head tilted over to one side and his breathing stopped.

Times goes by. Ever so slowly. Then it stops.

Agent Cefalu got up from his chair and went to the door that opened into the living room. He motioned with his hand, calling someone. Then, to Doe, he said, "There's someone here to see you."

"Me?"

Into the doorway stepped Benjamin and Anna Peterson.

"We're here for you if you need us."

www.ingramcontent.com/pod-product-compliance
Lightning Source LLC
Chambersburg PA
CBHW021233250626
47155CB00008B/2984